Praise for *The Forgotten Recipe*

"Clipston delivers another enchanting series starter with a tasty premise, family secrets, and sweet-as-pie romance, offering assurance that true love can happen more than once and second chances are worth fighting for."

—*RT Book Reviews*, 4 1/2 stars, top pick!

"In the first book in her Amish Heirloom series, Clipston takes readers on a roller-coaster ride through grief, guilt, and anxiety."

—*Booklist*

"Clipston is well versed in Amish culture and does a good job creating the world of Lancaster County, Penn. . . . Amish fiction fans will enjoy this story—and want a taste of Veronica's raspberry pie!"

—*Publishers Weekly*

"[Clipston] does an excellent job of wrapping up her story while setting the stage for the sequel."

—*CBA Retailers + Resources*

Praise for Amy Clipston

"Clipston brings this engaging series to an end with two emotional family reunions, a prodigal son parable, a sweet but hard-won romance, and a happy ending for characters readers have grown to love. Once again, she gives us all we could possibly want from a talented storyteller."

—*RT Book Reviews*, 4 1/2 stars, top pick!
on *A Simple Prayer*

". . . will leave readers craving more."

—*RT Book Reviews*, 4 1/2-star review of
A Mother's Secret, TOP PICK!

"Clipston's series starter has a compelling drama involving faith, family, and romance."

—*RT Book Reviews*, 4 1/2-star review of
A Hopeful Heart, TOP PICK!

"Authentic characters, delectable recipes, and faith abound in Clipston's second Kauffman Amish Bakery story."

—*RT Book Reviews*, 4-star review of *A Promise of Hope*

". . . an entertaining story of Amish life, loss, love, and family."

—*RT Book Reviews*, 4-star review of *A Place of Peace*

"This fifth and final installment in the 'Kauffman Amish Bakery' series is sure to please fans who have waited for Katie's story."

—*Library Journal* review of *A Season of Love*

"[The Kauffman Amish Bakery series'] wide popularity is sure to attract readers to this novella, and they won't be disappointed by the excellent writing and the story's wholesome goodness."

—*Library Journal* review of *A Plain and
Simple Christmas*

"[*A Plain and Simple Christmas*] is inspiring and a perfect fit for the holiday season."

—*RT Book Reviews*, 4-star review

A Dream of Home

ALSO BY AMY CLIPSTON

THE AMISH HEIRLOOM SERIES

The Forgotten Recipe
The Courtship Basket
The Cherished Quilt
(available November 2016)

THE HEARTS OF THE LANCASTER GRAND HOTEL SERIES

A Hopeful Heart
A Mother's Secret
A Dream of Home
A Simple Prayer

THE KAUFFMAN AMISH BAKERY SERIES

A Gift of Grace
A Place of Peace
A Promise of Hope
A Life of Joy
A Season of Love

YOUNG ADULT

Roadside Assistance
Reckless Heart
Destination Unknown
Miles from Nowhere

NOVELLAS

A Plain and Simple Christmas
Naomi's Gift included in *An Amish Christmas Gift*
A Spoonful of Love included in *An Amish Kitchen*
A Son for Always included in *An Amish Cradle*
Love Birds included in *An Amish Market*

NONFICTION

A Gift of Love

A Dream of Home

HEARTS OF THE LANCASTER GRAND HOTEL

BOOK THREE

AMY
CLIPSTON

ZONDERVAN

A Dream of Home
Copyright © 2014 by Amy Clipston

This title is also available as a Zondervan ebook.
Visit www.zondervan.com.

Requests for information should be addressed to:
Zondervan, *Grand Rapids, Michigan 49546*

ISBN: 978-0-7180-8000-6 (Mass Market)

Library of Congress Cataloging-in-Publication Data

Clipston, Amy.
A dream of home / Amy Clipston.
pages cm
ISBN 978-0-310-33585-6 (trade paper)
1. Amish—Fiction. 2. Domestic fiction. I. Title.
PS3603.L58D74 2014
813'.6—dc23
2014015375

Printed in the United States of America

16 17 18 19 20 21 22 / QGM / 22 21 20 19 18 17 16 15 14 13 12 11 10 9 8 7 6 5 4 3 2 1

For all the brave women who are serving
or have served in our military

GLOSSARY

ach: oh
aenti: aunt
appeditlich: delicious
Ausbund: Amish hymnal
bedauerlich: sad
boppli: baby
brot: bread
bruder: brother
bruderskinner: nieces/nephews
bu: boy
buwe: boys
Christenpflicht: Amish prayer book
daadi: granddad
daed: dad
Danki: Thank you
dat: dad
Dietsch: Pennsylvania Dutch, the Amish language (a German dialect)
dochder: daughter
dochdern: daughters
Dummle!: Hurry!
Englisher: a non-Amish person
fraa: wife
Frehlicher Grischtdaag: Merry Christmas

freind: friend

freinden: friends

freindschaft: relative

froh: happy

gegisch: silly

Gern gschehne: You're welcome

grank: sick

grossdaadi: grandfather

grossdochder: granddaughter

grossdochdern: granddaughters

grosskinner: grandchildren

grossmammi: grandmother

Gude mariye: Good morning

gut: good

Gut nacht: Good night

haus: house

Ich liebe dich: I love you

kapp: prayer covering or cap

kichli: cookie

kichlin: cookies

kind: child

kinner: children

kumm: come

liewe: love, a term of endearment

maed: young women, girls

maedel: young woman

mamm: mom

mammi: grandma

mei: my

mutter: mother

naerfich: nervous

narrisch: crazy

onkel: uncle

Ordnung: the oral tradition of practices required and
forbidden in the Amish faith

schee: pretty

schtupp: family room

schweschder: sister

Was iss letz?: What's wrong?

Wie geht's: How do you do? or Good day!

willkumm: welcome

wunderbaar: wonderful

ya: yes

NOTE TO THE READER

While this novel is set against the real backdrop of Lancaster County, Pennsylvania, the characters are fictional. There is no intended resemblance between the characters in this book and any real members of the Amish and Mennonite communities. As with any work of fiction, I've taken license in some areas of research as a means of creating the necessary circumstances for my characters. My research was thorough; however, it would be impossible to be completely accurate in details and description because each and every community differs. Therefore, any inaccuracies in the Amish and Mennonite lifestyles portrayed in this book are completely due to fictional license.

ONE

Madeleine Miller's heart pounded in her ears as she knelt next to the stretcher and held on to its side. "It's going to be all right," she cooed. She was wearing earplugs, but she knew the wounded soldier in front of her, barely clinging to life, couldn't hear her words any more than she could hear his moans. Every other sound was drowned out by the deafening thunder of the C-130's engine.

Suddenly she realized the cargo hold was filled with stretchers bearing soldiers and airmen hooked up to a tangle of oxygen canisters and IVs. Now their groans and pleas for help were nearly drowning out the roar of the aircraft. Madeleine let go of the stretcher, stood, and spun around, searching for her medical crew director, the other flight nurse who was supposed to have flown this mission with her. But Madeleine couldn't find her. The loadmaster, who was responsible for the aircraft's cargo, was also missing. Yet the number of patients on stretchers was still multiplying, and the entire fuselage was closing in on her.

Now, even with earplugs, Madeleine could hear the chorus of agonizing screams, and they overwhelmed her as she stared helplessly at the scene around her. She had no medicine, no support, no strength.

She was all alone.

Madeleine took a step backward and bumped into something. Turning, she looked down to see a body bag, and then cupping her hand to her mouth, she gasped as she read the tag: T. ROBINSON.

"Travis! No! No! No!" Madeleine screamed though grief nearly suffocated her. But the sound of her voice was again drowned out by the roar of the engine . . .

Madeleine's eyes flew open. She rolled onto her side and stared at the empty wall.

It was just a dream.

Another nightmare.

Madeleine released a shuddering sigh as she ran her hands down the sweat-drenched T-shirt and boxer shorts that served as pajamas. She kicked off the home-made quilt, sat up, and studied the large bedroom. It was the same room that had been her grandparents' master bedroom. It was still decorated the way they'd left it—with a double bed, two dressers, and four plain white walls.

She looked at the battery-operated clock on the nightstand. The bright green digital numbers indicated it was only 5:15. She sighed and ran her hands through her long, dark hair, which was also sweaty from the dream that had rocked her to her core. Memories of her time as an air force flight nurse haunted her, despite her attempts to leave it all behind. And then there was Travis.

Her gaze moved to a single stream of light that broke

through the tiny sliver where the green window shade didn't quite cover the bottom of the window. Madeleine's feet hit the cold floor, and she shivered as she walked to the window. She lifted the shade and stared out at the small, dark field behind the house. She'd spent nearly every summer in this house from the time she was five until she was twelve, while her mother served in the military. She could be with her mother as she was transferred from place to place—with Madeleine moving from school to school—but her happiest childhood memories were created during those summers in this small house in Paradise, Pennsylvania. Therefore, it only made sense when her mother suggested Madeleine move here.

Madeleine studied the two-story farmhouse and line of barns that sat across the field, beyond her single barn and the house she lived in now. She remembered when her grandparents owned both properties and ran a dairy farm. Then nearly ten years ago, they sold the land to an Amish man, who now ran a business on that land.

She turned back toward the bed and gave up on the notion of eight hours of sleep. She hadn't enjoyed a full night of sleep since she'd lost Travis, and it was apparent she wasn't going to enjoy that luxury anytime soon. Instead, she decided to do the one thing most likely to calm her when the nightmares came.

Soon Madeleine pulled her hair into a thick ponytail before changing into a long-sleeved sweatshirt, shorts, and her favorite running shoes. When she stepped out onto the front porch, the chilly September air hit her like a wall of ice. She shivered as she loped down the steps and began jogging toward the paved road at the end of her rock driveway, the one she and her neighbor shared.

Before long, thoughts of the crisp air evaporated as she fell into the zone. All that mattered was the sound of her feet pounding the pavement. She ran a route she had mapped out when she first moved into the house nearly eight months ago. She moved through the community, taking in the patchwork of farms, large homes, and barns. Cows lowed in the fields, and the aroma of a nearby pig farm overpowered her senses. The scenery was peaceful and inviting, just what her soul had craved. She wanted to find a place where she could release all the stress that had built up inside her since joining the military right after earning her nursing degree.

Her faith was shaken after she lost Travis. She'd always felt a close relationship with God, but when Travis died, she was left with nothing but loneliness and doubt. She prayed that coming back to Pennsylvania would help her find her faith again.

She ran until her legs were sore and her mind was free of the images that haunted her—the wounded service members, the body bags, the suffering. Madeleine's route circled through Paradise. The sunrise burst in colorful hues of orange, pink, and yellow as she ran past the Heart of Paradise Bed-and-Breakfast, which was located down the street from her house.

She slowed to a jog and then walked, allowing her breathing to return to normal as she walked up her driveway. She looked past her modest one-story home to the Beiler farm, the land that had once belonged to her grandparents. A large sign down by the street and another next to one of the barns read Beiler's Cabinets, and Madeleine considered walking over to introduce herself. Being an *Englisher*, she'd never thought she should disturb her Amish neighbors. But she longed to take a peek at Mr. Beiler's work. She planned to make a few minor changes to the house, and she had been considering updating the cabinets. She wondered what his prices were, but she assumed he was too expensive for her budget; most Amish-made items were astronomically priced.

Madeleine climbed the steps, to her back porch this time, leaned on the railing, and breathed in the wonderful autumn air. As she stared toward the Beiler farm, she saw a girl walking from one of the barns toward the farmhouse. Madeleine had noticed her before, but they'd never been close enough to make eye contact, not even when they passed her house in their buggy. She guessed she was eleven or twelve. She was wearing a prayer covering and a blue dress with a black apron, and she was carrying a basket.

The girl turned toward Madeleine and then waved vigorously. Surprised, Madeleine smiled as she waved back. She couldn't help but think that the little girl reminded her of herself at that age. Madeleine had spent so much time helping her grandmother in the yard and barn, carrying baskets just like that one.

She walked through her small mudroom into the kitchen and glanced at the clock on the wall. She had less than an hour to shower, eat, and get ready for her part-time job as a housekeeper at the Lancaster Grand Hotel. She'd been glad to find a job where she could earn some money without a lot of stress.

The fog of grief consumed her as she walked through the kitchen and family room toward the bathroom. Moving to Pennsylvania wasn't her original plan. She was supposed to have been married a year ago, but everything abruptly changed when her fiancé, Travis Robinson, died. After losing him, she needed a place to call home, and now she wondered if that place truly was in Amish Country. Had her mother thought so?

As Madeleine stepped into the shower, she pushed away any negative thoughts. Today was a new day, and she wouldn't let nightmares and grief smother the hope that was slowly blooming inside of her.

• • •

Saul stepped out of one of his workshop buildings and saw Emma holding a basket of eggs in one hand and waving her free arm toward the house adjacent to his farm.

"Emma!" he called as he approached her. "What are you doing?"

Emma continued to flail her arm while a woman standing on the porch across the field waved in return. "I'm waving to the *maedel* who lives in *Mammi's haus*." She faced him and tilted her head. "Who is she?"

"I don't know, and it's none of our business." He pointed toward their own house. "Are you ready for breakfast? You need to head off to school soon."

"*Ya.*" Emma watched the woman disappear into the house and then started for the back porch. "I'll go make breakfast, and you can finish your chores."

"*Danki.*" Saul's eyes followed his daughter as she climbed the steps and walked into the house. He looked toward the smaller home down the driveway, then finished feeding the horses and cows while questions about the new occupant swirled through his mind. Until she'd come nearly eight months ago, the home had sat empty since Martha Stoltzfus passed away. That was nearly two years ago, and her husband, Mel, had died two years before that.

Though Saul had become well acquainted with Martha and Mel, most of what he knew about the family's history was what older members of the community had told him. Apparently, their only child, the daughter he'd met at Mel's and then Martha's funeral, had left the community, but she frequently brought her own daughter to visit. Early in Saul's marriage, Mel and Martha had sold Saul their farm for a fair price. Soon after, he converted one of the large barns into a shop for his cabinet business, adding two more buildings a couple of years later.

Saul finished feeding the animals and then headed into the house. He shucked his light coat and hat and hung them on a peg in the mudroom before removing his boots. He watched Emma again, this time from the kitchen doorway. She was humming as she fried eggs and bacon on the stove, which was powered by propane.

The early morning sunlight streaming through the kitchen window gave her light brown hair a golden hue, reminding Saul of her mother, Annie. Memories of his marriage assaulted his mind while he watched Emma work. He wasn't Annie's first choice for a husband. Annie had settled for Saul after her boyfriend left the community and moved to a former Amish community in Missouri. He'd known Annie still loved her boyfriend, but Saul had believed he and Annie could somehow build a life together. He'd been blindsided when Annie's boyfriend came back for her and she walked away from both their marriage and their sweet and innocent four-year-old daughter.

He'd told Emma her mother had died to shield her from the painful truth, and somehow the truth had never come out. But the truth continued to haunt him daily because Emma looked like her mother with her sweet smile and pale blue eyes.

Emma turned and gave him a surprised look. "I didn't see you there, *Dat.*"

"Everything smells *appeditlich.*" He moved to a cabinet and pulled out two glasses.

"*Danki.*" Emma slipped the eggs onto a platter. "I'm getting better at making the eggs. They aren't brown at all."

"*Gut, gut.*" He put the glasses on the table and then took a pitcher of water from the refrigerator.

Emma brought the platter of eggs to the table and then picked up a basket of rolls and a platter of bacon. "Breakfast is ready."

Saul sat at his usual spot at the head of the table, and Emma sat to his right. After a silent prayer, they began filling their plates.

"The *maedel* in *Mammi's haus* is obviously an *Englisher*. She doesn't dress like us, and she drives a red pickup truck. Who is she?" Emma asked as she buttered a roll.

"I told you I don't know. Why are you asking now when she's been there all these months? You've seen her before." Saul grabbed a roll from the basket.

"I didn't like it at first when someone else moved into *Mammi's haus*. But I'm curious now, I guess. That's why I waved to her when I saw her looking at me. Why would an *Englisher* want that *haus*? Esther told me *Englishers* have houses with electricity. *Mammi's haus* is just like ours, so there isn't any electricity. And, like our *haus*, it's heated with a coal stove. Esther says *Englishers* don't know how to take care of a coal stove. They'll think it's too much work. So why would she want a house with coal heat and no electricity?" She bit into the roll.

"Sometimes people buy houses and then change them."

Her eyes brightened with understanding. "Like when people have you make new cabinets for them?"

"*Ya*, exactly." He wiped his beard with a napkin. "Maybe she's going to make some changes to the *haus* to make it an *English haus*."

Emma's mouth formed a thin line. "She's going to change *mei mammi's haus*?"

Saul forked his eggs. "I told you it's none of our business. We can't tell someone what they can and can't do with their *haus*."

Emma was silent for a moment while she ate, but

Saul braced himself for more questions. She'd been asking a lot of questions lately, and he knew soon she'd ask ones he wasn't prepared to answer. Although he'd tried to be both mother and father to his daughter, he could never take the place of a real mother. He'd longed to find Emma a loving mother ever since he'd received word last year that Annie had passed away in an accident.

"Why does that *maedel* put on those shorts and run?" Emma suddenly asked. "Aren't those clothes uncomfortable? Wouldn't she be cold in them this time of year?"

"Some *Englishers* like to run to stay fit. It's exercise to them." Saul lifted a piece of bacon.

"Huh." Emma looked as if she were considering this. "I guess. Farmwork keeps you fit, right?"

"*Ya*, it does." He had seen the mysterious young woman running the other day. She was jogging on the street toward their properties when he returned from picking up supplies in town. Her dark hair bobbed behind her as her legs pounded the pavement, and she had determination in her eyes. She was in her own world, oblivious to his horse and buggy as it moved past her.

"I hope she doesn't change *Mammi's haus*," Emma continued. "I loved visiting her and helping in her garden. I miss her."

"I know you do." Saul had been grateful for Martha's interest in Emma; his daughter didn't have the luxury of knowing his parents or Annie's; they had all passed away. Martha accepted Emma as if she were her own granddaughter, which is why she let Emma call her *Mammi*.

"Do you remember seeing *Mammi's dochder* at her funeral?" Emma asked.

"*Ya*, I do," Saul said as he forked another bite of eggs.

"She dressed liked an *Englisher* too. *Mammi* told me her *dochder* left the community when she was a teenager." Saul kept from looking surprised. He hadn't known Martha told Emma that.

"I imagine that was hard for *Mammi*," Emma went on, "just like it was hard for you when your *bruder* left after your parents died."

"*Ya*." Saul swallowed a sigh as his thoughts turned to Annie once again. He'd never had the heart to tell Emma that her mother had left too; he didn't want her to blame herself for her mother's decision. Someday, he knew, he'd have to tell Emma the truth, but he refused to burden her with it now.

"I want to meet that *maedel*."

"Emma, you should leave her alone. I'm certain she is very busy." He glanced at the clock above the sink. "You need to get ready for school."

They finished their breakfast, and then they had a silent prayer before carrying their dishes to the sink.

"You go on, and I'll make your lunch," Saul said.

"*Danki*." Emma rushed up the stairs.

By the time she returned to the kitchen, Saul had her lunch pail packed. "Have a *gut* day." He handed her the pail, and she smiled up at him.

"You too, *Dat*." He leaned down, and she stood on her tiptoes and kissed his cheek.

Saul followed Emma out to the front porch and then watched her rush to meet her friends, who were waiting on the corner at the bottom of the driveway. As she passed Martha Stoltzfus's house, the young woman wearing a gray dress stepped onto the back porch. She and Emma exchanged waves again, and then Emma disappeared around the corner with her friends. The woman climbed into her red pickup truck and drove off.

For a brief moment, Saul wondered, too, why the *Englisher* would want to live in Martha Stoltzfus's modest house, but, as he had told Emma, it wasn't any of his business. Yet, like Emma, he was curious, and the question still lingered in the back of his mind: Who was this mysterious woman?

TWO

Madeleine steered her pickup truck up the rock driveway leading to Carolyn Lapp's house later that evening. She was excited when Carolyn had invited her to come for supper after work. After working her usual shift at the hotel, she headed toward Gordonville and the farm where Carolyn lived. She drove past the main house and parked in front of the smaller house out back. As Madeleine climbed out of the truck, Carolyn appeared on the porch.

"I'm thrilled you made it," Carolyn, a pretty blonde in her early thirties, said as she rushed over to the truck. "I just put the potpie in the oven."

"Thank you for inviting me." Madeleine glanced around the property. "This is beautiful."

"Thank you." Carolyn nodded. "This is my brother's dairy farm." She pointed toward the large farmhouse. "Amos lives there with his family, and I live here in the *daadi haus* with my parents and my son, Benjamin."

"This is lovely, but you won't be living here much longer." Madeleine grinned. "Your wedding day will be here soon."

Carolyn's smile broadened. "That's true." She motioned for Madeleine to come into the small house.

Madeleine followed Carolyn inside and breathed in the aroma of the potpie. "It all smells delicious. Can I help you with anything?"

"Oh no." Carolyn pointed toward the kitchen table. "Have a seat. We can visit before I need to put the carrots and corn on the stove." As Madeleine sat down, Carolyn poured two glasses of water, then brought them to the table.

"Where are your parents and Benjamin?"

Carolyn sank into a chair across from her. "My mom and my sister-in-law are working on a quilt project. My father is working with my brother, and Ben is working at Joshua's farm in Paradise."

"You must be excited about the wedding. How are preparations coming along?"

"They're coming along well. And I've been thinking about the move to Joshua's house after the wedding. I already have plans to expand his garden in the spring." Carolyn paused before going on. "I'm very thankful for Joshua. I've always dreamed of giving Benjamin a real family. I'll finally be able to do that."

"I bet he's excited too." Madeleine sipped her water. "Does he like working with Joshua?"

"He loves the horse farm. It's all worked out so well for us. I didn't think I deserved a real family because I wasn't married when I had Benjamin. I'm thankful the Lord had other plans for me." Carolyn tilted her head in question. "How are you adjusting to living here? Your grandparents' house must be very different from what you're used to."

"It's very peaceful here. I was tired of living on

military bases." Madeleine thought back to her apartment in California. "The most noise I've heard so far was made by a rooster. It's heaven. I'm certain that's why the town is named Paradise."

"You spent a lot of time with your grandparents when you were little, right?"

"That's right. My mother served in the military, and we moved around a lot. I went to school near the base where she was stationed, and I was in daycare when my mom was working. It wasn't always easy, but my mom did the best she could. We managed. She would bring me to Paradise, especially for summers. I loved it. I would help my *mammi* work in the garden and bake, help my *daadi* care for the animals, and play with the neighborhood children. It was a wonderful break from living on military bases."

Carolyn grinned.

"Why are you smiling like that?"

"You said those words correctly. Do you speak *Dietsch*?"

"I remember a little bit." Madeleine thought back to her childhood. "I loved pretending I was Amish. It was a lot of fun. But it was a difficult transition when I went back home. I remember one year I begged my mother to let me stay and go to school with the neighborhood kids."

"Did you really?" Carolyn looked intrigued. "How did your parents feel about that?"

Madeleine shook her head. "I never knew my father, and I have no idea what he would say. My mother looked sad when I told her."

"Why did she leave the community?"

"She had met my father, and she told me she fell hopelessly in love with him. She hadn't joined the church, so she wasn't shunned. But, at the same time, her parents were devastated. They never got over it. They were even more upset when she joined the military, but they grew to accept it after I was born." Madeleine ran her fingers over the cool glass of water and thought back to her childhood. "The farm has changed quite a bit since I was little. My grandparents sold most of the land to an Amish cabinetmaker."

"Oh, that's right. Your property backs up to Saul Beiler's land." Carolyn's expression became a little embarrassed. "He's good friends with *mei bruder*. He wanted to date me, but then I got to know Josh."

"I remember you telling me that." Madeleine nodded slowly while wondering what had happened to Saul's wife. "Saul has one child, right?"

"*Ya*. His wife died when his daughter was little. I believe she was four."

"Oh. That's sad." Madeleine shook her head. "That poor little girl. She must've been heartbroken."

"*Ya*," Carolyn said. "Emma is a sweet little girl. I connected with her right away. Saul's a really good father, though."

"That's nice. I haven't met them yet, but Emma always waves to me now."

"She's very friendly." Carolyn nodded. "I hope Saul finds a mother for her someday."

"*Ya*." Madeleine thought about her grandparents. "I was devastated when I got back from overseas and found out my *mammi* had passed away. Apparently I was on my way home when she died, and somehow my mother's messages didn't get to me. I was even too late for the service here."

"I'm sorry to hear that. I'm certain that was a tremendous loss for you."

"It was. My mother was very upset too. She and my grandmother always talked at least once a week."

"Do you think you'll stay in that house?" Carolyn asked.

"Why wouldn't I stay?" Madeleine was confused by the question. "I love that house. It has many wonderful memories in it."

"Well, it's like this one." Carolyn gestured around the kitchen. "No electricity and no modern conveniences like the microwave we have in the break room at the hotel."

"I don't mind. Right now I'm enjoying the quiet."

"You're not going to change the house at all?"

Madeleine shrugged. "I'm not sure yet about modernizing it, but I want to update it a little. The house hasn't been cared for in a while. I'm working at the hotel, and I have some extra money to do a few projects on the house. I want to paint the rooms, replace the cabinets, and maybe replace the bathtub too. I'm going to do a little at a time."

"That sounds nice." Carolyn stood. "I'm going to start making the vegetables."

"Can I help?" Madeleine followed her to the counter.

"Would you like to cut up the fruit for the fruit salad?" Carolyn asked.

"Sure." Madeleine gathered apples, pears, and oranges from the refrigerator and began cutting and slicing.

Carolyn worked on getting corn and carrots into pots. She looked over at Madeleine and frowned. "Josh doesn't want me to keep working at the hotel. He said he wants me at the farm with him."

"Oh." Madeleine wasn't sure what to make of Carolyn's expression. "I guess that makes sense. Most Amish wives don't work away from the home, do they?"

"It depends." Carolyn added water to the pots. "Sometimes they do, but there's also a lot to do at the house. I just can't imagine not working, though. I've done it for so long that it's become part of who I am."

"Are you saying you'll miss the job?"

"*Ya*, I will." Carolyn placed the pot of carrots on the burner and turned it on. "I'll miss seeing my friends too. This is really becoming an issue between Josh and me. We had an argument about it the other night."

"Oh, I'm sorry." Madeleine wasn't quite sure what to say, but she offered some advice that made sense to her. "Maybe you should compromise. Maybe you can cut your hours and only work one day per week or something?"

"No, I'm certain he won't agree with that, even though it's a *gut* idea. He is really adamant that I don't work there."

"Why is he against it?"

"I think he's concerned because of what happened to Hannah."

"Oh, I heard about this. Hannah met Trey at the

hotel and they fell in love. Is he afraid you'll decide to become *English* and break off your engagement?"

"I think so." Carolyn put the pot of corn on the burner next to the carrots. "I've tried to tell him I'm not going to leave the community, but he still seems very insecure about it. I'm not sure what I can do to convince him I'm not going to allow the hotel to influence me, but I guess we'll see what God has in store for us."

"That sounds reasonable." Madeleine nodded.

Madeleine and Carolyn continued to talk while they finished preparing the meal. Soon Carolyn's parents came in, and then Benjamin arrived home from working at Joshua Glick's horse farm. Madeleine felt at home while they ate supper. She enjoyed hearing about their day. They talked and laughed while they enjoyed the delicious homemade chicken potpie and vegetables and finished off the meal with fruit salad and apple pie.

After supper and dessert, Madeleine helped Carolyn and her mother clean up the kitchen before heading to the porch with Carolyn. They sat and talked while they sipped hot cups of coffee.

"Everything was delicious," Madeleine said as she moved the porch swing back and forth. "I really had a lovely time. Your family is wonderful."

"I'm glad you could come." Carolyn cradled her mug in her hands. "I could tell my parents really liked you."

"Oh good." Madeleine's thoughts turned to her grandparents. "Sometimes I wonder what it would've been like if I'd grown up here."

"What do you mean?" Carolyn looked curious.

"I used to wonder what it would've been like to have grown up here instead of in a city."

Carolyn studied Madeleine. "Are you saying you wondered what it would be like to grow up Amish?"

"Yeah." Madeleine nodded. "It's peaceful here. Do you ever wonder what it would be like to be *English*?"

"No, not really. This is all I've ever known."

"Do you ever crave more?"

"No, I've always felt like I have all that I need, but I'll finally have a home of my own. Joshua and I will build our own life on his farm."

"I remember that my grandparents hosted church twice a year. Before they sold part of their property, they had a big barn they used for church services. They always had services every other Sunday at someone's farm. My *mammi* loved the off Sundays from church when they went visiting. It was fun to ride around in their buggy and see all their friends. I've visited a few churches around the area, but I haven't felt a real connection to them."

"You should come to an Amish service sometime."

Madeleine couldn't stop her smile. "Really?"

"*Ya*, you should. Everyone would love to see you. I'm sure some of the members of the community would remember you from when you visited as a child. Many of my relatives remember your *daadi* and *mammi*."

"That would be fun. I'd love to come to a service."

"And you'd better come to my wedding."

"I definitely will." Madeleine sipped her coffee and thought about Hannah. "Did you say Hannah is running a bed-and-breakfast now, in Paradise?"

"*Ya*, I think it's called the Heart of Paradise Bed-and-Breakfast."

"That's right near my house," Madeleine said.

Madeleine visited with Carolyn until it started to get dark and then thanked her for the meal and headed home. She parked next to her house and headed up the back porch steps.

When she reached the back door, she stopped and looked out toward Saul Beiler's farm and noticed light spilling out from the largest barn near his house. Her heart ached for this stranger, knowing that he'd lost his wife and was raising his daughter alone. She decided to keep them both in her prayers. She glanced up at the clear evening sky and whispered a prayer right then.

"God, I know you're still there, but I haven't felt your presence since I lost Travis. Help me find my way back to you. Please take away my nightmares and heal the hole in my heart Travis left after he died. I should've been there for Travis when he needed me. I should have protected him, but I failed him. I know I'm not worthy of your love, Lord, but I need you now. Make me feel whole again. In Jesus' holy name, amen."

She walked into her house, hoping she could some-how enjoy a full night's sleep.

· · ·

Saul continued to sand the cabinet door that was part of an *Englisher's* order for his brand-new house. He was thankful that his business was booming, but he was also starting to feel overwhelmed by so many orders.

He desperately needed an assistant. Or possibly even an apprentice who could learn the trade and help him keep up with the volume of requests.

He had always loved the work, and though his father had taught him a lot about woodworking, he was grateful that his uncle, now deceased like Saul's parents, had taken him under his wing at a young age and taught him the craft of fine cabinetmaking. When he'd married Annie, he'd hoped that she'd give him a son who would want to follow in his footsteps. Although he adored Emma, he'd also prayed that she'd one day have a brother, but that wasn't in God's plan for him. At least not with Annie.

He considered his life while he worked. He'd never imagined he'd wind up divorced with a four-year-old, and it was against his beliefs for him to remarry while Annie was still alive. However, that all changed when Saul received the letter from her new husband telling him Annie had died.

The idea of remarrying was frightening because he couldn't even remember how to date. He'd thought he'd gotten the hang of it when he started visiting with Carolyn Lapp, but he'd failed miserably. Yet he wasn't going to give up. Emma deserved a mother, and he'd do his best to find her one—with God's help, of course. And maybe he'd even find a wife who'd want to try to give him a son. At the same time, he wondered if he could trust another woman. Would another wife also abandon him and Emma?

He finished sanding the door and then glanced at the clock on the wall. He had to get Emma into bed and then go to bed himself. The evening was passing too quickly. He'd get busy on his current cabinet project again tomorrow morning.

He flipped off the four battery-powered lanterns he used to light his shop and then picked up another one to guide his journey back to the house. Would the Lord see fit for him to marry again? He didn't know if he'd ever remarry, but he did know one thing for sure—some days he grew weary of being both mother and father to Emma and raising her all alone.

THREE

The following morning, Madeleine awoke with another nightmare. Only this time, with the roar of the C-130 closing in on her, she was giving CPR to a soldier who'd been injured in a land mine blast. And as she often did in these dreams, she wound up trying to revive Travis in the ER. Although the dream had left her shaking, she was grateful she'd slept until nearly seven, which was a new accomplishment. She changed into her running clothes and then set off jogging her usual route around Paradise. Once she hit her stride, she let her mind go, releasing all the stress that plagued her dreams.

As she rounded the bend, the Heart of Paradise Bed-and-Breakfast came into view. She slowed to a brisk walk as she approached the three-story, clapboard house. It had a large wraparound porch with a swing, and it was peppered with rocking chairs. A wooden sign with old-fashioned letters boasted the name of the establishment.

She remembered hearing Hannah's story. Hannah had left the Amish community and opened the bed-and-breakfast with her new husband. It made Madeleine think of her own mother, who would never discuss why she left her Amish life behind, saying the life just wasn't for her. Madeleine's grandmother also didn't want to discuss losing her daughter to the modern world, but Madeleine always saw tears in her eyes whenever she asked her about it.

Madeleine hoped to meet Hannah soon and find out more about her life and her decision to leave the Amish.

. . .

Madeleine stepped into the break room at the hotel later that day and found her coworkers, Carolyn Lapp, Linda Zook, and Ruth Ebersol, already sitting around the table and unpacking their lunches.

"Hello." Madeleine retrieved her lunch bag from the refrigerator and sat beside Carolyn. "I was running behind on my rooms. Several of them were a real mess. It looked like the guests had thrown a few parties."

"*Ach* no." Linda, a petite brunette in her early thirties, sighed. "That's terrible."

"I heard a sports team checked in a few days ago." Ruth polished a bright red apple with a paper napkin as she spoke. "Gregg mentioned they were loud last night, and a few of the guests complained about the noise."

"That's awful." Carolyn shook her head as she lifted her cup of water. "How could they leave such a mess? You should've called me. I would've come to help you."

"I would've helped you too," Linda offered. "My rooms were fairly easy this morning."

"It's fine, but thank you. I got it all done." Madeleine pulled out her turkey sandwich. "I went for a run this morning and passed Hannah Peterson's house. Do you think she'd want to talk to me sometime?"

As if on cue, Carolyn, Linda, and Ruth all nodded.

"Oh *ya*. Hannah is a sweet person. She'd love to meet you," Ruth replied, her graying hair peeking out from under her prayer covering. "I haven't visited her in a while, but I've been thinking of her."

"I wonder how she's adjusting to her new life." Madeleine tilted her head askance. "She's shunned, right?"

Linda frowned. "*Ya*, she is."

"Are you allowed to be friends with her even though she's shunned?" Madeleine bit into her sandwich while waiting for a response.

"*Ya*, we can still be her friend," Carolyn chimed in. "But we can't eat at the same table with her, and she can't shop at an Amish store."

"She also can't attend worship with us unless she confesses in front of the congregation first." Linda continued to look sad. "I miss seeing her at services, but I'm glad she's happy with her new life. I know it was a difficult decision for her."

"I wonder how her relationship is with her daughter Lillian," Ruth said. "Last I heard their relationship was still strained."

"That's so sad." Madeleine pulled a small bag of baby carrots out of her bag. "I hope she can work things out with her daughter. That has to be heartbreaking."

"I hope so too." Carolyn paused for a moment. "I'd

like to invite Hannah to my wedding." She turned to Ruth. "Do you think it would be too painful for her?"

Ruth shrugged. "I don't know. I guess you would need to ask her. I'm certain Joshua would want his nieces and nephew there. It wouldn't be right to not invite her too."

"*Ya*, that's what I was thinking." Carolyn pushed an errant lock of blonde hair back from her face and back under her prayer covering. "I'll discuss it with Joshua. Hannah never had a good relationship with Joshua's mother, but she's still part of the family."

"My mother left when she was eighteen, but she hadn't joined the church yet," Madeleine said.

"That means she wasn't shunned." Linda finished Madeleine's thought.

"Exactly." Madeleine lifted a carrot from the bag. "But I think it was still difficult for her."

"It's always hard." Ruth's gaze was trained on her sandwich as she spoke. "You never get over it when a child leaves the community behind. It's heartbreaking."

Carolyn's smile faded as she placed a hand on Ruth's arm. "I know you miss Aaron. I'm sorry, Ruth."

"I miss him every day." Ruth cleared her throat. "I always wonder how he is."

"I'm sorry, Ruth. I never meant to bring up a subject so painful for you." Guilt washed over Madeleine.

"Oh no, no." Ruth shook her head. "It's not your fault. I always think of Aaron. It wasn't anything you said."

Madeleine took a bite of her sandwich and thought about how Ruth must feel.

"I hope you hear from Aaron someday soon." Carolyn sliced a piece of homemade bread. "I'm certain God will bring him back to you."

"I don't know. It's been a long time." Ruth met Madeleine's gaze. "Aaron was only fifteen when he went off on his own. He said the Amish life was too restrictive. It's been almost seventeen years now."

"I'm sorry." Madeleine racked her brain for something positive and encouraging to say. "Maybe things will have changed if he has a family. My mother worked things out with my grandparents after I was born."

"*Ya.*" Carolyn's expression brightened. "That's a good point. A baby always changes people."

"Usually it does." Linda continued to scowl. "Sometimes people can't find a way to warm their hearts, no matter what happens."

"Don't give up hope." Madeleine made a mental note to add Ruth and Aaron to her prayer list.

FOUR

Carolyn hugged her cloak to her body as she moved the porch swing back and forth. The early evening air was brisk as she glanced over at Joshua and smiled. "I'm glad you came for supper tonight. I was hoping you would."

"I hadn't seen you in two days. It had been too long." He rubbed her arm.

"I was thinking the same thing." She shivered as a breeze seemed to cut right through her cloak.

"You're cold. Take my coat." He pulled off his coat and draped it over her shoulders. "You need this more than I do."

"*Danki.*" She hugged the coat to her body, breathing in his scent of soap mixed with earth.

"Just think," he said as he covered her hand with his warm fingers, "in less than a month we'll be married. You'll be Carolyn Glick."

"*Ya.*" Carolyn rested her head on his shoulder and smiled. "I'm very thankful."

"That brings up an important issue." Joshua's expression became serious. "You and I will be Glicks, but Ben will still be a Lapp. That may be confusing."

Carolyn's eyes widened as excitement filled her. Was he going to ask what she'd hoped he would?

"How would you feel about me adopting Ben?" Joshua's expression turned hopeful. "I'd like to give him my name, really be his father."

"I would love that." Tears filled Carolyn's eyes. "We should ask Benjamin, but I know he'll say yes."

"*Gut*." Joshua nodded. "I'll ask him before I leave tonight."

"This is more than I could have ever truly hoped for. *Danki*, Josh." She'd finally found someone who would accept both her and her son and love them completely. She gazed up into his blue eyes, and the question that had been haunting her all day surfaced in her mind. "Josh, I have something I want to ask you."

"You can ask me anything." He brushed his fingertip down her cheekbone.

"How would you feel about inviting Hannah to our wedding?" She held her breath in anticipation of his answer.

He hesitated, and she felt the urge to fill the silence.

"Hannah's my friend," she said. "Plus, we want the *kinner* there, and it wouldn't be right to invite the *kinner* and not Hannah. I know she'd want to come. It's only right to invite the whole family."

Joshua rubbed his chin as he stared toward her brother's house. "I don't know how *mei mamm* would take seeing her."

"But how would you feel about seeing Hannah again?"

"I'm fine with seeing her." He looped his arm around

her shoulders. "I just don't know how others would react because she's shunned. People are still upset about it."

"Are you thinking of Lillian?" She leaned into his embrace.

"Not only Lillian . . . ," he began. "But if it will make you *froh*, then you should invite Hannah."

"*Ya*?" She smiled up at him. "You mean that?"

"*Ya*." He nodded. "I'll talk to *mei mamm* and ask her to remember to be civil. It's our day, not hers."

"Right."

"Have you started thinking about how you want to decorate the *haus*?"

"Decorate the *haus*?" Carolyn tilted her head in question as she looked up at Joshua. "You want to change it?"

"I want it to feel like a cozy home. After Hannah moved out, when she married Trey and I moved in, there wasn't much of a woman's touch left." He pulled her closer. "My *haus* will be complete when you and Ben move in. It will be more than just the place where I sleep."

"I'll definitely try to think of a few touches to make it ours."

"Have you thought any more about quitting the hotel?" His voice was tentative as if he knew he was treading on uneven ground.

"Josh," she began with impatience radiating in her voice, "we've already discussed this. You know I enjoy my job. I look forward to seeing my friends, and I like contributing to my family financially. I'm going to want to contribute to our family too."

"You will contribute, just in other ways. You can take care of the house and the garden, as well as the books for me. I'll be able to expand the business with your help. We'll grow it together." Joshua angled his body toward her. "We're going to be partners, and that means I need your help running our business."

"I realize that, but you have to understand that this job means a lot to me."

"Does it mean more than our new life together?"

"No." Carolyn shook her head as frustration gripped her. "That's not fair to say. You know I'm looking forward to our life together."

"You want a family, right?" Joshua asked. "You want more *kinner*?"

"Of course I do. I want as many *kinner* as God sees fit to give us."

"*Gut*." Joshua's expression softened. "Let's not argue."

Carolyn heaved a heavy sigh. "Okay. We won't argue, but we'll discuss this more later."

Benjamin approached them from the barn, holding a lantern in his hand. Although he was quickly approaching sixteen, he was short and thin for his age. "You're still here, Josh. I thought you'd gone home already."

"Your *mamm* and I were just talking." Joshua patted the rocking chair beside the swing. "Have a seat for a minute. There's something I want to discuss with you."

Joshua pulled his arm back to his side, and Carolyn sat up straight.

"What did you want to talk about?" Benjamin lowered his body into the rocking chair.

"Your *mamm* and I were just discussing what's going

to happen after our wedding next month. You're both going to move into the house on the farm." Joshua glanced at Carolyn, and she smiled. "Your *mamm* is going to be Carolyn Glick."

"I know." Benjamin gave Carolyn a confused look. "That's pretty standard when someone gets married."

"How would you feel about becoming a Glick too?" Joshua asked.

Benjamin continued to look perplexed. "I don't understand."

"Ben, I'd like your permission to adopt you." Joshua's voice was thick with emotion. "I'd like to be your *dat*."

Benjamin's brown eyes widened. "Really?"

"*Ya*, really." Joshua patted Benjamin's shoulder. "I'd like us to be a family by name too—all of us. What do you think?"

Carolyn's eyes filled with tears as her most fervent prayer came true.

"I think it's a great plan." Benjamin nodded with emphasis. "I'd like that."

"*Gut*." Joshua turned toward Carolyn. "That's settled."

Carolyn wiped her eyes with the back of her hand.

"Are you okay, *Mamm*?" Benjamin asked.

"*Ya*." Carolyn cleared her throat in an attempt to temper her emotions.

"*Wunderbaar*." Joshua stood. "I better get home."

"*Gut nacht*," Benjamin said as he stood. "I'll see you tomorrow." He disappeared into the house.

Carolyn followed Joshua down the steps. She handed him his coat when they reached his buggy. "*Danki* for your warm coat."

"*Gern gschehne.*" He pulled the coat on. He opened his arms, and she stepped into his embrace. "*Danki* for supper."

"You know you're always welcome here." Carolyn rested her cheek on his chest. "It means the world to me that you want to adopt Ben."

"I can only pray that I can make you as happy as you and Ben have made me." He kissed the top of her head.

Carolyn looked up at him. "I better let you go. It's getting late."

"*Gut nacht, mei* Carolyn." He kissed her cheek. "Sleep well." He climbed into the buggy.

"Be safe going home." Carolyn waved as his buggy rattled its way down the rock driveway toward the road. She glanced up at the clear night sky and silently thanked God for blessing her and Benjamin by leading them to Joshua Glick.

. . .

Saul was sanding a cabinet when he heard the shop door squeak open, allowing a crisp breeze to penetrate the shop.

Emma stepped into the doorway. "*Dat*? Are you coming in? It's getting late."

"Is it?" Saul glanced at the clock on the wall and shook his head. "I didn't realize it was almost seven. I was trying to finish this one cabinet."

"You can finish it tomorrow." She placed her hand on her small hip, and he bit back a smile. At times she seemed like a little wife instead of a daughter.

"You're right, Emma." He placed the sanding block on his long workbench and then turned off the surrounding lanterns.

He followed Emma through the door and was surprised to see a buggy traveling up the driveway. "I wonder who that could be this late in the evening."

"It's Marcus!" she said, announcing the arrival of Saul's best friend. "I wonder if Esther is with him." She started jumping up and down.

"I doubt it, Emma. It's awfully late for visiting. She's probably getting ready for bed, which is what you need to be doing." Saul and Emma approached the buggy as Marcus Smucker brought it to a stop by the barn. "*Wie geht's?*"

"Hi, Marcus!" Emma stood on her tiptoes and craned her neck to see inside the buggy. "Did Esther come too?"

"No, I'm afraid not." Marcus climbed from the buggy. Saul had often thought it interesting that he and his best friend since childhood looked so much alike—dark brown hair and matching beard, about the same height.

"She was getting ready for bed when I left." Saul gave Emma a knowing glance, and Emma nodded her head.

"You'll see her at school tomorrow," Saul said gently.

"I have something for you, though." Marcus held up a basket. "Esther and her *mamm* made a casserole and pie for you and your *dat*."

"Oh." Emma took the basket and sniffed it. "It smells *appeditlich. Danki.*"

"*Gern gschehne.*" Marcus nodded at Emma.

"Take that inside and get ready for bed now," Saul told Emma.

"Okay." She looked at Marcus. "*Gut nacht*." Emma waved and then headed for the house.

"You can tell Sylvia she doesn't have to keep cooking for us," Saul said after Emma had disappeared through the back door. "Emma and I are doing okay by ourselves."

"Does that mean you're saying you don't like my *fraa's* cooking?" Marcus grinned as he leaned against the buggy.

"You know it's not that." Saul shook his head. "I appreciate everything you and Sylvia do for Emma and me, but we're doing fine. Please tell her thank you for us."

"I will. You know Sylvia feels bad that you're raising Emma alone."

"It's not her fault Annie ran off." Saul leaned back on the fence behind him.

"I know, but she still feels bad." Marcus folded his arms over his coat. "She talks all the time about how the four of us were dating at the same time and then were married within a month of each other. Sylvia and I are still together, and you're all alone. Sylvia still can't comprehend what Annie did to you and Emma."

Saul shrugged as if it didn't bother him, even though Annie's abandonment was still painful. "That was Annie's choice. I guess on some levels it was better for her to go than to stay here and be miserable."

"You don't mean that."

"No, I think I do. Emma would've been able to tell that her *mamm* resented her. I don't believe any *kind* should feel that kind of rejection from a parent."

Marcus frowned. "She still doesn't know the truth about her *mamm*, does she?"

"No, and she doesn't need to know—not yet," Saul insisted. "I'll tell her when the time is right. I don't know when that will be, but not now. She's too young."

Marcus glanced toward the house in front of Saul's property. "I see that *Englisher* is still living in Martha Stoltzfus's old *haus*."

"*Ya*." Saul spotted the woman standing on the back porch while talking on a cellular phone. Her slight body was illuminated by two lanterns.

"Do you know anything about her?" Marcus asked.

"No, she just appeared back in February, so she's been in the *haus* for almost eight months now." Saul rubbed his beard as he spoke. "I guess she's renting the *haus* from Martha's *dochder*. I never saw a For Sale sign go up."

"Is that right?" Marcus looked intrigued. "And you've never met her?"

"No, but I've noticed she likes to go for runs early in the morning." He didn't mention he'd also noticed she was fairly tall, only a couple of inches shorter than his nearly six feet. "She drives that red pickup truck, and she leaves a few times a week and is gone for extended periods of time. It seems like she has a job somewhere. She hasn't had any work done on the *haus*, so she's living without electricity. But she uses that cellular phone frequently."

Marcus raised an eyebrow. "You've been watching her?"

"Watching her?" Saul shook his head. "No, I've just

noticed her patterns. Her *haus* is right in front of mine, so it's difficult not to notice things. Emma wants to go meet her, but I keep telling her to mind her own business. We don't need to barge onto her property any more than she needs to barge onto ours."

"Interesting." Marcus motioned toward Saul's biggest shop. "How's business?"

"*Gut, gut.*" Saul rubbed his beard. "I'm trying to keep up with all the orders."

"Do you need some help?"

"Oh no. You're busy enough with your furniture orders."

"You know it's time you hired someone to help you," Marcus said. "Then you can expand and start supplying the local stores with your cabinets. They could take the orders for you, and you could concentrate on the work."

Saul stood up straight. "That's easier said than done, my friend. I'll expand someday, when the time is right."

"I've known you since we were the same age as our girls," Marcus began. "You always go the cautious way. You never try something new. When we all went camping when we were teenagers, you were afraid to jump off that tree branch into the water, even when the rest of us did."

"What does my business have to do with jumping into a lake?" Saul's brow furrowed. "I don't think that's a fair comparison. You're talking about taking a risk with my *dochder's* livelihood. I can't hire someone and run the risk of going bankrupt when my cabinet sales fall off."

"What makes you think your sales will fall off? You're known for your quality and craftsmanship. That's why your sales are very *gut*." Marcus opened the buggy door and climbed in. "Think about it, Saul. You sell yourself too short. You can expand. Just have faith."

Saul shook his head. "You were always the free spirit."

"I better go." Marcus closed the buggy door. "I'll see you soon."

"*Danki* for the food again. Tell Sylvia we appreciate her meals."

"I will." Marcus paused. "I heard Carolyn Lapp and Joshua Glick are getting married next month."

Saul nodded and rubbed his beard again. "I'm not surprised."

"Don't give up. I'm sure the Lord has plans for you." Marcus grinned. "If not, then you'll just have to start eating supper at my *haus*."

"I told you we're not starving, but we do enjoy the food." Saul waved. "*Gut nacht*."

Marcus returned the wave before guiding the horse back down the lane. Saul saw his neighbor wave as Marcus's buggy passed her house, and he wondered again who the mysterious neighbor was.

FIVE

Hannah scurried around the kitchen, her mind racing with preparations. She was running out of time before her guest was supposed to arrive.

The storm door opened and closed with a bang, and then Trey stood near the kitchen doorway. "Hannah? Are you okay?"

"*Ya*." She grabbed a bleach wipe and began to swipe it over the counter. "Carolyn called a little while ago. She's coming by to visit."

"Carolyn Lapp?" Trey looked surprised.

"That's right. She asked if she could come to see me. She'll be my first Amish friend to visit the bed-and-breakfast." She opened the china cabinet and studied her best dishes. "I have to make sure everything is perfect."

"Hannah, I'm certain she will be happy just to see you." He crossed the kitchen. "How can I help you?"

"Would you hand me those teacups up top?" She pointed toward her favorite set of teacups, which Trey had bought her as a wedding gift. "I'm going to serve hot tea and the cheesecake I made yesterday." She suddenly stopped as dread settled in. "Oh no. We can't eat together at the same table."

Trey stopped and studied her. "Will she really visit and not share a dessert with you?"

"She's not supposed to." Hannah scowled. "I don't know what to do. How can I not serve her some refreshments?"

"Why don't you set out the cheesecake and then see what she says. She may surprise you. After all, she is coming to see you. She wouldn't come over here and then refuse your food, would she? That would be awfully rude, and I haven't met many rude Amish folks."

Hannah smiled. "You're right."

"Why don't you start the hot water and get the cheesecake out of the refrigerator, and I'll set the table?"

She kissed his cheek. "*Danki*."

The table was ready by the time Hannah heard a car door slam.

"She's here!" Hannah's heart thudded in her chest.

"It will be fine." Trey touched her hand. "Trust me. Go see her. I'll serve the tea."

She rushed to the open front door, pushed open the storm door, and saw Carolyn walking up the front sidewalk with a basket over her arm as a van backed out to the street.

"Carolyn!" Hannah hurried outside and met her in the driveway. "It's wonderful to see you."

Carolyn hugged Hannah with her free arm. "You too." She handed the basket to Hannah. "I brought you some goodies that my *mamm* and I baked. I remember you liked our pretzels and pumpkin muffins."

"Oh, *danki*!" Hannah looped her free arm around

Carolyn's waist and led her back toward the house. "Please come in."

"Oh, Hannah." Carolyn caught her breath, cupping her hand to her mouth. "This *haus* is positively *schee*. You must be *froh* here."

"I am." Hannah dropped her arm from around Carolyn and touched her abdomen. "I'm very happy here. Please come inside, and I'll show you the rest of the *haus*."

Carolyn's eyes moved to Hannah's abdomen, and Hannah saw the flash of a question twinkle in her friend's eyes. She wondered if Carolyn suspected her secret, but Carolyn didn't ask. Instead, she simply smiled.

Carolyn started up the porch steps. "You look *gut*, Hannah."

"You do too."

Carolyn stepped into the front family room and looked delighted. "Hannah, this is lovely."

"*Danki*." Hannah pointed toward a hallway. "Our living quarters are down there. There's a three-bedroom apartment for us and the *kinner*."

Carolyn looked toward the light switch on the wall. "Did it take you awhile to get used to electricity all the time now, instead of only at work?"

Hannah shrugged. "It was a fairly easy adjustment, although I do feel a little spoiled." She gestured toward the stairs. "There are six bedrooms upstairs for the guests."

"It's fabulous." Carolyn nodded. "You must love it."

"We do. Please come into the kitchen." There they

found Trey putting finishing touches on the table. "Carolyn, this is my husband, Trey."

"Carolyn." Trey shook her hand. "It's nice to meet you."

"It's nice to meet you too." Carolyn glanced around the kitchen.

Hannah placed the basket on the counter. "Would you like some tea?"

"*Ya*, I'd love that."

"I'll let you two visit," Trey said. "I'll be working out in the barn." He gave Hannah a smile and then disappeared through the mudroom and out the back door.

"He seems very nice," Carolyn said.

"*Danki*." Hannah gestured toward the table. "Would you like a cup of tea and a piece of cheesecake?"

"That sounds wonderful. You always made the best cheesecake."

Hannah poured two cups of tea and then handed Carolyn a cup. "Did you want to sit here?" She motioned toward the table and hoped her friend would agree to sit with her.

"Well…" Carolyn looked at the table and then crossed to a window. "Do you have chairs on your porch?"

Hannah nodded.

"If we sit on the porch together, then we aren't technically eating at the table together, right?" Carolyn asked with a wink.

"I understand." Tension slipped from Hannah's shoulders as she took a serving tray from a cabinet and loaded it up with the teacups, sweetener, and two pieces of cheesecake.

They moved out to the porch, where they sipped the tea and enjoyed the cheesecake.

"It's lovely out here." Carolyn looked out over the large backyard. "I can see why you fell in love with this place."

"*Danki.*" Hannah cradled her teacup in her hands. "Trey likes to go out into the barn and tinker with woodworking. I think he's making a trinket box to give Amanda for Christmas."

"How nice." Carolyn took another sip of her tea and then turned toward Hannah. "I have some news."

"Oh?" Hannah placed her cup on the small table beside her. "What is it?"

"I'm getting married."

"Carolyn!" Hannah clapped her hands together. "That's wonderful news! Who is your fiancé?"

"You know him very well." Carolyn paused. "It's Joshua Glick."

Hannah gaped at her friend.

"That's fantastic!" she finally said. Hannah couldn't stop a smile. She'd prayed that Joshua would find his true love. She'd felt guilty for breaking his heart, but she knew it wasn't in God's plan for her to marry him.

"*Danki.* Joshua is a wonderful man, and he's been *gut* to my son. He wants to adopt Benjamin, and that means a lot to Ben and me."

Carolyn's smile faded, and a look of concern took its place. "I want you to come to the wedding. Please tell me that you will."

Hannah hesitated. "Did you talk to Josh about this?"

"Oh *ya*." Carolyn nodded. "We talked about it last night, and he agrees that you should come."

"I don't know." Hannah felt stuck. She wanted to see her friend and Joshua get married, but she also knew if she went to the wedding, she'd be in an awkward situation because she was shunned. "Would it be all right if I thought about it?"

"Of course." Carolyn's expression brightened. "You think about it and discuss it with Trey. Of course, Amanda and Andrew are also invited. I'm certain Lily will be there too." She reached over and touched Hannah's hand. "I know you've had a difficult time with Lillian. Josh has told me. We're praying Lillian will forgive you soon."

Hannah studied her teacup as she rubbed her abdomen again. "*Danki*. I pray that every day."

"How are Amanda and Andrew? I bet the *kinner* are getting big, *ya*?" Carolyn asked as she forked the cheesecake.

"They are, and they're doing well," Hannah said. "Amanda is taking college biology classes, and she worries about her grades all the time. She's doing great, though. Andrew is enjoying fifth grade. He has new friends, and he loves the school bus."

"This cake is *appeditlich*." Carolyn wiped her mouth with a paper napkin.

"*Danki*." Hannah sipped the tea. "How's Benjamin?"

"He's doing *gut*. He works on Joshua's farm, and he loves it."

Hannah took a bite of the cheesecake. "How are your parents doing?"

Carolyn talked about her family, and then Hannah asked her how work was going at the hotel. They discussed their friends and acquaintances in the community, paying no attention to the time.

Soon Trey emerged from his workshop and approached the porch. "I'm heading to the hardware store for stain and a few other things. Would you like me to pick up something for lunch?"

"Lunch?" Hannah asked with surprise.

He tapped his wristwatch. "It's almost noon."

"Is it?" Hannah stood. "I didn't realize that. Amanda will be home soon."

Trey pointed toward his car in the driveway. "Do you want me to pick up something from town?"

"No, thank you. We'll make some sandwiches." She turned to Carolyn. "Does that sound *gut* to you?"

"Oh no." Carolyn shook her head. "I don't want to be any trouble. I'll call my driver and have him come to get me. I just need to use your phone."

"Don't be *gegisch*." Hannah waved off the comment. "I insist you stay for lunch, and then we'll take you home later."

Trey headed to his car, and Hannah and Carolyn made sandwiches before returning to the porch with the sandwiches and glasses of iced tea.

"How is business?" Carolyn asked while lifting a chip to her mouth.

"It's *gut*." Hannah nodded. "We've stayed very busy. Right now we have two couples staying until Sunday."

"Are you enjoying it?"

"Oh *ya*." Hannah ate a chip. "I love telling them about

the Amish culture and pointing out the best places for them to visit."

"And Trey?" Carolyn asked. "How are things?"

"Things are wonderful between us." Hannah's hand dropped to her belly again before she could stop it. Carolyn's gaze moved down and then back up to Hannah's eyes.

"Hannah . . . ?" Carolyn's question was barely audible.

Hannah nodded, and her cheeks heated.

"Oh, Hannah." Carolyn's eyes filled with tears.

Hannah wiped tears that had formed in her eyes too. "I didn't think God would bless me or Trey again, but he has. I'm praying Lily will find out and realize things have changed, but we'll always be family."

"*Ya*," Carolyn agreed. "I think that is true."

"How's Josh's farm?" Hannah asked. "He's asked me to stop by, but I haven't gone to see it."

"He's been very busy." Carolyn shared stories about Joshua's horses and customers while they finished their lunch.

They were enjoying Carolyn's homemade pretzels when Amanda's blue Ford sedan steered into the driveway.

"Amanda is home!" Hannah said. "I'm glad you'll get to see her."

"Oh *gut*," Carolyn said.

Amanda and her boyfriend, Mike Smithson, climbed from her car and walked to the house.

"Hi, *Mamm*." Amanda climbed the steps and dropped her backpack onto the porch. "Hi, Carolyn.

It's great to see you. This is my boyfriend, Mike."
She gestured between them. "Mike, this is my friend
Carolyn Lapp."

"It's nice to meet you." Carolyn stood and shook his
hand. "Would you both like a pretzel? I made them this
morning."

"Oh, I'd love one." Amanda took one and passed it
to Mike. "These are the best."

"Thanks." The young man smiled as he took a bite.
"Oh wow. These are amazing."

"Told you." Amanda grinned and then sat down
next to Hannah.

"How was your day?" Hannah asked.

"Oh, it was good." Amanda gestured toward Mike.
"Mike is going to help me study for my test tomorrow.
We were wondering if we could use the kitchen table
for a while."

"Of course you can. Carolyn came over to tell me
some news." Hannah smiled at Carolyn. "Would you
like to tell Amanda?"

"Oh *ya*." Carolyn wiped her hands on a napkin. "I'm
getting married next month."

"Oh!" Amanda's eyes widened. "That's wonderful
news! I had no idea you were engaged. Who are you
going to marry?"

"You know him very well," Carolyn teased.

"I do?" Amanda pushed her long, thick, blonde braid
behind her shoulder while she contemplated the riddle.
"I'm not certain who that could be. Tell me."

"Your *onkel* Josh." Carolyn's smile was wide.

"*Onkel* Josh?" Amanda gasped. "That's fantastic!"

She turned to Mike. "My *onkel* owns the horse farm where we used to live."

"Oh, right." Mike nodded. "You mentioned that when I walked you home from the deli that one time."

"You need to come by," Carolyn said. "Josh tells me all the time that he wants you all to visit." She turned toward Hannah. "All of you need to visit."

"That would be fun." Amanda pulled the pretzel apart. "I know Andrew would love to see Huckleberry." She looked at Mike. "Huckleberry is Andrew's favorite horse."

"Oh." Mike chewed another piece of pretzel. "I haven't been riding in a long time."

"It would be a blast to show you where I grew up. It's beautiful there. You'd love all the horses."

Amanda shared stories about the farm, and Hannah smiled as happy memories filled her. She'd wanted to visit the farm, but she was afraid the memories might be too emotional for her. Yet now that she was happy with Trey and her new life, the memories of her old life felt more like warm blankets from her past than frozen nightmares. And knowing Joshua was happy with Carolyn made the idea of visiting much easier.

Hannah, Carolyn, Amanda, and Mike visited for about an hour.

"We need to go," Amanda finally said as she tapped Mike's arm. They headed into the kitchen to start studying.

Hannah and Carolyn were still sitting on the front porch when a bright yellow school bus rumbled to a stop in front of the bed-and-breakfast. Hannah and

Carolyn walked to the driveway and met Andrew as he hopped down from the bus.

"Hi," Andrew said.

"How was your day?" Hannah took his backpack from his hands.

"It was great. I had pizza for lunch." He smiled up at Carolyn. "Hi. You're Carolyn, right?"

"That's right. How are you, Andrew?" Carolyn asked.

"I'm fine. Are you staying for supper?" he asked as they walked back to the house.

"No, I need to get home and make supper for my family." Carolyn touched his arm. "But I wanted to see you before I went back home. I've spent the day with your *mamm*."

"Oh. Well, it's good to see you." Andrew held the storm door open for them once they reached the porch.

"Carolyn brought homemade pretzels and muffins too," Hannah said as she walked into the family room.

"Oh wow! Thank you!" Andrew beamed. "They're my favorites."

"You're welcome," Carolyn said. "I'll see you next month."

"Next month?" Andrew tilted his head in question. "What's next month?"

"I'm marrying your *onkel* Joshua next month," Carolyn told him. "Will you come to our wedding?"

"Of course I will! That's cool!"

Carolyn laughed. "I'll see you then."

"Where are the pretzels?"

"In the kitchen," Hannah told him. "You can have a quick snack, and then you need to start your homework."

"*Ya, Mamm.*" Andrew ran out of the room.

"He's such a *gut bu.*" Carolyn crossed her arms over her apron. "I'll have to get used to seeing him in *Englisher* clothes and with a short haircut. Amanda looks different, too, but she's still the same sweet *maedel.*"

"*Ya,* they're still my *gut kinner.*" Hannah sighed. "I guess you need to get going."

"*Ya,* I do. I'll call my driver."

"No, you won't." Hannah shook her head. "Amanda can take you home."

"Are you sure it's not any trouble?" Carolyn asked.

"Don't be silly. Amanda loves to drive. She picks up Mike and takes him to their classes most days." Hannah started for the kitchen. "I'll get her for you."

Hannah poked her head into the kitchen and asked Amanda to take Carolyn home. After Amanda agreed, she retrieved Carolyn's basket from the counter and then returned to the family room, where Carolyn was gazing at the family photos lined up on the mantel.

Hannah sidled up to Carolyn and handed her the basket. "She said she'll be ready in a minute."

"*Danki.*" Carolyn pointed to the family portraits. "I like these photos."

"They're Trey's family." Hannah pointed out Trey's parents and also his daughter, who had passed away from carbon monoxide poisoning four years earlier.

"Are you ready?" Amanda walked into the family room, her car keys jingling in her hand. Mike stood beside her with his backpack over his shoulder.

"*Ya*, I am." Carolyn smiled at Hannah. "*Danki* for having me over."

"I'm glad you came." Hannah hugged her friend. "Please come visit me again soon."

"I will, and you need to come to the wedding." Carolyn touched Hannah's arm. "Please consider it. Joshua and I want you and your *kinner* there. You're part of our family."

"*Danki*," Hannah said, her voice thick with emotion. "I appreciate that."

Carolyn started for the door. "I'll see you soon."

"I'm going to drop Mike off at work after I take Carolyn home," Amanda said. "I'll be back soon."

Hannah waved good-bye as they all walked out the door. The need to pray gripped her: *Please, God, let my Lily spend the day at the bed-and-breakfast with me just as Carolyn did. I need Lily back in my life, Lord. Thank you. Amen.*

. . .

Hannah sat in the sitting area of her apartment while reading her Bible later that evening. Although her eyes were scanning the book of John, her mind was still stuck on her visit with Carolyn. She was thrilled that Carolyn and Joshua were going to be married, but she wasn't certain if she should go to the wedding. Would it cause more heartache if she went and had an unpleasant discussion with Lillian in front of the whole community? The question churned through her mind while she tried to study the Word.

The door creaked open, and she looked up as Trey entered the room.

"Hi." Trey sat down on the chair across the room from her. "How are you?"

"Fine." She closed the Bible and rested it on her lap. "Andrew is asleep and Amanda is studying for her exam."

"Good." Trey leaned back in the chair. "I was talking to the guests on the front porch. They seem to be enjoying their stay. They appreciated your suggestions for sightseeing, and they said they'd recommend our bed-and-breakfast to their friends."

"That's great news." Hannah knew her voice didn't match the sentiment in her words.

"Is something on your mind, Hannah?" Trey's eyes were full of concern. "You look upset about something."

"I'm not upset." Hannah shook her head. "I'm just confused."

"How do you mean?"

"Carolyn is getting married next month, and she wants us all to come to the wedding."

"That's wonderful." Trey's expression brightened. "We'll go."

"It's not that simple." Hannah sighed. "Carolyn is marrying Josh."

"Oh." Trey nodded slowly.

"I'm very happy for Josh, but I don't know if I belong at his wedding."

"Are you allowed to go even if you're excommunicated?" Trey asked.

"*Ya*, I'm permitted to go, but it may be awkward and painful for my family."

Trey's expression softened. "You mean it may be awkward for you to see Barbie and Lillian." He filled in the blanks.

"*Ya*." She nodded. "You know me well."

"How would an excommunicated church member be treated at a wedding?"

"I would simply have to sit with the *Englishers* and eat with the *Englishers*. So I could still attend, but it would just be . . . awkward." Hannah ran her fingers over the worn cover of her Bible. "I don't want to cause any more heartache for Lily than I already have."

"But you have a right to be there." Trey crossed the room and sat beside her. "You want to go. I can see it in your eyes. But you don't have to decide tonight. Why don't you pray about it and then make your decision? Talk to Amanda too. I'm happy to go with you and stand by your side. You won't be alone."

"Okay." She smiled up at him. "Thank you."

"You're welcome." He hugged her. "Now let's get some sleep." He patted her belly. "You both had a long day."

She laughed. "*Ya*, we sure did." She looked down and wondered what God had in store for the little person growing inside of her.

SIX

Madeleine leaned against the porch railing while balancing her iPhone between her shoulder and her ear. She listened to the ringing until her mother finally picked up.

"Hello?"

"Hey, Mom. How are you?"

"Maddie! How are *you*?"

"Fine, fine." Madeleine gazed toward the Beiler farm and breathed in the crisp air. "I'm enjoying this gorgeous day. You and Jack need to come out and see me. You can leave sunny California and experience some real fall weather for the first time in a long time."

"Oh, I know." Mom sighed. "I want to visit, but we're both very busy with work."

Madeleine rolled her eyes. She loved her mother, but she had every excuse not to come back to Pennsylvania. "I promise you can stay in a hotel so you'll have electricity."

"You still haven't had it installed in the house?" Her mother's voice was full of surprise. "I thought you would've had electricity put in by now."

"I'm not sure if I want electricity. I sort of enjoy the quiet. I had enough noise when I was working at the hospital." She noticed the little girl on the Beiler farm stepping onto her own porch. The girl waved, and Madeleine returned the gesture. "I wish you could see this adorable girl who lives next door. She and her dad live on the farm that your parents used to own. You know, the property behind *Mammi's* house."

"Oh yes. I remember seeing them at the funeral. Maybe at my dad's funeral too. They seemed nice." Mom paused for a moment. "From what I remember, the father is very reserved and quiet. He's like most of the Amish men I remember from my childhood. But the little girl is outgoing. I think she talked my ear off at the funeral."

"She always waves to me now," Madeleine said. "I should go meet them, but I always seem to have something to do. And I don't want to be an intrusive *Englisher*."

"How is the hotel working out? Are you still working there part time?"

"It's fine, thanks." Madeleine lowered herself onto the top porch step. "I'm working there three days a week. The other housekeepers are Amish, and I'm enjoying getting to know them."

"Really?" Mom sounded intrigued. "I didn't realize Amish women would work at a nice hotel like that."

"I find it interesting too. They all seem to have a unique story. I'm going to my friend Carolyn's Amish wedding next month."

"Wow. That's nice that they accept you."

"Yeah, I was wondering what would be an appropriate gift. You'll have to coach me on that."

"Oh, I don't know if I can remember what an acceptable wedding gift would be," Mom said. "You might want to ask one of your other friends. It's been a long time since I went to anything like that."

"I'll talk to Ruth—"

Madeleine thought she heard a scream, and she stood up. The shriek sounded again, and she looked over toward the Beiler farm, where the little girl sat on the ground. It looked like she was shaking, probably crying. "Mom, I have to go! Someone is hurt. I'll call you later."

"Maddie?" her mom asked just before Madeleine disconnected the call.

Madeleine took off running toward the farm, shoving her phone in her pocket as she rushed down the rock driveway toward the field where the girl screamed again and was most certainly sobbing now. When she reached her, Madeleine squatted next to her and found her cradling her foot in her hand. The girl looked up in surprise.

"Hey, sweetie," Madeleine said gently. "Are you okay? What happened?"

"I fell," the girl managed to say between sobs.

"Will you let me help you?"

The girl hiccupped and then nodded while tears continued to sprinkle down her pink cheeks. Her eyes were wide as her lower lip trembled.

"My name is Madeleine, and I'm a nurse," she explained. "Would you let me look at your foot?"

"It's my ankle. I think I broke it." The little girl pointed toward a hole in the ground. "I stepped in that hole on my way to the barn."

"Let me have a look." Madeleine hesitated. "Is it okay if I touch your ankle?"

The little girl nodded. "You're a nurse?"

"That's right." Madeleine gently removed the girl's shoe and sock and examined her small ankle. "I normally find out the names of my patients." She glanced up at the girl's pretty pale blue eyes and smiled. "What's your name?"

"Emma Beiler."

"Well, Emma Beiler, it's nice to meet you." She studied the small red spot on her ankle and then moved the girl's ankle slightly. When she looked up again, she saw Emma had jammed her eyes shut.

"You can open your eyes now. I don't think your ankle is broken. I'd say you have a slight sprain. All you probably need is some ice, but if the pain gets worse, then your daddy should take you to the doctor." Madeleine pointed toward her house. "I have a truck, and I can take you to the hospital if your dad wants you to go."

"Okay." Emma tried to stand up and then winced before sitting down on the ground again. "It hurts too much to stand."

"I can carry you." Madeleine turned and pointed to her back. "Climb on."

Emma studied Madeleine. "You want to give me a piggyback ride?"

"Sure." Madeleine shrugged. "Why not?"

"Okay." Emma carefully climbed onto Madeleine's back, wrapping her arms around Madeleine's neck and peeking over her right shoulder. "This will be fun!"

"Where's your dad?" Madeleine asked as she stood up, carefully grasped Emma's legs around her waist, and started to make her way to the farmhouse.

"In his big shop over there," Emma said near Madeleine's ear. "He makes cabinets. That building over there is where he stains the wood, and the other shop is the showroom. This big shop is where he builds the cabinets. He makes the best cabinets in Paradise."

"Really? Who told you that?"

"Marcus did. He's my *dat's* best friend." Emma loosened one arm and pointed. "His big shop used to be a dairy barn, but now it's where he does most of his work."

"I remember when it was a dairy barn."

"You do?" Emma's voice was full of surprise. "How do you know?"

"I know this property really well."

"How?" Emma asked as Madeleine approached the shop.

"I spent a lot of time on this farm when I was little."

"Does that mean you knew my *mammi*?" Emma asked as she craned her neck to look at Madeleine's face.

"Your *mammi*?" Madeleine stopped in front of the shop door and turned her head to look into Emma's eyes.

"*Ya.*" Emma nodded with emphasis. "Martha Stoltzfus lived in your *haus*. She was *mei mammi*."

"How was she your *mammi*?" Madeleine studied the girl. "I don't understand."

"She lived in the *haus* where you live now. I used to visit her all the time. We cooked, worked in her garden, and sewed together," Emma said as she tightened her hold. "Why are you living in her *haus*? It's not an *Englisher haus*."

"I inherited the house because she was my *mammi* too."

"She was?" Emma asked, her eyes wide.

"That's right. Now let's get your *dat*." Madeleine pushed open the door and stepped into the large woodworking shop.

The smell of wood dust filled her senses. The soft yellow light from lanterns perched around the large former barn illuminated the shop. A fairly tall man with dark brown hair and a matching beard stood at a workbench and sanded a cabinet while a diesel generator hummed. An array of tools cluttered a line of surrounding workbenches. A pile of wood sat beside cabinets in various stages of development that were sitting on the benches in the corner.

"*Dat*!" Emma called.

The man stopped working and turned toward Madeleine and Emma. His eyes rounded and his brow furrowed as he stared at them. He turned off the generator.

"What's going on? Who are you? Why are you holding my *dochder*?"

"This is Madeleine." Emma took one arm from around Madeleine's neck and tapped her shoulder. "I fell outside and she came to help me. She says my ankle isn't broken, but it's sprained."

"I'm Madeleine Miller." Madeleine moved a hand out from under Emma's leg and held it out to him. "I live next door."

"I know where you live." Saul wiped his hands on a shop towel and ignored her hand. Madeleine still waited for him to shake it, but he continued to study her with a scowl on his face. "I'm a nurse," she continued in hopes of softening his accusatory stare. "I heard Emma scream, and I immediately ran over to help her. I examined her ankle, and I think she's going to be just fine. It's painful for her to walk on it, so I carried her in here."

Saul remained silent, and she kept talking to fill the awkward space between them. "I believe it's sprained and not fractured. She should elevate it and use ice. The ice will stop the swelling, and a pain reliever would help too. You could give her Tylenol or Motrin if you have it. I have some pain relievers at my house if you need them. If the pain worsens or the swelling continues, then you may want to take her to the hospital and have X-rays done just to be certain her ankle's not broken. I can always drive you if you need help getting to the hospital."

"Fine."

"Do you have an Ace bandage?" she asked.

"*Ya*," he said. "I believe I do."

"Do you want me to carry her into the house?" Madeleine offered. "I can make up an ice packet and get her settled in a chair or on your sofa so you can keep working."

"No, no. That won't be necessary." Saul took Emma

from Madeleine and held her in his arms. "I will handle things from here."

Madeleine studied his stoic face. Why was he being cold to her? After all, she'd helped his injured daughter. She'd never met someone who was that curt or unwelcoming. How had Emma become sweet and friendly with such a quiet and rude father?

"Okay." Madeleine tried to draw him into a conversation. "I can come and check her ankle tomorrow if you'd like me to. I don't mind. I worked in the trauma unit at a military hospital before I came here."

"That won't be necessary." Saul's expression remained stony.

"Madeleine is Martha Stoltzfus's *grossdochder*," Emma said.

"Oh." Saul started for the door. "Let's get you inside and get some ice on your ankle." He exited, and Madeleine trailed behind him.

Madeleine stepped out into the sunlight and stood by the shop door as Saul carried Emma toward the house.

Emma peeked over his shoulder and waved. "Thank you, Madeleine!"

Madeleine waved. "*Gern gschehne*."

Emma's face brightened. "You speak *Dietsch*?"

Madeleine nodded. "*Ya*, I do."

Emma looked at her father. "Did you hear that, *Dat*? She speaks *Dietsch*!"

Saul grunted in response.

"Bye!" Emma waved to Madeleine again. "I'll see you soon!"

"I hope so." Madeleine waved again.

Saul and Emma disappeared into the house, and Madeleine shook her head. What had happened to Saul to make him such a cold man? His frosty demeanor most likely had something to do with the death of his wife. Her irritation toward him softened slightly. Still, he had no right to be so rude to her when she was only trying to help his daughter.

. . .

Saul stopped just inside the mudroom door and watched Madeleine walk back to her house. His scowl deepened as he studied her tight jeans and snug, long-sleeve shirt. He didn't appreciate that she paraded her inappropriate clothes in front of Emma. She had a lot of nerve marching over to his property and touching his daughter.

"*Dat?*" Emma's voice pulled him from his thoughts. "My ankle is throbbing. Would you please get me the ice? Madeleine said it would stop the swelling and make it feel better."

"*Ya.* I'm sorry." Saul pulled his gaze away from Madeleine and carried Emma into the family room.

He placed her on the sofa and then gathered a bottle of Tylenol, an Ace bandage, and a glass of water. After giving her the painkiller, he wrapped her ankle and then filled a plastic storage bag with ice. She winced when he placed the ice pack on her little ankle. Then he sat in a chair beside her.

"What happened?" he asked.

"I was running to the barn to check on that new litter of kittens, and I stepped in a hole and fell." Emma brushed her hand over her knee.

"Why did that *Englisher* come over? Did you call her?"

"No." Emma shook her head. "I screamed because I was in pain, and she came running."

Saul pushed a stray lock of Emma's hair under her prayer covering. "She just came to check on you?"

"*Ya*," Emma said. "She ran over and asked if she could help me. She told me she was a nurse, and she checked out my ankle. She was very nice. Can you believe she's Martha's *grossdochder*? I wanted to ask her if she's going to change the *haus* at all, but I didn't have a chance. I'll ask her the next time I see her."

"No, you won't. Remember what I told you about staying away from her. You can't go prying into her business, Emma." Saul's tone was gentle but firm. "You need to mind your own business."

"Then I can't go visit her?" Emma frowned. "I want to find out more about her."

"No, that's not a *gut* idea. We need to keep our distance. She's not a member of our community."

"But she's nice." Emma folded her hands as if she were saying a prayer. "I want to be her friend, *Dat*. I think she likes me."

"No." Saul shook his head. "You need to leave her alone."

"Okay." Emma sighed. "I'll stay away."

"*Danki*." He touched her leg. "How's your ankle now?"

"It still hurts."

He grabbed her copy of *Little House on the Prairie* and handed it to her. It was her favorite book. "You stay here and rest. I'll finish what I was doing and then start supper. Sound *gut*?"

"*Ya*." She opened the book and smiled. "*Danki, Dat*."

He nodded and then headed back outside. As he descended the porch steps, he looked toward Madeleine's house. Guilt filled him as he considered how rude he'd been to her. He'd reacted in an impolite manner because he was shocked to see that *Englisher* woman standing in his shop holding his daughter.

Saul walked back to his shop. If the opportunity presented itself, he would offer a proper thank you for her help. It was only the right thing to do.

. . .

Saul cleaned up the kitchen after supper and then helped Emma hobble to her room. After she was settled in bed with a new ice pack, he headed outside to take care of the animals. He was exiting the barn when he saw a light on Madeleine's back porch. She was sitting in a chair and talking on her cell phone. Now was the time to go and apologize to her. He took a deep breath and started up the driveway to her house.

Madeleine looked up as he approached the porch steps, and her eyes widened. With her youthful face, he surmised she was in her midtwenties.

"Hey, Mom," she said into the phone. "I need to go.

I'll call you soon, okay? All right. Tell Jack I said hello. Good night." She disconnected the call and then stood. "Hi. Please come up."

"Is this a bad time?" he asked as he climbed the steps.

"No, no. Not at all." She pushed her dark hair behind her ears. "Is Emma okay?"

"*Ya, ya*." He nodded. "She's fine."

"Oh good." Her smile was tentative. "Did you want to have a seat?" She pointed toward a chair. "Would you like a drink or something?" She gestured toward the door. "I have some iced tea and cookies."

"No, thank you. I can't stay long."

"Oh. Okay." She fingered her phone as if she were self-conscious and didn't know what to do with her hands. "What brings you over here tonight?"

He cleared his throat and tried to remember what he'd wanted to say to her. "I didn't thank you properly earlier. I appreciate that you helped my Emma."

"You're welcome." She waved off the comment as if her help were nothing. "I'm just glad I was outside and heard her crying out."

"*Ya*." Saul fingered his beard. "I didn't hear her over the noises in the shop, and if you hadn't come, she may have been stranded there for a while. So, thank you."

"You're welcome," she said. "Emma is a sweet girl."

"*Ya*, she is." He paused. It was time to apologize, but he wasn't good at expressing his feelings. Annie's abandonment had stolen his ability to express himself. "I had no right to be rude to you earlier. I'm sorry." He held out his hand. "I'm Saul Beiler."

"It's nice to meet you, Saul." She shook his hand. "I'm glad to officially meet my neighbors."

"*Ya.*" He gave her a stiff nod, and because he didn't know what else to say, he thought it was best to just go home. "Good night then." Before she could answer, he turned and started down the steps.

"Saul," she called after him.

He spun and faced her. "*Ya?*"

"Feel free to come and get me if you ever need anything." She pointed toward her red pickup truck sitting in the driveway. "I can always give you a ride somewhere if you have any emergency."

"*Danki.*" Saul quickly started down the driveway toward his house. He felt awkward when meeting new people. Madeleine Miller seemed like a perfectly fine person, but he wasn't comfortable interacting with women, especially *Englishers*. He appreciated her help tonight, but he didn't expect to interact with her again, except for the occasional neighborly wave. They had no business being friends.

As he climbed his porch steps, he looked back toward her house and was surprised to see Madeleine watching him from her own porch. She waved, and he responded with a halfhearted, stiff wave before disappearing into the safety of his house.

. . .

Saul Beiler stalked down the rock drive toward his house, and Madeleine shook her head as she stared after him. That was the strangest introduction she'd

ever experienced. He'd come over to introduce himself,
thank her, apologize to her . . . and then he just hurried away. She'd hoped to draw him into a conversation
and possibly have some refreshments too. She'd always
enjoyed getting to know her neighbors, but Saul didn't
seem to want to get to know her. He just wanted to do
the proper thing and then run away.

Saul seemed like a nice man under that crusty exte-
rior. He looked to be in his early thirties, and she also
noticed that his deep brown eyes were full of sadness.
He must have led a lonely life with Emma, but she knew
the Amish took care of their community members too.

When Saul reached his house, he looked back toward
Madeleine's place, and she waved. He halfheartedly
waved back. Madeleine almost laughed out loud. *When
was the last time he laughed?* she wondered. *He looks
like he could use loosening up.* But she was certain she
would never have the opportunity to get to know him
very well.

Still, questions about the man echoed in her mind as
she stepped back into the house.

SEVEN

Madeleine sat in the back of the large family room in Joshua Glick's house. She couldn't believe how quickly a month had passed since Carolyn asked her to come to her wedding. Bright sunlight streamed through the window beside her on this Thursday morning. She glanced around the room and estimated about two hundred members of the community had gathered to witness the wedding.

It felt strange to Madeleine that she had to ask for a Thursday off from work. Most non-Amish weddings were held on Saturdays. However, Carolyn explained that Amish weddings were always held on Tuesdays and Thursdays in the fall.

The wedding ceremony reminded Madeleine of the church services she had attended as a child. The benches were set up in the same manner, with the men and women seated separately. The women looked lovely in their best Sunday dresses and prayer coverings. Madeleine was struck by the brightly colored dresses the young ladies wore—a rainbow of teals, blues, purples, and pinks. The men were also in their best Sunday suits with suspenders and crisp white shirts.

Madeleine leaned over toward Ruth, who was seated beside her. "Where are Carolyn and Josh?"

"The bride and groom always meet with the minister before the wedding service," Ruth explained. "We'll sing hymns until they join us."

Ruth handed Madeleine a copy of the *Ausbund* just as the congregation began to sing. Madeleine successfully followed along with most of the hymns, and she was pleased she could still remember some of the Pennsylvania Dutch and German her grandmother had taught her.

After the hymns, Carolyn and Joshua joined the congregation and sat with their attendants. Ruth pointed out Carolyn's sister-in-law, Sarah Ann; her brother, Amos; her niece, Rosemary; and her son, Benjamin. Carolyn, with her attendants by her side, sat facing Joshua, Amos, and Benjamin.

Madeleine studied Carolyn's navy blue dress, which matched Sarah Ann's and Rosemary's. They were the typical Amish dresses Madeleine had seen women wear around the community, and they were nothing like the dresses she had seen in *Englisher* weddings she'd attended when her friends were married.

She leaned over to Ruth again and whispered, "Their dresses are beautiful. I love how simple and elegant they are."

"They made them themselves," Ruth said softly. "Carolyn did the majority of the work with her mother's help, but Rosemary and Sarah Ann helped her finish them up last week. Aren't they lovely?"

"They are." Would her mother's wedding have been

like this if she had stayed in the community? Of course, it was a silly thought. If her mother had remained Amish, then Madeleine wouldn't have been born.

The men in the wedding party wore their traditional Sunday black-and-white clothing. Madeleine studied Benjamin, struck by how his blond hair and cocoa-colored eyes matched Carolyn's. He was truly a handsome young man.

Madeleine sniffed and wiped her eyes as the bride and groom recited their vows, standing before members of their community. She was struck by how no one was taking photographs, but she reminded herself that the Amish didn't allow photographs because they were considered graven images.

Weddings always made her cry, even the *English* weddings she'd attended. She couldn't help but wonder what her wedding would've been like if she and Travis had gotten married. She tried to ignore the sad thought, but it lingered in her mind.

Ruth leaned closer to Madeleine and pointed. "We're going to sing another hymn, and then the minister sitting over there will talk. He'll give a sermon based on the Old Testament stories of marriages."

Madeleine nodded. She did her best to follow along with the hymn but lost her place a few times. Whenever she became confused, she'd glance over at Ruth, who'd point to where they were in the hymn.

Once the hymn was over, the minister began talking. Madeleine occasionally understood German words here and there during the sermon, but she wasn't really listening anyway. She was consumed with thoughts of Travis and her military career. She'd served nearly four years as a flight nurse and then spent the rest of her career working at a medical center on her home air force base in California, where she'd met Travis. They'd quickly fallen in love, and they were engaged after only a year.

"It's time to kneel for the prayer," Ruth whispered into Madeleine's ear, pulling her back from her memories.

Madeleine followed the rest of the congregation, kneeling for silent prayer and then rising for the minister's reading of Matthew 19:1–12.

"That's our bishop," Ruth explained as an elderly man with a long white beard stood. "His name is Elmer Smucker. He'll preach the main sermon now."

The older man began to speak, and Madeleine tried to concentrate on his words. "He's talking about the book of Genesis," Ruth explained in a soft voice. "He's discussing the story of Abraham and the other patriarchs included in the book."

"*Danki* for explaining it to me," Madeleine said with a smile.

Ruth grinned. "*Gern gschehne.*"

Madeleine scanned the crowd of young, unmarried ladies during the sermon and spotted Linda from work. A modestly dressed *English* woman with deep red hair sat a few rows behind her. She was sitting with people Madeleine thought must be her husband and children.

Madeleine touched Ruth's arm and leaned toward her. "Ruth, is that Hannah?" She nodded toward the woman.

"*Ya*," Ruth said. "And that's her husband, Trey, and her children Amanda and Andrew. I'll introduce you after the service."

Hannah's expression was sad. How did Hannah feel to be back at an Amish service but not a part of the congregation? Was that how her mother felt when she attended *Mammi's* funeral? Hannah met Madeleine's gaze and raised her hand as a greeting. Madeleine nodded in reply.

She looked back toward the soon-to-be newlyweds. Carolyn was radiant in her blue linen dress with her white *kapp*. She beamed at her groom, Josh, whose eyes shone with love for her.

I wonder if I'll ever find such a powerful, all-consuming love again in my lifetime. Does God have a soul mate in mind for me, or did my opportunity to find love die with Travis in that emergency room?

The thought caught Madeleine off guard. She'd resigned herself to enjoying life in Pennsylvania alone, but she hoped God still had a plan for her. She wanted a husband and a family.

She watched the bride and groom as they studied the bishop. She leaned over to Ruth once again. "What is he saying now?"

"He's telling them about the apostle Paul's instructions for marriage included in 1 Corinthians and Ephesians," Ruth whispered. "Now he's instructing Carolyn and Josh on how to run a godly household. Next he'll move on to a forty-five-minute sermon on the story of Sara and Tobias from the intertestamental book of Tobit."

When the sermon was over, the bishop looked at Carolyn and Joshua. "Now here are two in one faith. Carolyn Rose Lapp and Joshua Eli Glick." The bishop then asked the congregation if they knew any scriptural reason for the couple not to be married. Hearing no response, he continued. "If it is your desire to be married, you may in the name of the Lord come forth."

Madeleine was thankful she could understand the bishop and follow along. Next Joshua took Carolyn's hand in his, and they stood before the bishop.

Madeleine sniffed and wiped her eyes again as the bride and groom recited their vows. The bishop read "A Prayer for Those about to Be Married" from an Amish prayer book called the *Christenpflicht*. When the second sermon was over, the congregation knelt while the bishop again read from the *Christenpflicht*. After he recited the Lord's Prayer, the congregation stood, and the three-hour service ended with another hymn.

Once the ceremony was over, the men began rearranging furniture while the women set out to serve the wedding dinner.

"I'll introduce you to Hannah before going to help." Ruth took Madeleine's arm and led her to where Hannah stood with her family.

Hannah's face brightened as they approached. "Ruth, hi. It's so *gut* to see you."

"It's wonderful to see you," Ruth said. "I'd like you to meet my friend Madeleine Miller. She works with me at the hotel. Madeleine, this is Hannah Peterson."

"Hi, Hannah." Madeleine shook Hannah's hand. "We're neighbors, actually. I live a few streets away from your bed-and-breakfast. I inherited my grand-parents' house and moved into it back in February."

"How nice." Hannah touched the arm of the man next to her. "This is my husband, Trey. And this is my daughter Amanda and my son, Andrew."

"It's nice to meet you all," Madeleine said as they smiled at her. "I like to run a few mornings a week, and I jog past your bed-and-breakfast a lot. I've thought about stopping in to say hello."

"Oh, you should," Hannah insisted.

"Thank you. I would really like that." Madeleine excused herself before turning back to Ruth.

Women began bringing trays of drinks and food out of the kitchen.

"Should I help with setting out the dinner?" Madeleine asked Ruth.

"No, no." Ruth shook her head. "You're a guest." She pointed toward a corner. "You can sit with the other *Englishers*. I'll join you if you'd like."

"Oh no." Madeleine touched Ruth's arm. "You go and enjoy your family. Thank you for explaining the service to me."

"Did you understand any of it?" Ruth asked.

"I actually did. My *Dietsch* is coming back to me."

"That's *wunderbaar*." Ruth smiled.

Madeleine smoothed her hands over her long blue skirt and hoped her plain blue blouse and skirt were modest enough for the wedding. She wanted to blend in and not offend any members of Carolyn's com-munity. She touched her bun, making sure her thick hair had stayed in place. She'd used nearly half a can of hairspray on it that morning. She also had forgone any makeup, which seemed freeing. She used to worry about choosing the right colors of lipstick and eye shadow, but lately she felt most comfortable without any makeup at all.

"Madeleine!" Emma appeared beside her and grinned. "It's *gut* to see you!"

"It's nice to see you too, Emma." Madeleine touched her arm. "How are you? How's your ankle?"

"It's great!" She danced around. "See? It doesn't hurt at all. The ice and bandage really helped."

"Oh, that's great news." Madeleine touched Ruth's arm as well. "Do you know Ruth? She's my friend from work."

"*Ya*, I know Ruth." Emma smiled up at her.

"It's great to see you, Emma." Ruth nodded at her.

"How do you know Carolyn and Josh?" Emma asked.

"I work with Carolyn and Ruth at the hotel," Madeleine said.

"Oh." Emma nodded slowly. "You need to come by the farm. One of our barn cats had another litter of kittens, and they are cute. I've been naming them. You can name one too. You can keep a couple of them if you want to. Do you like cats?"

"I do," Madeleine said. "I have cats living in the small barn on my property. In fact, I think there may be a new litter there too. You'll have to come and visit them someday."

"Oh *ya*. I'd love to see your kittens too." Emma glanced across the room. "There's my best friend, Esther. I better go. See you soon."

"How do you know Emma?" Ruth asked as Emma ran off.

"My property backs up to her father's," Madeleine explained. "Actually, my grandparents owned all of her father's property and sold it to him years ago."

"Oh *ya*. I had forgotten that."

Madeleine watched Emma meet up with another girl and walk over to her father.

Ruth's gaze moved across the room. "I see my son and his family over there. Would you like to meet them?"

"Oh, sure." Madeleine smiled. "I'd love to."

"Wonderful." Ruth led Madeleine across the room. "I can't wait for you to meet my family."

. . .

Saul was talking with Marcus when he saw Emma and Esther rushing toward them.

"*Dat!*" Emma began, out of breath from running. "You'll never guess who's here!"

"Who?" Saul glanced at Marcus, who shrugged.

"Madeleine! She's here," Emma said.

"That's nice," Saul said.

"She asked how my ankle is, and she told me she was happy to see me," Emma continued. "I told her about the barn cats, and she said she has barn cats too. She wants me to come over and see her new kittens."

"Now, Emma," Saul began. "What did I tell you about leaving Madeleine alone?"

Emma frowned. "I know, *Dat*."

"What did I say?" he asked again.

"I shouldn't bother her," Emma said, her voice lacking its previous enthusiasm.

"That's right," Saul said.

Emma turned to Esther. "Let's go help them serve the food."

"Okay!" Esther agreed.

The two girls headed to the kitchen.

Marcus sidled up to Saul. "Who's Madeleine?"

"She's the *Englisher* who lives in the *haus* in front of my property." He nodded toward where Madeleine was standing. "She's over there by Ruth Ebersol and her family."

Marcus looked toward the Ebersol family as Saul studied Madeleine. She looked different today. In fact, he almost didn't recognize her. Her dark hair was styled in a tight bun, and she was wearing a plain dark blue blouse and skirt. He was relieved to see her in appropriate clothing. At least she wouldn't give Emma the wrong idea about how a woman should dress.

"I take it that you finally got to meet her then?" Marcus asked.

"*Ya.*" Saul crossed his arms over his chest. "A few weeks ago, Emma fell and Madeleine came over to help her. I was in the shop and didn't hear Emma crying out."

"You never told me this." Marcus's eyes were wide with concern. "Was Emma hurt?"

"She sprained her ankle, but it healed up just fine. Madeleine told me how to care for it. She's a nurse."

"Oh. That's *gut* that Madeleine heard her."

"*Ya*, it was." Saul considered Emma's interest in Madeleine. "But I don't want Emma getting too friendly with this *Englisher*. I don't want her to influence Emma into thinking that it's a *gut* idea to leave the community."

"How would Madeleine do that?" Marcus looked incredulous. "She's just your neighbor."

"Right, but apparently Madeleine is Martha Stoltzfus's *grossdochder*. Martha's *dochder* left the community, and now Madeleine has come back. If Emma gets to know her better, she may influence Emma to leave."

"Just like your *bruder* did." Marcus finished his thought.

Saul sighed. "Exactly."

Marcus leaned over and lowered his voice. "Why don't you just say what you're really thinking? You're afraid she'll leave like Annie did."

Saul gave him a stiff nod. He couldn't admit the words out loud.

"Saul, you can't live in fear of that," Marcus said. "Emma is going to make her own decisions. You just keep doing what you're doing—being a *gut dat* to her. She'll make the right decisions. God has the perfect plan for her."

Saul prayed his best friend was right, but he couldn't stop that nagging fear at the back of his mind.

"Hi, Saul."

Saul turned and found Madeleine standing beside him. "Madeleine," he said with surprise. "Hi."

She stuck her hand out to Marcus. "Hi. I'm Madeleine Miller. I live next to Saul's farm."

"Nice to meet you." Marcus shook her hand. "I'm Marcus Smucker."

"Smucker." Madeleine tilted her head with surprise. "Are you related to the bishop?"

"*Ya*, I am, actually." Marcus nodded. "He's my *daadi*. I mean grandfather."

"I know what *daadi* means," Madeleine said with a smile. "My grandparents were Amish. They were Martha and Melvin Stoltzfus."

"You're living at your grandparents' house?" Marcus asked.

"That's right." Madeleine nodded. "I inherited it."

"I've seen you at Martha's *haus*. It's nice to finally meet you." Marcus turned toward Saul. "I'm going to go find my *fraa*. I'll see you both later." He nodded and then headed toward the other side of the room.

Saul wished his friend had stayed by his side. He had no idea what to say to Madeleine Miller.

"It's good to see you again, Saul," Madeleine began. "I spoke with Emma earlier. She said her ankle has healed nicely."

"*Ya*, she's all better now. *Danki* again for your help." He fingered his suspenders and tried to think of something else to say. "I didn't expect to see you at the wedding. I noticed you were talking to Ruth Ebersol. Do you know her and her family well?"

"I work with her at the Lancaster Grand Hotel." She glanced toward where Carolyn and Joshua were sitting and eating their wedding supper. "Carolyn also works with us."

"That's right," Saul said. "I remember Carolyn worked at the hotel."

Madeleine smiled at him, and her eyes were the color of his morning coffee. "Well, it was nice to see you again, Saul."

"*Ya*, it was nice to see you too," he said, repeating the sentiment.

"Take care." She gave him a little wave and then headed toward a corner where other *Englisher* guests were talking.

Saul studied Madeleine as she approached another guest and began to talk to her. He was surprised she had taken a moment to speak to him. That was friendly of her, but at the same time, he didn't like the idea of Emma getting to know Madeleine. She was much too worldly for his liking, and he needed to shield his precious daughter from the *Englisher* world. After all, Emma was the only family he had left.

EIGHT

Hannah stepped out onto the porch and breathed in the brisk October air. It was surreal to be back at the farm where she'd lived with her first husband, Gideon. This was the same home where Gideon had brought her after their wedding and where she'd had her three children. It was also on this property that Gideon had succumbed to his massive heart attack nearly seven years ago.

Although she'd enjoyed seeing Carolyn and Joshua's wedding, she'd felt a bit claustrophobic surrounded by the members of her former community. No one said anything outright about her excommunication, but the sad expressions people tossed her way, even those who were kind enough to speak to her, were overwhelming. She felt like an outcast in the home that had belonged to her not very long ago.

She descended the porch steps and gazed off toward the barns where Joshua's horses and animals were housed. Her husband's shiny European car seemed out of place inside the sea of buggies clogging the field beside the pasture. It almost seemed like an analogy for her life—she was a lone anachronism when she visited her former community.

"Hannah?"

She glanced up toward the porch to where her former mother-in-law, Barbie Glick, was staring down at her. Her stomach tightened at the sight of the older woman, who had criticized her both while she was married to Gideon and when she decided to leave the community to marry Trey.

"Barbie." Hannah worked to keep her voice even despite her anxiety. "Hello. It was a lovely wedding, wasn't it?"

"*Ya*, it was." Barbie's blue eyes bored into her. "What are you doing here?"

"I was invited." Hannah crossed her arms over her dark blue dress. "Carolyn invited me, Trey, and my children."

Barbie studied her. "Well, I'm glad that your *kinner* came. I like to see my *grosskinner* as often as I can, you know."

"And you also know that you're welcome to see them anytime. I've never kept them from you." Hannah stood her ground, despite her frayed nerves. "All you have to do is call me, and Trey or I will bring them to your house. Amanda drives now, and she can come over on her own as well."

"Fine, then." Barbie nodded and then disappeared into the house.

Hannah blew out a deep sigh when the woman was out of sight. She'd hoped to speak with Lillian, and she'd spotted her across the room a few times after the service. She'd tried to approach her, but each time she started to cross the room, another kind member of the community stopped Hannah to speak with her.

A group of young people was gathered by the horse barn. Amanda smiled and laughed while surrounded by her former school friends. Although Amanda and her boyfriend, Mike, weren't dressed in traditional Amish clothing, she seemed comfortable with her friends. Hannah searched the sea of young faces for Lily's.

"Hannah?" Trey approached her. "I was wondering where you went."

"I'm sorry I left abruptly, but I needed some air." She hugged her coat to her body. "I knew coming here would be difficult, but I didn't imagine just how difficult it would be."

"I'm sorry." Trey rubbed her shoulder. "I'd hoped it would go better. Do you want to leave?"

Hannah sighed. "I don't know. It seems like Andrew and Amanda are having a good time. I hate to pull them away from their friends."

"Mike brought his car, remember?" Trey asked gently. "You can tell them we're leaving and ask Mike to take Amanda and Andrew home. I'm certain it won't be a problem." He continued rubbing her shoulder. "I don't want you to feel like you need to stay here if you're not comfortable. You came and you congratulated Josh and Carolyn. We can go now, okay?"

Hannah hesitated and stared toward the group. *Is Lily over there? If so, will she talk to me? Will today be the day she finally forgives me?* At these thoughts, her hand moved to her abdomen, which had begun to protrude more in the last few weeks.

"You wanted to talk to Lily." Trey said her thoughts aloud. "You were hoping she would want to talk today, right?"

Hannah nodded.

Trey's gaze moved toward the group of young people. "Do you want me to see if she's there?"

"No." Hannah shook her head. "I can't ask you to get involved in this."

"Maybe it's time I get involved," he suggested.

"I think that might make it worse. She might accuse me of trying to bully her into talking with me." Hannah turned back toward the young people, and her eyes quickly found Amanda and Lillian talking off to the side. Lillian was talking while Amanda nodded. Beside them, Mike chatted with Leroy King, the boy Lillian liked.

"I don't know how much longer I can watch you suffer," Trey said. He stopped rubbing her shoulder and turned her toward him. "I worry about you and how it could affect our unborn child."

"I'll be fine." Hannah forced a smile as she looked up at him. "I promise you it will all be fine." She laced her fingers with his. "Let's go home."

"Did you say good-bye to the bride and groom?" he asked.

"I congratulated them earlier." Hannah nodded. "It's all right if we leave."

"Sounds good." Trey led her toward his car, which was parked near the younger people. They stopped close to where Amanda, Lillian, Mike, and Leroy were talking.

"Hi, *Mamm*." Amanda smiled over at them while Lillian's smile faded.

Hannah studied Lillian, who looked down at her shoes.

"We're going to head home," Trey said. "Mike, would you please bring Amanda and Andrew home?"

"Absolutely," Mike said.

Hannah continued to stare at Lillian, who moved her eyes from her shoes to a nearby leaf.

"Do you know where Andrew is?" Trey asked Amanda.

"*Ya*." Amanda pointed toward the house. "He was with *Daadi* when I last saw him. I'll let him know you left, and I'll keep an eye out for him."

"Thank you," Trey said. "You all have fun, and we'll see you later."

"Lily," Hannah said while watching her daughter's eyes continue to look at anything but her. "Lily, please look at me."

Lillian scowled as she met her gaze. "What?"

"I'd like to speak to you in private before I leave." Hannah held her breath. *Please answer me, Lily. Talk to me!*

Lillian looked at Amanda, who gave her an encouraging expression.

"Fine." Lillian turned to Leroy. "I'll be right back."

Leroy nodded. "Take your time. I'm not going anywhere."

Hannah and Lillian walked past the car and moved

behind the large barn that housed most of the horses. "How have you been?" Hannah asked when they stood together.

"I'm fine." Lillian pushed her glasses farther up on her nose and lifted her chin in defiance. "I'm a *gut* teacher, and the school board is very satisfied with my work with the scholars."

"I knew you would be a great teacher." Hannah smiled. "I'm so proud of you."

Lillian continued to scowl.

"I see you're still friends with Leroy King." Hannah attempted to pull Lillian into a conversation.

Lillian shrugged. "We're getting to know each other."

"It looks like Leroy and Mike get along. That's nice, *ya*? The four of you can do things together. Maybe you can all have a buddy day."

"Why are you here?" Lillian narrowed her eyes. "You know you don't belong here anymore."

Hannah winced at her daughter's cruel words. "That's not true. Carolyn asked me to come and bring Trey and your siblings. I have every right to be here. You know that. People who leave the community come back for special celebrations."

"I don't understand why you would want to come back." Lillian spat out the words as if they tasted bad. "Everyone probably feels sorry for you and wonders why you left. It's not good for you to be here. It's hard on everyone—especially me."

"It doesn't have to be hard on you, Lily." Hannah reached for Lillian's hand, but Lillian took a step back, out of her reach. "It doesn't have to be this difficult between us. We can repair what's broken, if you help me."

"No." Lillian shook her head. "That's not possible."

"Does that mean you'll never forgive me?" Hannah's voice was thick while she blinked through her tears.

"I don't think I can." Lillian shook her head. "I need to go. Leroy is waiting for me." She started to walk away.

"Lillian! Please wait. Just give me another minute." Although it wasn't customary for Amish women to discuss something this personal, she had to tell Lillian about her pregnancy. Perhaps this little life growing inside her would be the link they needed to repair their broken relationship. "Lillian, I need to tell you something. It's important."

"What?" Lillian faced her.

Hannah rested her hand on her belly. "I'd like for you to get to know your new sibling."

"You're—you're . . . ?" Lillian stuttered as her eyes widened.

Hannah nodded. "*Ya*, it's a miracle. I'm seeing a doctor who specializes in high-risk cases, and everything is fine so far. This is a tremendous blessing from the Lord. Trey and I are thrilled, and Amanda and Andrew are too."

Lillian's eyes glistened with tears. "I need to go." Her voice broke. She rushed away, leaving Hannah staring after her.

Hannah heaved a heavy sigh and then looked up at the clear blue sky. Tears sprinkled down her hot cheeks as she opened up her heart to God and allowed her most fervent prayer to spill out.

Please, God, help me find a way to prove to my daughter that I love her and need her back in my life. Please help Lillian find a way to accept her new sibling and forgive me. Lord, I miss her, and I love her. Please, God, help us.

· · ·

Lillian didn't want to cry in front of her friends, especially Leroy. Things had been going well between them, and she didn't want to scare him away with her family issues. Even though he said he understood how she felt, he could never fathom the pain of her mother leaving the community and abandoning her.

She rushed past her friends, trying her best to avoid their confused stares, and she quickly hurried up the porch steps.

"Lily?" Amanda called after her. "Lillian?"

Lillian headed into the house and up the steps toward her former bedroom, the room she'd shared with her twin until her mother left the community nearly two years ago and she'd moved in with her grandparents. She opened the door and found the room clogged with boxes. A lonely chair sat in the corner by the window. She weaved past the boxes, sank into the chair, and allowed her tears to flow.

"Lily." Amanda appeared in the doorway and closed the door behind her. "What happened?" Her twin pushed a box marked BOOKS over to Lillian and sat on it.

Lillian wiped her eyes. "I'm fine."

her sleeve and her emotions were raw. She wanted to cry, scream, and curl up in a ball like one of the cats that lived in her grandparents' barn.

"It will be okay." Amanda gently squeezed Lillian's arm. "Just open your heart and let God lead you. Give him a chance to heal your heartache."

Lillian began to sob, and Amanda hugged her. Lillian rested her head on her sister's shoulder and prayed that God would help her sort through her confusing and painful emotions.

. . .

Trey glanced over at Hannah as they drove home. He couldn't stand to see her cry. He wanted to fix everything. He wanted to make her happy, as happy as she was on their wedding day. He needed God's help to figure out how to make that happen.

"Do you want to talk about it?" He slowed the car to a stop at a red light.

She shook her head and sniffed.

The light changed to green, and he accelerated through the intersection. He racked his mind for something to say to lighten her mood.

"The service was beautiful." He gave her another sideways glance and found her staring out the window. "It was very different from our ceremony. It was strange to not see any flowers or candles."

She nodded but didn't turn toward him.

"I also found it fascinating that all the women in the

wedding party were dressed the same, even the bride," he added.

"Carolyn made the dresses," Hannah said. "The bride always chooses the color and makes the dresses." Her voice was raw with emotion, but he was happy to hear her speak.

"Really?" he asked with a smile.

"*Ya.*" Hannah swiped her hand over her pink cheeks. "When I married Gideon, my dresses were blue too."

"Were you married at the same house?" he asked.

"No." She shook her head. "We were married at my parents' house, and then we lived with them for about six months before we moved into that house."

"I never knew that." He steered the car through another intersection. "I also found it interesting to not have any music during the service, but I quickly realized you don't need music. The ceremony was still nice without it." He paused and then considered the food. "And the meal was delicious. That was superb chicken with stuffing. And I really enjoyed the mashed potatoes, gravy, pepper cabbage, cooked cream of celery . . ."

"That's the traditional meal." Hannah cleared her throat and turned back toward the window.

They sat in silence as he drove the rest of the way to the bed-and-breakfast. After parking in the driveway, Trey turned and took her hands in his.

"Hannah," he began, "I know you're hurting. It's apparent in your beautiful green eyes, and it's breaking my heart."

She sniffed as fresh tears filled her eyes. "I thought

telling her about the baby would help, but it only made her run away from me. I don't know what else to do, Trey. I've tried everything."

"I know you have. It's time for you to step back and let God work on Lily. Let her come to you."

"What if she doesn't?" Hannah asked, her voice cracking as the tears spilled down her cheeks.

"She will. I know she will." He pulled her into his arms and held her as she cried. The sound of her sobs shattered his heart. He had to do something. He would talk to Lillian. When the moment was right, he'd have a heart-to-heart with her and hopefully make her realize that she needed her mother as much as Hannah needed her.

NINE

Madeleine stood in her bedroom. She held a chip with shades of yellow against the wall and then one with blues. A knock sounded, and she jumped with a start.

With the paint chips still in her hand, she went to the back door and pulled it open.

"Emma." Madeleine smiled at her through the storm door. "What a pleasant surprise."

"Do you like cookies?" Emma held up a plate. "These are chocolate chip. I just made them. Would you like to share them with me?"

"I'd love to. Please come in." Madeleine held the storm door open. "Would you like some milk to go with the cookies?"

"*Ya.*" Emma moved into the kitchen and sat at the table. "That's how I always eat *kichlin,*" Emma announced.

"I agree." Grinning, Madeleine nodded her head, placed the paint chips on the table, and gathered a half gallon of milk and two glasses. "Did you just get home from school?" She poured the milk, returned the carton to the refrigerator, and fetched two small plates from a cabinet.

"I got home a couple of hours ago. I took care of my chores and then made the *kichlin*." Emma pointed toward the paint chips. "What are those?"

"Paint chips." Madeleine placed the glasses and plates on the table and sat down across from Emma. "You use them when you're choosing paint for a room. You decide which shade you like, and then you go back to the store and ask the paint people to mix up the color for you. You have to figure out, of course, how much paint you need." She bit into a cookie and closed her eyes. "These are *appeditlich*, Emma." She opened her eyes and found the little girl staring at her. "What's wrong?"

"You're going to paint *mei mammi's haus*?" Emma frowned. "You shouldn't change her *haus*. That's not right. She wouldn't like that."

Madeleine studied the girl, and her heart warmed. She suddenly lost any interest in painting the walls. "You were close with *mei mammi*, weren't you?"

"I visited her every day. We cooked together and worked in her garden. She taught me how to make a dress." Emma pointed to her green dress. "I made this dress using *Mammi's* instructions."

"You're a great baker and a wonderful seamstress." Madeleine imagined her grandmother standing at the counter teaching Emma how to make cookies and pies, and her eyes filled with tears. She dabbed at her eyes with a finger and took another bite of her cookie.

"Madeleine?" Emma asked. "Are you *bedauerlich*?"

"No, no. I was just thinking of *mei mammi*. She was a special lady." Madeleine smiled and finished the cookie. "You did a wonderful job on these. Did your *dat* help you make them?"

Emma shook her head. "No, he's working in his shop. He's always working. I'm allowed to bake and cook easy things by myself, but he helps me with things that are harder. He lets me make *kichlin* as long as I'm careful." She lifted a cookie and examined it. "I'm always careful."

"I bet you are." Madeleine dunked a second cookie into the milk and then took a bite. Saul was a good father to Emma. She wished her father had been around to do things with her like Saul did with Emma.

"Why weren't you at *Mammi's* funeral?" Emma's words were gentle and not accusatory.

The question was simple, but the words weighed heavily on Madeleine's heart. "I was traveling back from overseas when she passed away, and I missed the service too."

Emma tilted her head. "Where were you?"

"I was in Europe when it was time to come home." Madeleine took another bite of her cookie. "I had to go for work, and I didn't even know *Mammi* was ill. I found out too late."

"Oh." Emma nodded. "Have you traveled a lot?"

"I was in the air force, and I went all around the world."

"You were a nurse in the air force?" Emma asked.

"That's right." Madeleine smiled. "I went to school to become a nurse and then joined the air force."

"Your *mamm* left the church, and that's why you aren't Amish, right?" Emma asked.

"That's true." Madeleine finished her second cookie. They really were good.

"Why did she leave?"

"My *mamm* doesn't talk about it much, but it was because she met my father. He wasn't Amish, and she fell in love with him. She wanted to get married, and so she had to leave the church." Madeleine paused. "My *mamm* was in the military too. That's why I joined after I became a nurse. I wanted to serve my country like my mother did."

"*Mei mamm* died when I was four. I don't remember her very well."

"I'm sorry to hear that," Madeleine said. "I never knew my father."

"You didn't?" Emma's eyes were wide. "Why not?"

"He left before I was born, and I only had my *mamm* growing up. It's difficult when you have only one parent. But at the same time, I felt blessed that I had a mother who loved me. I know your dad loves you. I could tell by the way he was worried about you when you fell."

"*Ya*, he's a *gut dat*. He just works too hard." Emma bit into her second cookie.

"He has to work hard so he can provide for you." Madeleine took a sip of her milk. "My *mamm* had to work a lot, and I was here with my *mammi* and *daadi* in the summers. I did the same things you did with *Mammi*. We sewed, worked in the garden, baked, cooked, and sang. I also went to church with her."

"Just like I did." Emma smiled as she chewed another bite. "That means you were Amish when you were with *Mammi*."

"Right. I even dressed Amish. I had my own dresses and aprons that I kept in the spare room." Madeleine pointed toward her former bedroom. "I left my *English* clothes in my suitcase, and I wore a prayer covering and apron."

"Do you like to cook?"

"Yes, I do." Madeleine pointed toward a cabinet. "I have all of my *mammi's* cookbooks."

"Oh, you do?" Emma's eyes lit up. "We should cook together sometime. Would you like to do that?"

"I'd love it. You let me know when you want to cook. I usually work at a big hotel Tuesdays, Thursdays, and Fridays, but sometimes I go in for extra hours if my coworkers need to have a day off." Madeleine pointed toward the window. "If you see my truck outside, then you know I'm here. You're welcome to come over here anytime, as long as your *dat* says it's okay."

"Great." Emma ate another bite and then tilted her head again. "My *dat* said you might change *Mammi's haus* to make it like an *Englisher haus*." She frowned. "Are you going to change her *haus*?" Emma picked up the paint chips. "Are you really going to paint the rooms? And add electricity and update the heating system?"

Madeleine shook her head. "The coal stove is enough to heat the little house for now."

"You don't mind having to check the stove twice a day?"

Madeleine shrugged. "Well, I did have to get used to cleaning out the ashes and taking them down to the creek. It's a lot of work, and I had to learn how to adjust it right so that it runs all night long. Once I got that straight, I really started to appreciate the coal heat. It's cozy, and it's economical. I don't think I'm going to add electricity, but I was thinking about painting the rooms."

"I hope you don't paint, unless you paint them white again," Emma said. "The walls should be white."

Madeleine studied the girl. This meant a lot to her. Emma had been close to her grandmother, and Madeleine wanted to respect her wishes. *I can't bear the thought of breaking this sweet little girl's heart.* "Okay. I won't paint if that makes you *froh*."

Emma giggled. "It's funny hearing you speak *Dietsch*."

"Why is that funny?" Madeleine asked with a grin. "I've been told my accent isn't too bad."

"No, it's not bad, but you're wearing jeans and a sweatshirt, and your hair isn't covered."

"Does that mean an *Englisher* shouldn't speak *Dietsch*?" Madeleine asked. "I don't think that's fair."

"You're not a regular *Englisher*, though. You wear *English* clothes and drive a truck, but you don't have electricity."

"I guess I am unusual."

"I saw television once." Emma lowered her voice. "*Mei dat* doesn't know. I was at my friend Rachel's *haus*, and we went to visit her *English* cousins. We actually watched a television show. It was funny."

Madeleine felt like the girl's confidante, and she loved it. "Your secret is safe with me, Emma. I won't tell anyone."

"*Danki.*" Emma picked up one more cookie. "Do you miss electricity? I've heard *Englishers* can't live without it."

"I don't really miss electricity too much. I like using lanterns, and I never watched much television. But I do miss my computer a little."

"Oh." Emma sipped her milk. "And you like your phone, too, right?"

"I do." Madeleine nodded. "But you also use a phone, don't you? The only difference is that I can carry mine with me."

"That's true." Emma lifted her glass. "Do you like to toast? My friend Rachel likes to say a toast. She learned it from her *English* cousins."

Madeleine lifted her glass. "What should we toast?"

"New friends." Emma tapped her glass against Madeleine's.

"Yes, to new and special friends." Madeleine laughed. She was thankful for her special new friend, Emma Beiler.

• • •

Saul bowed his head in silent prayer later that evening and then filled his plate with meat loaf and mashed potatoes.

"How was your day?" he asked as he glanced over at Emma.

"It was *gut*." Emma passed the green beans. "I made *kichlin* and took them over to Madeleine's *haus*. We sat and ate them, and we talked about *Mammi*. She would dress Amish and speak *Dietsch* when she stayed with *Mammi*."

Saul studied Emma as he frowned. "You went to see Madeleine?"

Emma nodded. "*Ya*, we had a nice time. She said she was going to paint the rooms, but I talked her out of it."

"Emma, I told you to leave her alone. I know you heard me because you repeated it back to me." How would he ever overcome his daughter's stubborn streak? He opened his mouth to yell at her and then stopped. He didn't want to make her cry tonight. She yearned for a female adult with whom to spend her time, but he preferred her female role model not be an *Englisher*.

Emma's smile evaporated. "I'm sorry, *Dat*. I wanted to bake, and I decided to take some cookies over to Madeleine. She was very *froh*, and we had a very nice visit." She paused for a moment. "We're going to cook and bake together. She has *Mammi's* cookbooks." Emma's face radiated with her excitement. "She served in the air force. She said her *mamm* was in the military too."

Saul gnawed his lower lip, then pointed to the table. "You should stay on this farm, not go spend time with an *Englisher*."

"But you're always working." Emma's eyes suddenly widened as if she realized she'd been disrespectful to him. "I'm sorry, *Dat*. I know you have to work so you can provide for me." She quickly changed the subject to her friends at school and spent the rest of supper telling him about what she learned and all the fun she had on the playground.

After supper Emma took care of cleaning up the dishes, and Saul stepped out onto the back porch. He shivered in the night air while he looked toward Madeleine's place. A single light burned at the back of the house.

It didn't make sense for her to live there. She wouldn't stay.

He knew one thing for certain—he needed to shield his daughter from more heartache. He had to keep Emma away from Madeleine before the *Englisher* put the house on the market and left.

Saul stepped back into the kitchen, where Emma was drying a pot. "Emma, you need to spend your afternoons here at our farm. Do you understand me?"

Emma's pale blue eyes were round as she nodded. "*Ya*, I do, *Dat.*"

"*Danki*," Saul said. "I'm going to work for a little bit. I'll be in my shop." He stepped back outside and looked over at Madeleine's house one last time as he walked. He'd talk to her tomorrow and make it clear that she was to stay away from his daughter.

• • •

Madeleine stepped out onto her porch the morning after Emma's visit. She hefted her tote bag farther up on her shoulder just before she suddenly remembered her lunch was still on the kitchen counter. After rushing back into the house, she grabbed her lunch bag, shoved it into her tote bag, and glanced at the clock. She gasped. She had to hurry or she was going to be late for work.

As she stepped back outside, she saw Emma hurrying by on her way to school. "Hi, Emma!" Madeleine called. "Have a great day at school."

"Hi, Madeleine!" Emma waved and kept rushing past toward her friends, who were waiting at the corner.

Madeleine descended the porch steps and headed for her truck.

"Madeleine."

She turned as Saul approached. "Oh. Good morning, Saul. It's nice to see you." She opened the driver's side door and tossed her tote bag into the truck. "I'm late for work, and I have to run. I hope you have a nice day."

"Wait." He held up his hand. "Do you have just a couple of minutes?"

His brown eyes seemed determined, and she couldn't bring herself to say no to him.

"Sure." She closed the truck door and faced him. "What did you want to talk about?"

Saul heaved a heavy sigh. "Emma told me she visited you yesterday."

"She brought over some cookies she'd made, and we shared the cookies and glasses of milk." Madeleine smiled. "We had a wonderful time. Emma's a very special little girl. You should be proud of her."

"I'm not comfortable with her spending time with you." Saul's words were simple, but they sliced through her like carving knives.

"Excuse me?" she asked.

"I'm not comfortable with her spending time with you," he repeated. "I don't want her to come over and cook with you, either."

"I don't understand." Madeleine studied him. "I thought Amish weren't supposed to judge others. You don't even know me."

"Exactly." He pointed toward the house. "I don't know why you're here or how long you'll decide to stay. I don't want her to be upset if you suddenly sell the house and move away."

Madeleine pointed to the house too. "This was my grandparents' home. I'm not planning on moving anytime soon."

"I know how you *Englishers* are. Your plans can change minute to minute, especially because you were in the military. You have no roots." Saul crossed his arms over his wide chest. "Emma doesn't need to get to know you or find out more about your life. I don't want her visiting here, and you don't need to come and visit her at our *haus*. It's best if we keep our distance. *Englishers* and Amish shouldn't mix anyway. The results are never *gut*."

Her spirit deflated as she stared at her neighbor. "I'm sorry to hear you say that. Emma and I have a lot in common."

"Really?" He shook his head. "I find that difficult to believe."

"It's true. Emma and I both loved my *mammi*."

He gave her a stiff nod. "Martha was a *gut* woman."

"Yes, she was." Madeleine held her head high despite her disappointment. "And that's not all. Emma said she lost her mother when she was four. I never knew my *dat*. I know what it's like to have only one parent. Emma and I could learn a lot from each other."

He paused, and for a quick moment, she thought she saw his expression warm. However, he remained stoic.

"I'm her father, and I don't want her to visit you. Please respect my wishes." Saul turned and started back toward his house.

Madeleine stared after him. How could a man who was so warm to his daughter be so frigid to her? She'd never been so insulted in her life. Disappointment and heartache flooded her as she climbed into her truck, started the engine, gripped the wheel, and drove toward the hotel.

TEN

Madeleine rushed into the break room and stowed her tote bag and lunch before pulling on her apron and name tag.

"Madeleine?" Ruth stepped into the room. "I was beginning to worry about you."

"I've been running late all morning." Madeleine shook her head and checked her hair in the mirror next to the lockers. "It's just been one of those mornings when everything goes wrong. My alarm didn't go off, so I got up late, which is unusual for me. I normally wake up before the alarm." She frowned. "And then I had a run-in with my neighbor."

"You had a run-in with your neighbor?" Ruth crossed the room and stood in front of her. "Do you mean Saul Beiler?"

"Yes, I mean Saul Beiler." Madeleine scowled. "He is the most coldhearted, cruel person I've ever met. I always thought all Amish people were tolerant of *Englishers*, but I guess that's not true in his case." She started for the door. "I'm sure Gregg is upset that I'm not cleaning yet."

"Wait," Ruth said. "You have a minute to talk."

Madeleine stopped and faced her. "What is there to talk about?"

"Sit with me for a minute." Ruth pointed toward the table, and they sat down across from each other. "What happened with Saul?"

"Emma came to visit me yesterday," Madeleine said. "She brought me cookies, and we talked for a while. She's a lovely young lady."

Ruth nodded. "*Ya*, she is."

"Emma asked me if we could cook together, and I told her I have my *mammi's* cookbooks. She loved the idea of our using them together." Madeleine ran her finger over the wood grain on the table as she spoke. "I realized Emma was very close to my *mammi*. We have some other things in common too. I really enjoyed talking to her. She's very mature for her age. I assume that's because she lost her mother when she was young."

"I'm certain that's why," Ruth agreed.

"This morning I was leaving for work, and Saul came over just as I was about to get into my truck. He told me he doesn't want Emma spending any time with me."

Ruth's expression was unreadable.

"He basically said that, because I'm an *Englisher*, I could leave anytime, and he doesn't want Emma to get attached to me and then wind up hurt." Madeleine grimaced. "I haven't done anything to make him think I'd hurt her. I don't understand why an Amish person would be so judgmental to assume things about me that aren't true. I would never deliberately hurt anyone, especially a sweet, innocent little girl."

"It's not you." Ruth frowned.

Madeleine studied Ruth's expression. "You know something."

"I do." Ruth rested her hands on the table. "Saul has been hurt."

"I have too." Madeleine folded her arms over her chest. "But I don't treat people the way he does. He really offended me."

"I don't think you understand," Ruth began. "His wife died, but she didn't die seven years ago."

"What? I'm not sure what you're saying, Ruth. You've lost me."

"Annie didn't die seven years ago," Ruth said. "She left Saul and Emma."

Madeleine gaped at Ruth. "She left him? I didn't think Amish divorced."

"Normally, we don't, but sometimes it happens. We just don't talk about it because it's against our beliefs."

"What happened?" Madeleine asked.

"Annie left Saul and moved to the same former Amish community in Missouri where, from what I heard, her boyfriend had gone several years before. He came back to get her once he had settled and established his life there." Ruth shook her head. "Saul was devastated. Emma was only four years old."

"What a minute." Madeleine held her hand up. "Saul's wife had a boyfriend? How does that work?"

"I believe Annie was in love with this other man before she married Saul, but he left the community."

"Does that mean she married Saul simply because he was willing to marry her?" Madeleine asked.

"That's right." Ruth nodded. "And they had Emma together. But then it all fell apart when her boyfriend came back for her. Annie left Saul, divorced him, and I assume she married this other man."

"Oh no." Madeleine gasped. "That's heartbreaking. Emma thinks her mother died. She has no idea what really happened."

"That's right. And because our community doesn't talk about divorce, Saul has been able to keep the truth from her." Ruth continued to frown. "I heard Saul received a letter last year telling him Annie died in an accident. I assume that's why he started dating again. He was seeing Carolyn for a while, but she married Joshua, as you know."

"Now it all makes sense," Madeleine said. "He doesn't trust me because he thinks I'll leave like Annie did. Like my mother did."

"I can understand his fear, even though I know you would never deliberately hurt Emma."

Madeleine considered this. "I guess he doesn't trust women at all. I don't blame him, but it's sad he feels that way." She paused and thought about Saul and his sweet daughter. "I'll miss Emma, but I can't go against him."

"That's a *gut* plan." Ruth pushed back her chair and stood. "We'd better get to work."

"Thank you, Ruth." Madeleine followed her to the door. "I'm glad I know the truth."

"You're welcome." Ruth touched Madeleine's arm. "Please keep it to yourself. I only know because I'm close friends with Sylvia Smucker's mother. Sylvia is married to Saul's best friend, Marcus. I'm not certain who in the community knows what really happened with Annie. He doesn't talk about her at all, and I don't want word to get back to him."

"I understand. I'll keep it to myself." Madeleine walked to the supply closet. As she filled her cart with fresh towels, she thought about Saul and Emma. She was sorry to hear how hurt Saul had been. She prayed that somehow he would see she'd never hurt him or his daughter.

. . .

Saul guided his horse up the driveway leading to Marcus's farm. He stopped the buggy in front of the wood shop where Marcus created the dining room tables and chairs he sold to local stores. After hopping out of the buggy, Saul crossed the driveway to the shop and wrenched open the door. He found his best friend sanding a long table.

Marcus removed his respirator and smiled. "Saul. *Wie geht's*? What brings you here this morning?"

"I was in the area, and I thought I'd stop by." Saul leaned against the workbench and studied the table. "That is a *schee* table. Your work gets more and more impressive. Pretty soon it will be almost as *gut* as mine," he teased, and Marcus chuckled.

Marcus shook his head. "You're avoiding my question. What brings you over here on a Thursday morning? You never stop by during the week unless you need something or something is wrong."

Saul crossed his arms over his middle. "I can't

concentrate on my work. I think I made a mistake, and I need to talk to someone. I suppose you'll do."

Marcus laughed again and took two bottles of water from the small cooler under his bench. "Here. Take a sip, and then tell me what's bothering you."

"*Danki*." Saul took a long gulp and then wiped his mouth. "I told you Emma likes to talk to my *Englisher* neighbor."

"Madeleine Miller." Marcus nodded. "I remember her from the wedding. She seemed pleasant."

Saul explained how Emma had spent the previous afternoon with Madeleine and wanted to cook with her. He also told Marcus about the conversation he'd had with Madeleine earlier in the day. "I told her I don't want Emma over at her *haus*, and I don't want her to come to see Emma at *mei haus*, either."

Marcus grimaced.

"You think that was too much, huh?" Saul asked. "I crossed a line, didn't I?"

"I don't know." Marcus shook his head. "I can't judge you." He paused. "How do you feel about what you said?"

"I think I may have been too abrupt with her." Saul rubbed his temple as he remembered the hurt expression on Madeleine's face. He could tell his words had completely crushed her. Guilt soaked through him. How could he be that cold and cruel to that young lady? "I'm just very confused. Parenting all alone is just too much for me sometimes. I don't know if I'm *gut* at being a *dat*."

"Of course you are."

"I'm worried about Emma. I want her to make the

right choices and not leave the community like *mei bruder* did." Saul gripped the bottle of water. "But I don't know if I'm holding her too close or pushing her away. How do I find the right balance, where I'm not pushing her away *or* smothering her?"

"You need to trust God to lead her down the right path. You just raise her the best way you can, the best way you know how, and leave the rest to God." Marcus gulped another drink of water. "You worry too much. You're a *gut* parent, just like your parents were. They are the best examples you can follow."

"But *I* need to lead her down the right path. I have to be actively involved in her life, and I have to make sure she makes the right decisions." Saul shook his head. "I have to do more than my parents. They couldn't convince *mei bruder* to stay."

"His decision to leave wasn't their fault." Marcus leaned forward on the table he was building. "Stop being so hard on yourself. It's not your fault Annie left, either. Stop punishing yourself for Annie's and your *bruder's* decisions to leave."

Saul nodded, even though he didn't agree with his friend's words. He had to do all the right things to convince Emma to stay Amish. But what exactly were those right things? He needed to pray more and ask God for the right words to say to Emma. He needed answers. He had to know how to be the best parent he could be—for her.

"How are your projects going this week?" Marcus asked. "Are you still drowning in cabinet orders?"

"I'm finally getting caught up." Saul lifted his hat

and raked his hand through his thick hair. "I still need to find a way to hire an assistant. I need to find a way to stay more organized with all the orders."

"I know what you mean. I'm considering hiring an apprentice. The furniture stores are calling me every day now." Marcus tapped the table. "After this one, I have three more to make before I'm caught up."

"You do fantastic work. I'm sure an apprentice would be happy to learn from you."

"You too," Marcus countered. "You're the best cabinetmaker in the county."

"No, not really." Saul shook his head. "I've seen better."

"Marcus?" Sylvia appeared in the doorway. "Oh, hi, Saul. How are you?"

"I'm well, Sylvia." Saul nodded. "How are you?"

"Fine, fine. I saw your horse and buggy, and I was wondering who was visiting." Sylvia smoothed her hands over her apron. "Would you like to stay for lunch?"

"Oh no." Saul shook his head. "I don't want to impose."

"Don't be *gegisch*, Saul." Sylvia smiled. "We have plenty. Come and join us. We'd love to have you."

Saul glanced at Marcus, who nodded.

"Absolutely. Have lunch with us." Marcus started for the door. "I'm starved."

As Saul followed Marcus and Sylvia to their house, he prayed God would someday bless him with a wife who would be a good mother to Emma and a loyal helpmate to him.

. . .

Madeleine steered her pickup truck into her driveway that afternoon. She'd spent the entire day thinking about Saul and Emma and wondering what she could do to help them. His marriage wasn't any of her business, but she couldn't help thinking of him. She knew what it was like to feel abandoned. And even though she and Travis were never married, after pledging her heart and her future to him and then losing him tragically, failing him, she was afraid she could never love anyone again—or let anyone love her. Was that how Saul felt? Did he also feel unworthy of love?

Madeleine killed the engine and yanked her key from the ignition. She gathered up her tote bag and headed for the back porch. As she climbed the steps, her phone began to ring. She dug it out of her bag and found her mother's number on the screen.

"Hi, Mom," Madeleine said as she held the phone to her ear.

"How was your day?" Mom asked.

"Not that great," Madeleine admitted with a sigh.

"What's wrong? I haven't heard you sound this depressed since you moved to Paradise."

Madeleine shared the story of her visit with Emma, her heartbreaking encounter with Saul, and then her conversation with Ruth.

"I've never been accused of being a bad person, Mom." Madeleine sank onto the porch swing. "You know I always believe the best in people, and I try to consider others' feelings. It hurts to hear someone say I would deliberately break a child's heart. How could he say that about me?"

"Oh, Maddie." Her mother's voice was warm. "I don't think his anger and disappointment were directed at you. From what you've told me, I think he's hurting because of what his wife did to him and their child. He's afraid his daughter will be hurt again. All you can do is respect his wishes and wait for him to come to you. Maybe he'll realize you're the best neighbor he could hope to have."

"You think so?" Madeleine asked as she ran her fingers over the cold armrest. Her mother's encouraging words gave her a glimmer of hope. Maybe she could convince Saul she was a good person.

"Of course I do," Mom insisted. "You have a wonderful heart. People see that as soon as they get to know you. But you worry about what people think of you. Even in kindergarten, you came home in tears when someone didn't like you. You always wanted everyone to be your friend. Don't give up hope. Saul will see what his daughter sees in you, and you'll wind up good friends."

"Before meeting my friends at the hotel, I did think the Amish tried to stay away from *Englishers*. And for the first eight months I was here, I took that to heart and didn't even introduce myself to Saul." Madeleine stared toward Saul's house as she spoke. "Do you think he'll want to be friends with me, even if he changes his mind about me?"

"My mother had plenty of *English* friends. She used to sew for the *English* neighbors. She had her own seamstress business. I think you helped her with her sewing a few summers, didn't you?"

"That's right. I remember neighbors coming in to

see *Mammi* and dropping off their clothes. She taught me how to hem trousers one summer." Madeleine hoped her mother was right. "I don't know why this is bothering me so much. I don't even know him."

"You just want him to know the truth about you—that you're a good person."

Madeleine sighed. "You're absolutely right. Thanks." She stood and unlocked her door. "How's Jack doing?" She stepped inside and started unpacking her tote bag.

"He's fine." Her mother launched into a long discussion of her stepfather's business and how busy they were.

"Well, I should let you go," Madeleine finally said. "Thanks for calling."

"It was good talking to you. Just pray for Saul. Everything will be fine," Mom insisted.

"I will." Madeleine disconnected the call and sent up a prayer for the man she hardly knew.

ELEVEN

Madeleine was flipping through cookbooks the following Monday afternoon when a knock sounded. She went to the back door and found Emma standing on the porch with a basket in her hand.

Regret washed over Madeleine as she studied the little girl's eager smile. She pulled the storm door wide open and leaned against the door frame. "Hi, Emma."

"Hi." Emma lifted the basket, revealing bright red apples. "I thought we could make an apple pie. We can use *Mammi's* recipe. I remember which cookbook it's in."

Madeleine hesitated while she internally debated what to do. She wanted to let the little girl in and spend the rest of her afternoon cooking with her. However, Saul's instructions were explicit—Emma wasn't permitted to spend time with Madeleine either in Madeleine's house or at his house.

"Emma, I would love to cook with you, but your father told me he doesn't want you spending time with me. I'm sorry." Madeleine couldn't stop her frown.

Emma's eyes widened. "He told you that?"

"Yes, he did." Madeleine nodded. "He came to visit

me last Thursday before I left for work. He asked me not to spend time with you. I'm not allowed to come to your house, and he doesn't want you here."

"He told me I shouldn't bother you, but I didn't think he really meant it if we could be friends." The disappointment in Emma's expression caused Madeleine's heart to crumble.

Madeleine recalled her conversation with Saul and tried to think of a way to summarize it without causing Emma more disappointment or hurt. "I think he's afraid that you and I might become close friends and then I might move again."

"You're moving already?" Emma gasped.

"No, no, *no*," Madeleine emphasized the word. "I'm not planning to move, but your *dat* doesn't want you to get close to me and then feel bad if I do move."

"But you're not moving?" she asked.

Madeleine shook her head.

"That means it's okay, right?" Emma's smile was back.

Madeleine paused. "I don't know, Emma. I don't want to upset your *dat.* It might be a good idea if you go home, sweetie."

Emma paused and then smiled again. "I know what would make him *froh.*"

"What's that?"

"He would love it if we made him a special supper." She held up the basket. "We could also make apple pie for dessert. If we make him a meal, then he'll see that you're our friend. He'll say that I should visit you more often because we make him *appeditlich* meals. *Mei freind* Esther's *mamm* says the way to a man's heart is through his stomach."

Madeleine laughed and shook her head. "You don't give up, do you?"

"*Mei dat* calls me stubborn for a reason. What do you think?"

Madeleine stepped aside to let Emma through. "Come on in."

"Wonderful!" Emma stepped through the mud-room and to the kitchen table, and Madeleine trailed behind her.

"I was thinking you could decide what we make for supper because I picked the dessert." Emma set the basket of apples on the table. "Does that sound like a *gut* idea?"

"That sounds like a perfect idea." Madeleine moved to the counter and pointed to a page in the cookbook she'd just opened before Emma arrived. "I was thinking of making spaghetti and meatballs. What do you think?"

"Oh *ya*. I've never made meatballs. I bet my *dat* will love that." Emma pushed a stool over to the counter and hopped up onto it. "What do we do first?"

"Let's see. I'll get out the ground beef and the spices. We have to mix it all up and then roll the meatballs." Madeleine pointed to the recipe. "You read the ingredients, and I'll pull them out."

Soon they were sitting side by side at the table, rolling out the meatballs and dropping them into a glass pan.

"This is fun." Emma grinned. "I like cooking with you."

"I like cooking with you too." Madeleine hoped Saul would forgive her for breaking his rule. "What's your *dat* doing today?"

"He's installing cabinets at a house over in Bird-in-Hand. He left me a note saying he'd be home by six." Emma hesitated a moment, then asked, "What was it like to grow up without a *dat*?"

"I didn't know any different." Madeleine considered the question. "I guess it's difficult to miss something you never had."

"Do you know what he looked like?"

Madeleine nodded. "My mother has photos of him. I have a couple of photos from when they eloped and when they moved into their first apartment."

"What does *elope* mean?"

"It's when a couple gets married alone. They don't invite anyone to the wedding. Instead, they go to the city courthouse and get married in front of a judge."

"Oh." Emma considered this. "Do you look like your *dat*?"

"My mom once told me I have his hair and his eyes."

"That's like me with *mei mamm*. I have her hair and eyes too." Emma smiled up at Madeleine. "We have that in common."

Madeleine smiled back. "You're right."

"Where does your *mamm* live now?"

"She's in California," Madeleine said. "I used to live there too."

"I saw a map at school. California is really far away." Emma formed another ball.

"It is, but it's nice there. I liked living there." Madeleine thought about her mom. "My mother remarried when I was about twelve."

"I'm almost twelve, so you were my age," Emma said.

"That's true."

"How did you feel when your *mamm* remarried?"

"It was fine." Madeleine shrugged. "I was in the wedding, which was special. I was my mother's maid of honor."

Emma tilted her head and scrunched her nose. "What does that mean?"

"Oh, it's like being an attendant in the wedding. I was able to stand next to my mom during the service, and I held her bouquet of flowers." Madeleine gathered more of the meatball mixture in her hand. "I like my stepfather. His name is Jack, and he's really nice."

"Did your *mamm* have more *kinner* after she married him?" Emma asked.

"No, she said she was too old, and she was happy to have just me." Madeleine wondered why Emma had so many questions about her mother's second marriage.

"I'm hoping *mei dat* gets married again." Ah, there it was. Emma was thinking about her father.

Emma dropped another ball into the pan. "I'd like to be a big *schweschder*. Remember Carolyn from the wedding?"

"Yes, I do. I work with her at the hotel."

"She and *mei dat* were dating before she met Josh. I was hoping they would get married. She would've been a nice *mamm*."

"I imagine your *dat* will find someone nice to marry, and you'll have a nice *mamm*." Madeleine turned to look at Emma. "Don't give up hope yet. Your *dat* is young. He'll find someone nice to marry. I'm certain there are plenty of nice young ladies in the community who would jump at the chance to have a husband like your *dat*."

"You think so?" Emma looked up at Madeleine.

"Of course I do." Madeleine added two more meatballs to the pan before the stove buzzed, indicating the oven was preheated. "Let's finish up these meatballs and then put them in the oven."

"Okay." Emma seemed to be thinking as she made her last two meatballs and then wiped her hands on a paper towel. "Do you ever wonder what it would've been like if your *dat* had stayed with your *mamm*?"

Madeleine was caught off guard by the question and took a moment to contemplate her response. "No, not really." She paused again. "I suppose I used to wonder why he didn't want to get to know me. But I never really thought about what would've happened if he stayed because I didn't know him. I used to make up stories about him when I was little, though."

"Really?" Emma asked. "What kind of stories?"

"Let's see." Madeleine chuckled to herself. "I used to tell my friends my father was an astronaut or a ship captain or an airplane pilot to make up excuses for why he wasn't around."

Emma laughed. "That's *gegisch*."

"Sometimes I imagined he was a king of a foreign country and that he would come to visit me and bring me lots of expensive presents." Madeleine dropped one more meatball into the pan. "I knew it was all pretend and I would never meet him."

"Have you ever met him or even talked to him on the phone?" Emma asked, her voice full of hopefulness.

"No, I haven't." Madeleine shrugged. "Really, it's okay. Jack has been like a father to me."

Emma was quiet for a moment. "Sometimes I wonder what life would've been like if my *mamm* had lived."

Madeleine reflected on the story Ruth had shared with her, and she tried her best not to frown as she stood, put the pan of meatballs into the oven, and set the timer on the oven. Then she turned back to Emma with a smile. Emma seemed to be thinking.

"I wonder if *mei mamm* and *dat* would've had more *kinner*," Emma finally said, her expression not sad but more curious. "I remember *mei mamm* a little bit."

"Do you?" Madeleine moved to the sink and started filling it with frothy water.

"Oh *ya*. She was *schee*." Emma touched her covering. "Just like *Dat* says, she had light brown hair like mine and light blue eyes like mine. *Dat* says she was the prettiest *maedel* in his youth group."

Madeleine smiled. "I imagine she was."

Madeleine began scrubbing the utensils and dishes they used for making the meatballs. She worked in silence for a minute or two. Emma seemed to be lost in thought again.

"Her name was Annie," Emma finally continued.

"That's a nice name."

"*Ya*, it is. Do you have a middle name?" Emma stood, grabbed a dish towel, and began drying a platter.

"I do." Madeleine placed a bowl in the drain board. "It's Dawn."

"Dawn." Emma repeated the name. "That's *schee*. Some of my friends have nicknames. Do you have a nickname?"

"My mother calls me Maddie."

"Maddie." Emma nodded. "I like that. May I call you Maddie?"

"Sure." Madeleine put the last utensil in the drain board and dried her hands. "Shall we start on the apple pie?"

"*Ya*! I can find the recipe." Emma dried the last spoon and hurried over to the cookbooks.

Madeleine put away the clean dishes and utensils and pulled out the supplies for the apple pie.

"I found the recipe." Emma began to read the ingredients, and Madeleine pulled them from the cabinets.

"I have a couple of premade crusts I was going to use for a pie." Madeleine pulled one of them out of the refrigerator. "It will save us some time."

Emma nodded. "That sounds like a *gut* idea."

"I'm glad you agree." Madeleine smiled.

Soon they were peeling and coring the apples and reminiscing about baking with Madeleine's grandmother. When the meatballs were done, Madeleine put them on top of the stove, and when the apples were ready, Emma had another question.

"Did you like being a nurse?" Emma asked.

"Yes, I did, but I was ready for a change. It's hard work and very stressful." Madeleine mixed their apples with the rest of the filling. After it was all combined and she had poured everything into the piecrust, she slipped the pie pan into the oven and then pulled a tin of cookies from one of her cabinets. "Should we have a snack?"

"*Ya*, let's do that." Emma took the milk from the refrigerator.

They sat down at the kitchen table and ate their cookies and drank milk while the aroma of meatballs and apple pie filled the kitchen.

"Do you want to get married and have a family someday?" Emma asked while they ate.

Madeleine nearly choked on the cookie. "You really get to the point, don't you, Emma?"

"Oh." Emma's eyes were wide. "Am I being too nosy? *Dat* tells me I'm too nosy sometimes."

"No, it's okay. I don't mind answering the question." Madeleine wiped her hands on a napkin. "I would like to get married and have a family someday if that's what God has in store for me."

"Oh," Emma said. "Have you ever had a special friend, someone you might want to marry?"

"Yeah, I have." Madeleine picked up another cookie. "I did have a special friend once, and we were going to get married."

"What happened?" Emma's eyes were full of curiosity.

"He died." Madeleine tried her best to ignore the way her voice thickened when she said the words out loud.

"Oh." Emma grimaced. "I'm sorry."

"*Danki*," Madeleine said, overwhelmed by the sympathy in Emma's expression.

"I bet you get sad and miss him," Emma said.

"I do. Some days are worse than others." Madeleine

pointed toward a bag of yarn in the corner of the kitchen. "When I have bad days, I like to crochet. I picked up that yarn at the store the other day. I'm working on an afghan. I have a place to crochet in the spare room."

"Oh." Emma nodded with interest. "*Mammi* taught me how to crochet."

"She taught me too."

"I'm sorry you get sad sometimes." Emma frowned again. "That has to be hard since you're here alone."

"*Danki*, but I'm fine. I'm happy here, and that's what matters." She glanced at the clock. "Let's eat up our snack and then finish making supper. We'll put it all together, and then you can surprise your *dat* with a nice meal. We need to add the tomato sauce to the meatballs. I'll get the jar out of the pantry."

They finished their cookies and milk, and then Madeleine showed Emma how to cook spaghetti to go with the meatballs. By the time all the food was ready, it was close to five o'clock.

"You'd better get going," Madeleine said. "It's almost five."

"Oh no," Emma said. "I can't be late."

"I'll help you carry everything to your house." Madeleine pulled out serving platters and bowls and loaded up the meatballs with tomato sauce, spaghetti, and apple pie, first slicing one piece of pie for herself. "You can take most of the pie. I just want one piece." She pulled a gallon of vanilla ice cream out of the freezer. "Have you ever had apple pie with ice cream?"

"No." Emma's eyes were wide with excitement. "That sounds *appeditlich*."

"It is." Madeleine put a few scoops of ice cream into a refrigerator jar. "You can take some of this too." She put the ice cream and container of spaghetti into Emma's basket. "Let's carry all this over to your house."

When Madeleine and Emma reached the large farmhouse at the end of the driveway, they climbed the back porch steps, entered the house through the mud-room, and stepped into the large kitchen.

Madeleine placed her basket and bowl of meatballs on the counter and glanced around the room. She gasped as she ran her hands over the beautiful walnut cabinets.

"Emma, these are gorgeous." She opened a cabinet door and examined the craftsmanship. "Did your *dat* make these?"

"*Ya*." Emma bobbed her head up and down, causing the ribbons from her prayer covering to dance over her little shoulders. "He made the cabinets and the counters." She pointed toward the long table in the middle of the room. "His best *freind*, Marcus, made the table and chairs a long time ago. It was a wedding gift for my parents. Marcus makes tables and chairs. His *dochder*, Esther, is my best *freind*. We go to school together. I think you met them at Carolyn's wedding."

"Yes, I did. Wow." Madeleine couldn't take her eyes off the cabinets. "I'd love something like this for my kitchen."

"You should talk to my *dat*."

"No." Madeleine shook her head. "I'm certain I couldn't afford his work."

"I'm sure you could," Emma insisted. "He does a lot of work for *Englishers*, and they can afford it."

"I'm certain they have more money than I do." Madeleine looked at the table. "Your friend Marcus does nice work too." She pointed toward the food on the counter. "Do you need help setting the table or anything?"

"Oh no, *danki*. I can handle it. I do it every day."

Madeleine grinned. "You're a very special little girl."

"I'm not little." Emma shook her head. "I'm eleven."

"Oh, I'm sorry." Madeleine tried to suppress her smile. "You're a young lady, and I'm glad you're my friend." She started for the door. "I better get home. Please tell your *dat* that I hope he enjoys his meal."

"I will." Emma waved. "*Danki*, Maddie!"

Madeleine's smile widened when she heard her nickname. "*Gern gschehne.*"

While she walked home, Madeleine felt the urge to pray. *Lord, I know I went against Saul's wishes today by cooking with Emma, but I couldn't bring myself to break her sweet little heart. Please soften Saul's heart toward me, and let him see that I only have the best intentions in mind. Don't let him be angry with Emma. I hope this meal brings him happiness. I also pray that Saul will allow me to be both his friend and Emma's. In your holy name, amen.*

. . .

Saul stepped into the mudroom and shucked his coat, hat, and boots. "Hello," he called as the aroma of meatballs filled his senses. "What's for supper?"

"It's a surprise." Emma stood in the doorway and grinned. "*Kumm! Dummle!*"

Saul lifted an eyebrow as he followed her into the kitchen. He found the table set with bowls of spaghetti, meatballs, salad, and carrots. He studied his daughter. "You did this by yourself?"

"No." She shook her head. "I had help." She pointed toward the sink. "Wash up and we'll eat. I can't wait to try it."

Saul washed his hands and then sat down at the table. After a silent prayer, he began to fill his plate. "This smells wonderful, Emma. How did you do this?"

"A *freind* helped me." She piled salad on her plate. "I went to visit Maddie, and we cooked together all afternoon." Her expression was tentative.

"Who's Maddie?" he asked.

"Madeleine Miller." Emma's voice was small and unsure.

"You went to visit Madeleine Miller?" Saul snapped. "Emma Kate, I've told you time and again to stay away from her. It's not right for you to barge into her home." He slammed his fist on the table, and Emma jumped.

Emma's lip quivered, and regret coursed through him. He couldn't stand it when Emma cried, but she had to learn to respect him.

"I was home alone, and I decided to go see if I could make an apple pie with Maddie." She sniffed and wiped her eyes with a napkin. "We had all of those *schee* apples, and I remembered that *Mammi* had an *appeditlich* recipe. Maddie had told me she had all of *Mammi's* cookbooks, and I went over to see if she could help me make the pie. We decided to make you a nice meal too." She made a sweeping gesture toward the spaghetti and meatballs. "Spaghetti and meatballs were Maddie's idea."

Saul stared at the food. "Why would she want to make me a meal?"

"Maybe she wants to be our *freind*."

Saul forked a meatball, put a bite in his mouth, and savored the taste.

"Do you like it, *Dat*?" Emma leaned forward, her blue eyes filled with hope.

Saul wiped his mouth and beard with a napkin. "It's very *gut*." Actually, it was outstanding. He'd never had such delicious meatballs before. He ate a few more forkfuls and then wiped his mouth again. "But I told you to stay away from her, and you defied me, Emma. If you don't respect my wishes, then you'll have to spend your afternoons at Esther's *haus*. That would mean you'll have all your chores still to do when you get home later in the day. I need to know I can trust you here alone. You're supposed to do your chores, not visit with neighbors."

"But making supper is one of my chores." She twisted spaghetti around her fork as she spoke. "Maddie said you told her not to spend time with me, but I convinced her to cook with me today. She was helping me out."

"Why do you keep calling her Maddie?" Saul asked before taking a sip of water.

"That's her nickname." Emma was still winding spaghetti around her fork. "Her *mamm* calls her Maddie. Did you know she never knew her *dat*? He left before she was born. Oh, and she has her *dat's* eyes and hair, like I have *Mamm's*." Emma began a long monologue about Madeleine's life, including where she had lived and that she had a stepfather.

Saul continued to eat while he listened. His fear was already coming true—his daughter was becoming attached to this *Englisher*, and he didn't know what to do about it.

"Maddie was wearing pants," Emma continued. "They were lightweight with a stripe down the side. I think I've seen her running in those before. And she also had her hair in a ponytail. I wonder what my hair would look like in a ponytail."

Saul gritted his teeth. Was this Madeleine Miller making his Emma rebellious? "You're not to try on any *English* clothes, Emma. You're not going to change how you look."

"I know." Emma nodded. "I was just saying that Maddie dresses so different from how I dress." She pointed toward the meatballs. "Do you like the food, *Dat*? Did Maddie and I do a *gut* job?"

He nodded. "*Ya. Danki.*"

"Wait until you see dessert." She sat up a little taller. "We have apple pie and vanilla ice cream. I can't wait to try it." She then talked on about Madeleine and how much fun they had together.

When Emma brought out the pie and ice cream, Saul enjoyed them despite his frustration with Emma and Madeleine defying his wishes. He had to admit it was nice to enjoy a delicious meal that was different from what they normally ate.

"What do you think of the pie?" Emma asked.

"It's *appeditlich*. It's the best apple pie I've ever had."

Emma clapped her hands. "I'm glad you like it!"

Saul saw the happiness in his daughter's eyes, and he couldn't bring himself to punish her. He was thankful that Madeleine had made her happy, but he prayed she wouldn't break Emma's heart. Maybe God had brought Madeleine into his daughter's life for a reason, but Saul hoped the reason had nothing to do with stealing his daughter away from the community he loved.

TWELVE

Madeleine couldn't stop thinking about Saul's kitchen as she cleaned hotel rooms. The memory of the beautifully crafted cabinets floated through her mind. Although she adored her grandparents' house, the kitchen had needed attention for quite some time. Her grandmother had loved her little house just as it was and seemed set in her ways, but Madeleine suspected she also wanted to keep the house the way it had been when her mother was growing up and her grandfather was still alive.

Although her grandmother never discussed how heartbreaking it was for her when Madeleine's mother left the Amish community, Madeleine knew she missed the days when her daughter was home. She'd kept all of her clothes, which Madeleine wore when she visited as a little girl.

She was still thinking about her small kitchen when she returned her cart to the supply closet.

"Hi, Madeleine," Linda Zook said while pushing her own cart toward the closet. "How did your morning go?"

"It went fine, thanks. I finished the second floor. How about you?" Madeleine asked.

"I finished my rooms too."

Madeleine thought of her kitchen ideas. "Linda, do you know of an affordable cabinetmaker?"

"A cabinetmaker?" Linda shook her head. "I know of a few around the community, but I don't know them personally. What do you want a cabinetmaker for?"

"I want to do some renovations in my grandparents' house. It's needed some upgrades for a while." Madeleine leaned against a shelf that held paper products. "I want to keep the spirit of my grandparents' house, but the cabinets are falling apart. Last night I was in my neighbor's house, and I was really astounded by the cabinets in his kitchen. He makes cabinets for a living, but I'm certain I can't afford his work."

"What's his name?" Linda asked.

"Saul Beiler."

"Oh." Linda nodded. "He's one of the best in the area, from what I've heard."

Madeleine smiled. "That's all the more reason I can't afford him."

"You don't know that unless you ask."

"But we don't make that much money here. My grandmother left me some money, but I need it to last as long as possible. I'm actually working to earn extra money for home projects."

"That's true. We don't earn a lot here." Linda pointed toward the office. "You might want to talk to Gregg. He can give you some names, or you can look them up on his computer."

"That's a great idea." Madeleine stood up straighter. "Thank you, Linda."

Linda shrugged. "You're welcome. I really didn't do much."

Madeleine headed to her boss's office and found him squinting at his computer screen. Gregg Larson was a short, plump, balding man in his midfifties, with thick glasses and small, dark eyes.

She knocked on the door frame, and Gregg peered at her over his computer. "Hi, Gregg." She gave him a little wave. "I was wondering if you could give me a recommendation for kitchen remodelers. I want to replace my kitchen cabinets."

"Sure thing." Gregg nodded. "I'll see what I can find. I can also ask my wife to put a list together for you and then get it to you before the end of the day. She knows the contractors in the area because she works at a store in town."

"That would be fantastic. Thank you." Madeleine headed back to the supply closet with a smile on her face.

• • •

Later that evening, Madeleine sat on the sofa in the family room and sipped a can of Diet Coke while she examined the list of contractors she'd called. She'd set up times for representatives from three different companies to stop by and give her estimates during the next couple of days.

She finished the soda and then walked into the

kitchen. She stared at the cabinets. Two were missing the metal knobs on the doors, which had fallen off before Madeleine came to live in the house. Another was missing a door that had fallen off with a loud clatter just yesterday.

As she made her way to the bedroom, Madeleine imagined how pretty the house could be if she renovated it the way she wanted to. She prayed she could make that a reality in memory of her precious grandparents.

. . .

Madeleine stood in the driveway as she watched the last contractor drive away. She stared down at the estimate and shook her head. After meeting with the three contractors, she didn't know which company to choose. She had thought she'd know whom to hire by the end of the week, but she was still as confused as she had been on Tuesday when she'd called the first contractor.

"Maddie!" Emma hurried up the driveway with a piece of paper in her hand. "Do you want to cook? I have *mei mamm's* recipe for chicken and dumplings."

"How did your *dat* like the food we made on Monday?" Madeleine asked, shivering in the cold November air. "I've been wondering if you were in trouble for cooking with me."

"He loved the food. He said it was the best apple pie he'd ever had." Emma held out her paper. "He would love this too."

Madeleine examined the recipe, which looked easy enough. She would have to go to the grocery store for most of the supplies, but she always did her grocery shopping on Fridays, so it wasn't really a problem. Yet, at the same time, she couldn't keep the voice in the back of her mind from warning her not to go against Saul's wishes again. Would cooking with Emma cause more problems between her and her neighbor, who lived in such close proximity?

"How would your *dat* feel about you coming over to my house again?" She studied Emma's pretty face. "Are you certain you're allowed to spend time with me?"

Emma shrugged and then shivered. "I think he'd be happy to have another delicious meal." She smiled, and Madeleine felt her worries evaporate.

"When will your *dat* be home?" Madeleine asked.

"His note said he'd be home around five thirty."

"We'll have to go to the grocery store before we start cooking." She nodded toward the house. "Let me go in and get my purse and keys. Come inside for a minute." Madeleine hoped it would also be acceptable to Saul for her to take Emma along to the store.

"Okay." Emma skipped ahead of Madeleine and opened the back door. "Who was that man in the truck?"

"He gave me an estimate on my cabinets." Madeleine followed Emma into the kitchen and placed the estimate on the counter next to the other two.

"He has a cabinet company?" Emma asked.

"That's right." Madeleine grabbed her purse and keys from the kitchen table. "He told me how much it would cost to replace my cabinets."

"You should talk to *mei dat*." Emma folded her arms over her cloak. "He's the best."

"I might talk to him. Maybe he can give me some guidance." Madeleine jingled the keys in her hands. "Let's head to the store, and then we'll start cooking."

"Yay." Emma clapped her hands. "I love cooking with you."

Madeleine smiled. "I love cooking with you too."

. . .

"I think it turned out well." Madeleine closed the lid on the last of the chicken and dumplings after she'd put most of it into a large refrigerator jar. The delicious aroma caused her stomach to growl. "Hopefully your *dat* will enjoy this as much as he enjoyed our creation on Monday."

A knock sounded at the door, and Madeleine glanced at Emma. "Would you please see who that is?"

Emma went through the mudroom and looked out the window. "Oh, it's my *dat*," she called back. "We can ask him what he thinks of the meal."

Madeleine's smile faded as she walked in behind Emma. She hoped he wasn't angry.

Emma wrenched the door open. "Hi, *Dat*! We were finishing up—" She backed up as Saul quickly opened the storm door and stepped inside.

"I have been worried sick about you." Saul wagged a large finger millimeters from Emma's nose while the girl's eyes widened. "I told you to stay home today, but you still came over here. I explicitly told you not to come over here and bother Madeleine."

"But you said you liked the meal we made you on Monday. I thought it would be okay if we made you another one." Emma's voice was tiny, as if she were five instead of eleven.

"You still insist on breaking the rules. I don't know what to do to make you realize that I want you at home, not here with this *maedel*." He looked over at Madeleine and then back at his daughter. "You are supposed to come home from school and take care of your chores."

Madeleine felt like an intruder watching Saul reprimand his daughter. Should she leave? But that was a silly notion. After all, they were in *her* house.

"We made you chicken and dumplings," Emma offered. "It's your favorite recipe."

Saul shook his head. "You're avoiding the issue here. You disobeyed me. It's your job to follow my rules." He pointed to his wide chest. "I'm the *daed*, and you're the *kind*." His voice was gruff, and his face was full of frustration.

Madeleine scowled. He was overreacting. After all, the girl only wanted to cook for her father. What was so wrong about that?

"Let's go!" Saul bellowed as he pointed toward the door.

Emma glanced back at Madeleine and then turned toward her father. "I told Maddie to talk to you about building new cabinets for her kitchen." She pointed toward the counter. "She's gotten some estimates, but I told her that you're the best."

Saul's expression softened a little. "I said it's time to go."

"*Ya, Dat.*" Emma started to leave.

"Emma, wait!" Madeleine said, causing Saul to glare at her. "Your chicken and dumplings are here." She ignored Saul's frown and went back into the kitchen to get the container she'd just filled.

Saul walked into the kitchen behind her and took the container. "*Danki,*" he muttered. His eyes moved to the counter, and he stared at the pile of estimates. "Are these the estimates Emma was talking about?"

"Yes."

He looked up at the cabinets and grimaced. "I see. These must be the originals from when this place was built." He touched a door and opened and closed it. "You want to replace them?"

"That's the plan." Madeleine crossed her arms over her hooded sweatshirt.

"Is it all right if I look at the estimates?"

"Sure." She shrugged.

He placed the container on the counter and began studying the paperwork.

"I told Maddie you would give her a better price and do better work for her," Emma said.

"That's true," Saul said before looking up at Madeleine. "Do you know what you want your cabinets to look like?"

"Yeah." Madeleine pointed toward his house. "I

want ones like you have in your kitchen. I love walnut, and I really like the simple design."

"My kitchen?" He turned toward Emma. "Madeleine was in our kitchen?"

"She helped me bring the food to our *haus* on Monday." Emma turned to Madeleine. "That reminds me. I need to return your dishes to you."

"There's no rush." Madeleine waved off the comment.

Saul's expression softened, and he seemed embarrassed. "Those were the first kitchen cabinets I made without *mei daadi's* help. I had just gotten married, and I was starting my own business. They aren't my best work."

Madeleine shook her head. "If those aren't your best work, then I can't imagine how amazing your cabinets really are. Those are exactly what I want."

"Really?" he asked. "Those are exactly what you want?"

As he studied her, she took in his bottomless brown eyes. They were warm and comforting, like the hot chocolate she and her grandmother made when she was a child. She pushed the thought away and realized he was awaiting her response.

"Yes," she repeated. "Those are exactly what I want, but I'm certain I can't afford you."

He blanched. "Why would you say that?"

"I know Amish work is the best, and you get what you pay for."

Saul held up the medium price estimate. "I won't charge you much more than this company."

"Really?" Madeleine was intrigued. She moved closer

to him and looked down at the paper. She realized he was only a couple of inches taller than she was, and she estimated him to stand at just under six feet. "You can really keep your price in that range?"

"*Ya*, I can." He gestured toward his property. "Do you want to come over to my shop and talk about the design?"

"Why don't we eat first?" Emma suggested.

Madeleine looked at Saul. "Would you like to eat here, and then we can talk about the cabinets?"

He hesitated and then gave a quick nod. "*Ya*, that sounds *gut*."

"Great." Madeleine looked at Emma. "Would you please set the table? I'll warm up the chicken and dumplings." She glanced at Saul. "You can go clean up if you'd like. The bathroom is down the hallway to the left."

"*Danki*." Saul shucked his heavy coat and hung it on a peg just inside the mudroom before disappearing down the hallway.

Madeleine hoped her taking Emma to the grocery store wouldn't come up.

. . .

Saul washed his hands in the bathroom and then stepped back into the hallway. He had visited this home dozens of times when Martha and Mel lived in it. After Mel passed away, Saul frequently stopped by to see if Martha needed any help. He'd taken care of minor household projects, such as fixing her leaking kitchen sink, and also major repairs, including repairing her roof. He was happy to assist her and wouldn't take no for an answer when he asked her if she needed help.

He took a step and stood in the doorway of the master bedroom, which looked nearly identical to how it had looked when Martha lived in the house. The same quilt was on the bed, and the walls were still bare except for a small mirror and a faded wreath. Why hadn't Madeleine decorated it like the *Englisher* homes he'd visited while installing cabinets? Or was getting new cabinets the beginning of a plan to make the house more *English*?

Then he peered into the spare room, which included a small desk, a chair, a rocking chair, and a pile of boxes with BOOKS written on them in black marker. Beside the rocking chair were a plastic drawer unit filled with yarn and what looked like a half-crocheted, pastel-colored blanket. He was surprised. Crocheting didn't seem to fit with her *English* life.

Saul moved to the kitchen where his daughter and Madeleine were still preparing the meal. Emma was folding napkins while Madeleine carried a pan of chicken and dumplings to the table.

"I hope my *dat* likes this meal," Emma said with her back to Saul. "I made it once before, but I think I cooked it too long."

"I think he'll enjoy it." Madeleine turned toward Saul and gasped. "Oh, I didn't see you there." Her cheeks blushed a light pink. "You can have a seat anywhere you'd like. What would you like to drink, Saul?"

"Water is fine. *Danki*." Saul sat at the head of the table and folded his hands in his lap.

"I'll get drinks." Emma scurried over to the cabinet for glasses and began preparing the drinks. "Do we have anything for dessert, Maddie?"

"Oh." Madeleine rested her hand on her hip while considering the question. "I believe I have some ice cream." She glanced at Saul. "Do you like vanilla fudge ice cream?"

He nodded. "That would be fine."

"Great." Madeleine examined the table. "I think we're all set. Let me help you with that." She rushed over to Emma and took two glasses of water from her.

She set one next to Saul and smiled at him. He suddenly realized that she had a beautiful smile that caused her dark eyes to sparkle in the natural, late afternoon light flooding the kitchen. He nodded and quickly looked down at the glass.

Madeleine sat to his right and Emma was at his left. After a quick silent prayer, they began to eat.

"What do you think, *Dat*?" Emma asked after Saul had taken his first bite of chicken and dumplings.

He wiped a napkin across his beard and nodded. "It's fantastic."

"Yay!" Emma clapped her hands. "He likes it, Maddie."

Madeleine smiled at Emma, and Saul was stunned by the love in her expression as she looked at his daughter.

"I told you he'd like it. You worry too much, Emma." Madeleine filled her plate. "You're a very good cook. You don't need my help."

"*Ya*, I do," Emma said.

"Why?" Madeleine's expression became facetious. "You need me to buy the groceries, right?"

"No, I need you to reach the spices that are high in the cabinet." Emma giggled.

Madeleine feigned a gasp, and Saul couldn't stop his own chuckle.

"What are we going to make next?" Emma asked. "Have you ever made a ham loaf?" She glanced at Saul. "That's one of my *dat's* favorites."

"No, I haven't made a ham loaf." Madeleine turned toward Saul. "We'll have to see if your *dat* will allow us to try to make one together." She seemed to be awaiting his approval, and he felt obligated to agree.

"Perhaps we can choose a night for that," he said, and Emma smiled.

Not only was supper delicious, but Saul couldn't get over how Madeleine interacted with Emma. They discussed recipes like old friends. They laughed and talked about everything from barn cats to gardening. His daughter had bonded with the *Englisher*, and it sent conflicting emotions swirling through him. He was amazed at how happy his daughter was, but he also was still concerned about Madeleine's influence.

After supper, Emma and Madeleine cleaned up the kitchen while Saul drank a cup of coffee he'd allowed his hostess to make. He sat at the table, still marveling at how well the two got along.

"Madeleine," he said once most of the dishes were clean, "would you like to look at cabinet samples in my showroom? I have a catalog and some sample cabinets in the smaller shop near my *haus*."

Madeleine nodded. "Yes, I'd like that."

"All right." He started for the door.

"I'll finish up," Emma offered. "We just have these utensils and pots left. You and *Dat* can go to the shop. I'll probably be home before you will, *Dat*."

"Are you sure?" Madeleine asked while scrubbing the first pot.

"I can do it," Emma insisted.

"All right." Madeleine dried her hands on a towel. "Just leave everything else in the drain board. I can put them away when I get home." She moved to the mudroom and pulled on her coat, grabbing a flashlight as well. "Thank you, Emma," she called back.

Saul held the door open for Madeleine, and she stepped out onto the porch. "*Danki* for supper," he said as they walked side by side down the porch steps. The setting sun sent bursts of oranges, purples, reds, and yellows across the sky, and the cold air tickled his nose.

"*Gern gschehne*," she said.

He glanced at her. "You really do speak *Dietsch*."

"*Ya*, I do. Is that so difficult to believe?" She gave him a slight smile as they made their way down the rock driveway toward his shop, their shoes crunching against the stones.

"No, it's not difficult to believe," he explained. "It just seems ironic for an *Englisher* to speak *Dietsch* that well."

"I'll take that as a compliment," she teased. "I'm glad you liked supper. I think cooking for you makes Emma happy."

He nodded. "She is eager to please."

"I think she likes to see you smile."

Her comment caught him off guard, and the words hit him square in his heart. Talking about his daughter always touched him deeply. Speechless, he kept walking toward the shop.

"Did I say something wrong?" Madeleine asked.

"No," he said. They approached the showroom, and he wrenched the door open. "It's going to be cold in there."

"I'm not afraid of the cold," she quipped. "I served in Afghanistan with some challenging conditions."

He nodded while studying her young face in the remaining light of the day. How could a sweet young lady like her serve in the military and go to a place where war had been raging for years? She was brave to travel so far without family to protect her. Madeleine was more than she seemed. In fact, she was a mystery. He was certain he had a lot to learn about his neighbor.

"Let me turn the lanterns on." He slipped past her and flipped on the four lanterns located around the shop before picking up a copy of the full-color catalog he'd had designed by a local print shop. He placed it on the workbench closest to the door for her to study. "These are my most popular designs." He pointed toward the wall. "There are more samples there."

Madeleine stood beside him and flipped through the catalog. Her arm brushed his, and he instinctively took a step back. He glanced at her face and was struck by how her hair had a slightly reddish tint in the low light of the lanterns. Her eyes also seemed a lighter shade of brown, resembling milk chocolate.

He quickly looked away. Why would he admire an *Englisher*? Madeleine Miller was only a neighbor, an acquaintance. He was falling into the trap of believing Amish and *Englishers* could be friends. Their lives were too different for that, and he needed to remind Emma to keep her distance. He'd enjoyed their supper, and Emma obviously liked Madeleine, but it was still a mistake to let Emma get so close to this woman.

"I don't know," Madeleine said, wrenching him from his mental tirade. "These are all gorgeous, but I still like the cabinets in your kitchen the best." She closed the catalog. "Would you design something simple for me, like those?"

Saul rubbed his beard. "Are you certain that's what you want? Those are very plain."

"That's what I like, and I think that's what my *mammi* would've liked. She kept her life simple and plain, and I want to do something that would have made her *froh*."

He studied her, fascinated by her love and respect for her grandmother. "All right. I can do something like that. Are you certain you want walnut?"

She shrugged. "Why not?"

"Walnut is dark. Would you rather go with something lighter?" He crossed to the opposite side of the shop and began lifting wood samples. "Would you prefer a light walnut or maybe an oak?"

"Oh wow." She studied the samples. "I don't know." She ran her hand over the boards and then looked up at him. "What do you think? You're the expert."

"It's your kitchen. Whatever you want would be fine with me."

She smiled. "I still like your cabinets the best."

"Okay." He pulled out an order form. "What kind of countertop would you like?"

She grinned. "I already told you. I like what you have in your kitchen."

"Fine." He wrote down her name and address on the top of the form. "I can have an estimate to you in a week or so."

"When do you think you can start on my cabinets?"

"A few days after that. I'm finishing up a job now. I'll just have to coordinate with my plumber, but it shouldn't be a problem. Does that sound okay?"

"It's perfect. *Danki.*" She shivered.

"You should go back home and get warm." He placed the form on the workbench. "I'll come see you in a few days and take measurements."

"Sounds great." She hugged her arms to her chest. "I'm excited."

He extinguished the lanterns, picked up another to light their way, and followed her out of the shop. After locking the door, he faced her. "I'll see you soon."

"Great." She glanced toward her house and then looked back at Saul. "I had fun tonight. Thank you for sharing Emma with me."

For the second time that evening, her words tugged at his heart. "*Gern gschehne.*"

"*Gut nacht*, Saul," she said.

"*Gut nacht.*" He watched her start down the road with her flashlight shining in front of her, and he suddenly wondered what to call her. "Wait."

She spun and faced him, her pretty face filled with curiosity.

"I don't know what to call you," he said.

"I don't understand." She took a step toward him.

"*Mei dochder* calls you Maddie, but your name is Madeleine," he explained. "What should I call you?"

"My friends call me Maddie," she said. "You can call me Maddie."

"*Gut nacht*, Maddie." He said the words and couldn't help but think that the nickname fit her. She was the most complex *Englisher* he'd ever met.

Madeleine continued down the driveway, turning back once to wave at him. He waved back at her. Would she be a constant in his and Emma's life, or would she stay long enough to get to know them and then leave again? For a split second, he hoped she would stay, but thoughts like that were dangerous. She was only a neighbor who wanted him to design and build new cabinets for her. She would never be any more than an *English* customer. They could not—he could not—get too close.

THIRTEEN

Trey steered his BMW down a winding road. He had finished all the errands he'd planned to run today. At least, he'd crossed everything off his list that he'd told Hannah he'd do today, but he still had one stop he wanted to make. It was an errand he had pondered ever since he'd attended Joshua Glick and Carolyn Lapp's wedding. Something he had to do for his lovely wife.

He drove down another road, passing beautiful Amish farms on either side. The one-room schoolhouse came into view, and he slowed to a stop. Lillian stood by the doorway and waved as a line of children rushed out of the school, talking and laughing as they made their way down the steps and toward their homes. Another young lady, whom he assumed was Lillian's assistant, also waved and smiled as the children left.

Trey had spent two weeks considering what he would say to Lillian if he had a chance to talk to her alone. Now that moment was finally here. He had to find a way to make Lillian understand that Hannah still loved her and wanted—needed—her to be a part of her life.

He waited until it looked like the last child had left

the building before climbing from the car and making his way toward the school. Lillian and her assistant had disappeared inside, and as he approached, the other young lady reappeared on the front steps.

When she saw him, her eyes widened with panic. "May I help you?"

"Hi." Trey stopped before he reached the bottom step. "I was looking for Lillian Glick."

"Just a minute." The girl stepped back into the school, and he heard her call Lillian. She then returned to the top step and fiddled with the ties on her prayer covering. "She'll be right here."

"Thanks." Trey cleared his throat and leaned against the railing while he waited for his stepdaughter. The young lady studied him with a suspicious expression.

"Trey?" Lillian asked when she came through the door. "What are you doing here?" Her eyes widened as she looked down at him. "Did something happen to my sister?"

"No." Trey shook his head. "Your sister, your brother, and your mother are fine."

"Oh. Praise God. You scared me." Lillian rested her hand on her chest. "Then why are you here?"

"I'd like to talk to you." Her expression hardened, but he pressed on. "Please, Lily. Let me take you out for a cup of coffee or something."

"No." She pushed her glasses farther up on her nose. "I have things to do. I'm very busy."

The other young lady looked back and forth between them.

"I have things to do as well, but this is important

to me." Trey sighed. "Please, Lillian. Just hear me out. Let me take you out for coffee, and we'll talk for a few minutes. Then I'll drive you home. What do you say?"

Lillian's expression remained stoic. "I don't think so."

Trey stood there for a moment. Should he insist she go out for coffee with him, or should he just leave? His heart was torn, but he knew one thing for certain—he was determined to do anything to help Hannah heal her broken heart.

Lillian stepped back into the school, and the young lady stood on the top step watching Trey. Did she think Trey was going to try to hurt Lillian?

His stepdaughter reappeared with a tote bag slung over her shoulder. She locked the school door and then descended the steps with the other young lady close behind her.

"Lily," Trey began, "if you won't go with me, then I'm going to ask you to hear me out right here."

Lillian stopped in front of him and frowned. "I have nothing to say to you."

"That's fine. You don't need to speak, but I need you to listen to me."

The young lady said something to Lillian in Pennsylvania Dutch, and Lillian shook her head.

"It's okay," Lillian responded. "You can go. I'll be fine."

"Are you certain?" the girl asked.

"*Ya.*" Lillian nodded. "I'll see you tomorrow, Anna Mary."

Anna Mary nodded and then started down the street.

"What do you want to say to me, Trey?" Lillian crossed

her arms over her apron. "Did *mei mamm* send you here to speak to me?"

"No." Trey shook his head. "She has no idea I'm here. I've wanted to talk to you for some time, but I felt it wasn't my place to get involved. However, things have escalated to a point now that I feel I have to get involved." He took a deep breath. "Lily, I realize this change has been hard on you. What you don't realize is how hard this has been for your mother."

Lillian's frown deepened. "I can't imagine that it's been more difficult for her than it has for me. I lost everything—my home and my family. *Mei mamm* didn't lose anything."

"That's not true." Trey worked to keep his voice calm despite his raging frustration. "Your mom feels that she's lost you. She cries every night. Sometimes she cries during the day. She thinks I can't hear her, but I do. And it's breaking my heart."

"That was her choice." Lillian lifted her chin with defiance, but her green eyes shimmered with tears.

"But it wasn't an easy choice, and it doesn't have to be something that keeps you apart forever." He paused to gather his thoughts. "Lily, your mother loves you. I believe you love her too. I want you to think about giving her a chance. Just come visit us and talk to her. Let her show you how much she loves you."

"I can't do that." Lillian's voice cracked. "I just can't."

"Yes, you can. I can take you over to our house right now. You can stay for supper, and then I'll take you home."

"No." She shook her head. "I just can't."

"Fine. I can't make you want to visit us. When you're ready, you just let me know," Trey said. "I want you to consider something. Your mother is going to have a baby. She wants you to be a part of that baby's life."

Lillian wiped away a tear as it trickled down her pink cheek.

"I don't know if you know my story." Tears stung Trey's eyes. "I lost my first wife and my daughter to carbon monoxide poisoning. I was on a business trip, and they passed away while I was gone. I lost everything, Lily. They were gone, completely gone. I can't see them or talk to them on this earth ever again. But you haven't lost your mother. You've just chosen to ignore her and act like she died."

"It's not that simple," Lillian whispered, her voice thick.

"I think it is," Trey countered. "Your mother brought joy back into my life. And this child she's carrying represents our love. You, Amanda, and Andrew are my family now. I want you to *be* a part of our family. I'd like to bring us all together before this child comes into the world. It would make your mother very happy to have you back in her life. She may have stopped being Amish, but she never stopped loving you or being your mother."

Lily's lip quivered as more tears spilled from her eyes. "I have to go." She turned and walked away before Trey could respond.

"Lillian!" he called after her. "Please think about what I said. We're still a family, Lillian. Let's act like a family again."

Although she kept walking, Trey didn't give up hope that Lillian would consider his words.

• • •

Amanda yawned as she climbed the back steps toward the porch. She was exhausted after a day of sitting in classes and then working at a veterinarian's office in Paradise. She yanked open the back door, walked through the mudroom, and found Trey loading the dishwasher.

"How was your day?" she asked before yawning again.

"It was okay." He placed a plate with the others. "How was yours? How's the new job?"

"Exhausting." She let her backpack drop to the floor with a thump and then sat at the kitchen table. "I love working with the animals, but it's tiring. I had to chase one puppy through the office, and then I had to help pacify an angry cat." She pushed her long braid over her shoulder. "Where are *Mamm* and Andrew?"

"Andrew is taking his shower, and your mom is resting." Trey wiped his hands on a dish towel while facing her. "I have your supper in the fridge. I just have to warm it up for you."

"I can do it." She started to stand.

"Don't be silly. I'll get it for you." He pulled a plate from the refrigerator and then stuck it into the microwave. After he pressed a few buttons, the microwave hummed. He brought a glass of iced tea to the table.

"Thank you. Is *Mamm* okay?"

Trey frowned. "She had a rough day."

Amanda stood. "Should I go check on her? Does she need to see her doctor? Is the baby okay?"

Trey held his hand up to calm her. "She's fine now. Her stomach was upset." The microwave beeped, and he retrieved the plate with two slices of turkey roast, noodles, and spinach. He set it on the placemat in front of Amanda and then sat down across from her.

"Thank you." Amanda bowed her head in silent prayer and then began to eat. "I'm sorry *Mamm* isn't feeling well. Is there anything I can do?"

"No." Trey rested his chin on the palm of one hand. "She's also been upset about Lily."

"I know." Amanda ran her fingers over the cool glass of tea while she contemplated her twin. "I've been praying about Lily, and I've even tried talking to her. I don't know what else to say to help her forgive *Mamm*. I hoped she would have come to visit us and talk to *Mamm* by now." She cut up a piece of turkey roast. "I'm at the end of my rope with her."

"I know you've tried," Trey said. "I spoke to her today."

Amanda swallowed a gasp. "You spoke to my sister today?"

He nodded in response.

"How did you manage that?"

"I went to see her at the schoolhouse after I ran errands for your mother." He gave her a little smile. "And she looked about as shocked to see me as you look right now. I tried to convince her to go out for coffee and talk for a while, but she wouldn't go. So I talked to her right outside the schoolhouse."

"What did you say?" Amanda set her fork down beside her plate as her appetite evaporated.

"I told her your mother misses her and she cries for her just about every day. I explained that we want her to be a part of our family and also be a part of our new baby's life." He shrugged. "I said everything you and I have talked about. I told her we miss her and just because your mother is no longer Amish doesn't mean Lillian is no longer part of our family."

Amanda nodded slowly while digesting his words. "That's exactly right."

"I told her we want her to come visit us." Trey shook his head. "I don't know what else to say to her."

"What did she say?"

"Not much." Trey ran his finger over the table. "She cried a little, but she didn't say anything. She just walked off."

"That's my sister. Stubborn and headstrong." Amanda picked up the fork and moved the meat around on her plate. "She seems determined to stay miserable."

"I'm not giving up hope yet," Trey added. "She cried. I could tell this all hurt her deeply. She listened to me, and that was progress."

"Are you going to tell *mei mamm* about it?"

Trey shook his head. "I don't think I should. If Lily said she wanted to visit, then I think it would be beneficial to tell her I had talked to her. But I don't think telling her Lily refused to visit would be a good idea." He tilted his head. "Do you think I should tell her?"

"No, you're right." Amanda frowned. "I keep praying

Lily will soften her heart toward *Mamm*. I'm certain God will answer our prayer when he sees fit."

"He will." Trey stood. "Would you like me to get you something else? We have chocolate pie for dessert."

"No, thanks. I'm fine." Amanda smiled at him. "Thanks for talking to my sister today. You're very good to my mother."

"I try to be good to her." Trey started for the door. "I'm going to go check on her."

Trey disappeared toward their family quarters as Amanda picked at her supper. She hoped Lily would come around soon. If only Lillian could see what a good man Trey was. He wasn't Amish, but he was a good Christian man who made their mother happy and provided a good home for them.

While she picked at her supper, she whispered a prayer. "God, please open Lily's heart toward *Mamm*. We need Lily in our family again. Please let her see she needs us as much as we need her. Send her back to us before our new sibling is born. Thanks, God. In Jesus' holy name, amen."

. . .

Carolyn cradled a cup of hot tea in her hands while she sat on the porch. She smiled as Joshua walked from the barn toward the house.

My husband.

She loved the sound of that. They'd been married nearly four weeks now, and she was still basking in the newness of it all. She loved having a husband, a new name, and a home—a *real* home for her and her son.

"Carolyn." Joshua's handsome face glowed in the light of his lantern as he took the steps two at a time. "It's awfully cold for you to be sitting out here. You're going to get sick."

"I'm enjoying the *schee* night on the porch. Our porch."

He smiled, and her heart turned over in her chest. She enjoyed seeing his attractive smile every day. She wondered how different he'd look when his beard grew in.

"I'm thankful you're *froh* here." He sank onto the swing beside her, and his leg brushed against hers. "Do you want me to go get you a blanket?"

"No, *danki*." She rested her head on his shoulder. "The tea is keeping me warm. I was just admiring all those gorgeous stars in the sky. I love this time of year."

"I love every time of year now that you're here." He pushed the swing back and forth. "The animals are set for the night."

"That's *gut*." She closed her eyes and enjoyed the motion of the swing and the comfort of her husband beside her.

"Now that you're settled here, I'd like to have you help me with the books. I've really fallen behind on the paperwork for the recent horse sales. Would you help me with that?"

"Of course I will." She opened her eyes and looked up at him. "I'd be *froh* to help."

"*Gut*." He rested his hand on her leg. "You know that will take a lot of time."

She nodded. "I'm sure it will, but I'll learn it. I know I can do a *gut* job. I'm pretty *gut* with numbers."

"And in the spring, you'll have the garden to care for too."

"I realize that, but Rosemary said she still wants to help with that. She enjoys coming over here and visiting Danny. She likes your assistant a lot, and she also likes spending time with me."

"I'd like to see this farm become your priority." His words were gentle, but she knew where the conversation was leading. "Have you thought any more about quitting the hotel?"

Carolyn sat up. "I don't think I need to quit right now. I'll reduce my hours if I have to, but I want to work there for a while longer."

"Why is working at the hotel so important to you?" His eyes seemed to search her for an answer. "Why don't you want to make this farm your priority?"

"It is my priority," Carolyn insisted. "I just want to keep working there for a while longer. I enjoy my friends, and I like the work."

His expression hardened. "I don't understand, Carolyn. You told me you wanted a home and a family. Now you have a home, and hopefully we'll soon be blessed with *kinner*."

"I have faith that we'll be blessed with *kinner* soon. Until then, I'd like to keep my job."

He studied her. "I'm trying to understand, Carolyn, but I can't. What is it about the hotel that has you so determined to work there?"

Carolyn paused and contemplated her allegiance

to the hotel. "I guess it's because it's something that's mine. I've always contributed to the family by working there, and I want to keep making those contributions."

"But this business is now ours." He gestured toward the barns. "You're my *fraa*. It's our *haus*, our farm, and our business. You have my name. Why isn't that *gut* enough for you?"

"You're misunderstanding me." Carolyn tried to explain how she felt without causing an argument. "I never said this wasn't *gut* enough for me. I just want to keep contributing to the family through my own salary. That's all I'm trying to say."

His frown deepened, stealing his handsome smile. "I need you at home. I need you here to help me with the farm and care for the *haus*." He touched her hand. "And I like having you here with me. I don't want to share you with the *Englishers* at the hotel."

Carolyn studied Joshua's grimace and realized he was still nervous that working at the hotel would cause her to be tempted by the *English* life because Hannah had met Trey while working there. She needed to convince him she wasn't going to leave the community.

"Josh, I'm very *froh* here." She placed her cup on the small table beside her. "Working at the hotel isn't going to change how I feel about you or our life together. I'm just not ready to give up my job yet, and I need you to understand that."

He turned away and stared out toward the farm.

"Can you give me a few months to adjust to the idea of quitting?" she asked. "Just let me ease into it."

Joshua faced her and gave her a quick nod. "I'll give you until spring."

"Okay." She squeezed his hand. "That's fair."

He stood, took her hand, and eased her to her feet. "It's cold. Tea or no, your hand is like a block of ice. Let's go inside."

As she followed him into the house, she tried to accept the notion of giving up her job by spring. She wasn't sure why she wanted to hold on to her former life. What was she afraid of losing? She hoped she could get used to the idea of being a wife without her former independent life.

FOURTEEN

Madeleine was about to carry grocery bags into the house when someone called her name.

"Madeleine." Saul hurried up the driveway toward her pickup truck. "Do you need some help?"

"Hi, Saul." She nodded toward the truck. "There are two more bags in there if you don't mind grabbing them."

He got the bags and followed her up the path to her house. "I was wondering if I could measure for your cabinets."

"Oh, sure. That's fine." Madeleine climbed the porch steps and stood in front of the back door, balanced both bags with one arm, and attempted to dig the house key out of her pocket. "I was wondering when you need to take down the old cabinets so I'll know when to start emptying them." She started to drop one of the bags, and he reached for it.

"Let me take the bags from you," Saul said. "I can manage all four."

"Thanks." She handed him the bags, found her key, pulled open the storm door, unlocked the back door,

and pushed it open. "Go ahead." She stepped back, and
Saul moved past her.

He placed the grocery bags on the kitchen table
and then hung his coat on the peg just inside the mudroom door.

"Thank you." Madeleine placed her coat on the peg
beside his and then suddenly felt embarrassed that she
hadn't picked up the kitchen. A pile of bills and advertisements was on the counter and a laundry basket
filled with dirty clothes was on the floor by the family room doorway. "I'm sorry the house is a mess." She
pushed the basket of laundry into the family room. "I
was going to go to the Laundromat tomorrow."

"The Laundromat?" Saul raised an eyebrow. "Don't
you have a wringer washer out there?" He pointed
toward another small room off the kitchen.

"Yes, but I don't remember how to use it. The last
time I used a wringer washer I was twelve, and my
mammi helped me."

"Do you want me to show you how to use it?" he
offered.

"Oh no, thank you. I don't want to trouble you." She
waved off the question. "I can go to the Laundromat.
I just wait until I'm running out of clothes, and then I
spend the afternoon there. I take a good book with me."

He studied her and then gave a quick nod. "Fine,
then." He pulled a measuring tape and small notepad
from his pocket. "I'm going to take some measurements and make some notes. Is that all right?"

"Go right ahead." She began unloading her bags,
placing the groceries in the pantry, refrigerator, and

freezer while he worked. She tried to think of a way to engage him in conversation. "Did you have a good day?"

He didn't answer. Was he ignoring her, or was he so engrossed in his project that he didn't hear her?

"Saul?" she asked.

"Hmm?" He glanced over his shoulder at her. "I'm sorry. Did you say something?"

"Yes, I did." She laughed, and he gave her a sheepish smile. "I asked you how your day went."

"Oh." He paused as if puzzled by the question. "It went fine. I finished up a small job, so I can start on yours." He shrugged. "The usual—woodworking, sanding, and staining. And how was your day?"

"It was pretty good. I cleaned at the hotel and then, obviously, stopped at the grocery store." She carried a carton of eggs to the refrigerator.

"You know I have chickens, right?" Saul asked.

"You do?" she asked. Now that she thought about it, she realized she had seen Emma out feeding some chickens next to one of their barns.

"I can have Emma bring you some eggs." He pointed toward the carton in her hand. "Just save the boxes, and we'll refill them for you. We have more eggs than we know what to do with. We could eat scrambled eggs three meals a day and still have eggs left over."

"Oh." She was surprised by his thoughtful offer. "*Danki*. I'd love that."

He nodded and turned back toward the cabinets. She put away a few more items—a carton of milk, a package of cheese, and a package of ground beef—while waiting for him to say something else. He was very quiet, but he wasn't rude. *How can I bring him out of his shell? Last week he loved talking about his work while he gave me the tour of his shop. Would asking about his woodworking help him open up to me? Maybe asking about cabinets is the key to becoming his friend.*

"How long have you done woodworking?" she asked.

"I've created things with wood since I was a *bu. Mei daadi* taught me in his shop. He mostly tinkered in wood since he was a farmer by trade, but he and my *onkel* taught me almost everything I know." He continued to measure and write. "I became an apprentice to my *onkel* for cabinetmaking when I was fifteen. I opened my own business right before I was married."

"Oh." She silently admired his confidence. He wasn't arrogant, but he was comfortable with his skill. "Do you like working alone?"

Saul shrugged. "I prefer working alone, but I'd like to grow my business. I haven't had the money to do it, but I believe God will give me the means when the time is right. I'd like to be able to take more orders and not have to ask customers to wait too long for their cabinets."

"That makes sense." Madeleine put a bag of chips and a box of noodles in the pantry. "Emma is a great girl. Thank you for allowing her to spend time with me."

"I know she enjoys cooking with you," he said. "It will still be awhile before she gets home from school, but I told her to come here when she does. I thought she could keep me company while I work. It takes me awhile because I always measure everything at least twice, and I take pretty detailed notes. She was surprised but excited too."

"That's great. I'm looking forward to seeing her." Madeleine had finished putting her groceries away. "I'm going to go in the spare room to pay some bills."

Madeleine disappeared into the room she'd made into an office, a storage place for a pile of random boxes she hadn't yet unpacked, and a place for her crocheting supplies. She paid a couple of bills and then moved to the rocking chair to start working on the afghan she'd been crocheting for a couple of months.

But her eyes moved to the unpacked boxes, and she'd moved to sort through some of them when she heard Emma's voice in the kitchen. She longed to go and visit with her, but she thought she should wait for Emma to seek her out just in case the father and daughter wanted to talk privately first.

She'd just opened a box and found it was full of old photo albums and yearbooks when she heard Emma's voice in the hallway.

"Maddie?" Emma called. "Are you back here?"

"I'm in the spare room," Madeleine called. "Come on in."

Emma appeared in the doorway. "Hi. What are you doing?"

"I just started going through a few boxes I hadn't unpacked yet." Madeleine pulled out a stack of yearbooks from her elementary school. "I guess I need to put a bookshelf in here. Does your dad make bookshelves?"

"He can make them. He does special orders." Emma crossed the room and craned her neck to see the books. "Willard School?"

"That's my elementary school." Madeleine held up a yearbook. "I think this was when I was in third grade."

"What is it?" Emma asked.

"It's a yearbook. It has photos of my classmates."

Emma sank to the floor and crossed her legs. "May I look at it?"

"Sure." Madeleine opened the book to her class's page. "Can you find me?"

Emma giggled. "Those are funny clothes."

"That was a long time ago." Madeleine laughed. "Do you see me?"

Emma pointed to a few different girls and laughed each time Madeleine said she was wrong. Finally Madeleine pointed out where she was in the photo, and they both laughed.

. . .

Saul heard his daughter laughing down the hallway and found himself smiling while he worked. He loved the sound of Emma's laughter. It was light and airy— like the song of a little bird. He had decided it was okay for Emma to come to Madeleine's house only because he'd be working there, but he would have to restrict her contact with Madeleine after he finished the cabinet job. Meanwhile, he worked in the kitchen with the sound of Emma's and Madeleine's chatter and laughter as background noise.

"*Dat*!" Emma ran into the kitchen nearly thirty minutes later and shoved a large book into his line of sight. The book was open to a page of small portraits of young people. "Look at this photo! It's from when Maddie was a senior in high school." She pointed to a girl dressed in what appeared to be a formal-looking blouse with her hair down. "Wasn't she beautiful?"

Saul hesitated for a moment, uncomfortable because it was against Amish beliefs to make a graven image of a person. Emma's interest in the photographs reminded him of the risk of Madeleine's *Englisher* influence. But he gave in to his curiosity and studied the photo. Madeleine was beautiful, but he didn't feel comfortable commenting on the photograph. Words agreeing with Emma were stuck in his throat.

"I'm sorry." Madeleine appeared in the doorway and grimaced while her porcelain-colored cheeks flushed a bright hue of pink. "I told her you wouldn't want to see the photo, but she insisted. We've been perusing my yearbooks. Emma likes hearing about my childhood, moving from school to school while my mother was in the air force. That was my life until she married my stepfather when I was twelve."

Madeleine was apparently embarrassed, and he couldn't help thinking she looked adorable with her pink cheeks. He quickly pushed the thought away. She was an *Englisher*, and she was his client. Any thoughts about her otherwise were inappropriate and destructive.

"It's a nice photograph," Saul muttered before returning to his cabinet sketches.

"I'm hungry," Emma announced. "What should we make for supper?"

"Emma, Maddie may not want us to stay for supper," Saul said gently. "We shouldn't invite ourselves."

"It's no problem." Madeleine stepped into the kitchen. "What would you like, Emma?" She opened the freezer. "Let me see what I have in here."

"Pizza!" Emma pointed toward a frozen pizza. "Pepperoni sounds good."

"Frozen pizza?" Madeleine turned toward Saul. "Do you like pizza? It's not a very Amish meal."

He shrugged. "That sounds fine to me. Do you mind sharing your food with us again? It seems like you always get stuck with the cooking."

"We can cook at our house sometime soon too," Emma offered.

"That sounds like a plan." Madeleine read the back of the box and then preheated the oven.

Saul had finished up his measurements, sketches, and notes by the time the pizza was ready. Emma talked about school while they ate, and Saul watched Madeleine's reaction to his daughter's stories. She smiled and listened intently while Emma talked. Madeleine seemed like a genuine woman with a warm heart. He was grateful for her friendship, but she was *English*. Any relationship between them was forbidden.

When supper was over, Emma helped Madeleine clean up the kitchen and Saul sat drinking the cup of coffee Madeleine had insisted on making for him.

"Could I please go see the kittens in your barn?" Emma asked while she dried a dish. "I'll run out there quickly and then come back. I just want to see how big they've gotten since the last time I was here."

Madeleine glanced at Saul as if to ask permission. "It's okay with me if it's okay with your *dat*. I'll finish cleaning up if you want to go now."

Saul nodded. "*Ya*, you can go see the cats, but make it quick. It's getting late."

Madeleine nodded toward the pantry. "I bought a big bag of cat food, and there's a dish in the cabinet by the back door. You can take them some food if you want."

"*Danki!*" Emma filled the dish before pulling on her cloak, grabbing a lantern, and rushing out the storm door.

"I remember being quite excited about the barn cats, too, when I was her age," Madeleine said while scrubbing the pizza pan. "I would sit out in the barn for hours and talk to the kittens. Well, I only was allowed to do that after my chores were done." She glanced back at Saul and smiled.

He admired her smile and realized he needed a distraction. He stood, grabbed a dish towel, and picked up a plate.

"You don't have to help," she said. "I can put the dishes away."

"I don't mind." He busied himself with drying.

"*Danki*," she said. After a moment, she said, "I really love it here in Lancaster County. It feels like home. I moved a lot when I was a child, but I always came back here for the summers. Sometimes my grandparents were the only consistent part of my life."

He nodded and dried another dish.

"I guess that's difficult for you to relate to, right? You probably lived in the same house the whole time you were growing up."

"*Ya*, I did, but I went through some changes too."

"You did?" she asked. "What changes did you have?"

"My parents both passed away before I was married."

"Oh, I'm sorry." Her eyes were sad. "May I ask what happened?"

"*Mei dat* had kidney disease." Saul placed the dishes in a cabinet. "He was on dialysis for a long time. He succumbed to the disease when I was eighteen. *Mei mamm* had cancer. She died when I was twenty."

She reached out as if she were going to touch Saul's arm but then pulled her arm back. "That had to be very difficult for you."

"It was." He took the pizza pan from the drain board and began to dry it.

"Do you have any siblings?"

"I have an older *bruder*."

"You do? Does he live nearby?"

"No, he left the community when he was eighteen."

"Oh. Why did he leave?"

"He wanted to go to college. He was certain he was meant to be a doctor. He became a pediatrician, and he lives out in Oregon."

"Really?" She faced him. "Do you hear from him at all?"

Saul shrugged. "He sends a Christmas card every year with a picture of his family. He and his wife have four children. We talked about a year ago, and he mentioned coming out to visit. The plans fell through, though. I don't know what we'd talk about if we ever got together, but I would like for Emma to meet her cousins someday."

"Wow." Madeleine's eyes sparkled. "That's interesting that you have a brother who is a doctor. I had no idea."

"He went after his dream, and he's very *froh*." He held up the dry pan. "Does this go under the oven?"

"Yes." She pointed toward the drawer. "You've lost your parents, and your brother moved away. Do you miss your brother?"

He nodded and avoided her sympathetic eyes by stowing the pan.

"I'm very sorry." Madeleine was silent for a moment while she washed the utensils. "When I decided to leave the air force, I wasn't sure what I wanted to do. My *mammi* had left me a good amount of money and also this property. My mother convinced me to move here."

"She had to convince you?" Saul gave her a sideways glance. "I thought you said you loved it here."

"I do love it here, but it was more complicated than that."

He suddenly felt rude for being nosy. "You don't have to share it with me."

"No, it's okay." She pulled the stopper out of the sink, and the water gurgled and belched as it swirled down the drain. She grabbed a wet rag and began to wipe down the table. "I was supposed to get married, but after my fiancé passed away unexpectedly, my world sort of fell apart."

Saul turned and faced her. "Your fiancé?"

"Yes, I was engaged." She continued to wipe the table, even though it looked already clean to Saul. "Travis was also in the air force."

"That must've been so difficult for you." Saul suddenly related to Madeleine on a deeper level. She, too, had experienced heartache and loss when her fiancé passed away. Her beautiful dark, sad eyes mesmerized him, and the strong emotion made him nervous. He couldn't allow himself to be attracted to this woman. He didn't want to experience the same temptation that had taken Annie away from the community he cherished.

She finished wiping the table and then tossed the rag into the sink. "I've talked your ear off, haven't I? I'm sorry."

"You don't need to apologize for talking." He dried the utensils and slipped them into a drawer.

"What's next with the cabinets?" she asked. "I assume you still need to design them before making and installing them, right?"

"That's right." He pulled the notepad from his pocket. "I'm going to take these notes and sketches and draw formal designs from them. I'll bring them over to show you once they're done. It will take me a few days. I'll also contact the plumber and get on his schedule."

"Great." She pushed a thick lock of dark hair back behind her shoulder. "I can't wait to see them."

"All done!" Emma burst through the storm door, her cheeks rosy from the cold. "I fed the kittens and talked to them for a few minutes. They're doing well."

"Thank you." Madeleine touched Emma's nose and smiled. "You're cold. You need to get home and take a nice, warm bath."

"That's a *gut* idea." Emma hugged Madeleine. "*Danki* for a fun evening."

The tender moment between his daughter and Madeleine caused Saul to shift his weight from one foot to the other. The hug affected him deeply, his heart warming at the sight. He walked to the mudroom and pulled on his coat, hoping to make a quick exit.

Emma and Madeleine had followed, and Emma started for the door. "Let's go, *Dat*."

He turned to Madeleine and held out his hand. "*Danki* for supper."

"*Gern gschehne.*" She shook his hand. "See you soon."

As Saul followed Emma to their house, he tried to sort through his confusing feelings. Madeleine was only a neighbor and a customer, but he couldn't stop remembering her pretty smile and the way his daughter had hugged her.

FIFTEEN

Madeleine clipped the last pair of jeans to the clothesline with two clothespins and then pushed the line forward. She shivered in the brisk air, and her hands were numb from the cold fabric. She was thankful the laundry was finally done. Now she could go do what she'd been longing to do—crochet.

The nightmare that plagued her last night had been lingering at the back of her mind all day, and she needed to find some peace. When running didn't help clear her mind, she crocheted. It was the only way to escape the pain surging through her soul.

She padded into the spare room, sat in the rocking chair, and began to work on the afghan. She lost herself in the rhythm of the work, hoping to erase the dream that had stolen her satisfying sleep. After a while, she heard the back door bang. She'd seen Saul earlier and told him to just come on in when he came over with the designs he had ready. She knew she'd be in the spare room crocheting, and she didn't want to risk not hearing him knock.

After a moment, she heard him call out for her.

"Maddie? Are you in here?"

"I'm in the spare room," Madeleine called. "Come on back."

The sound of his work boots echoed in the hallway, and he appeared in the doorway holding a clipboard. He pointed toward the back of the house. "I see you figured out the wringer washer."

"Hi, Saul," Madeleine said. "Yes, I did figure out the wringer washer. My *mammi* would be very disappointed if she knew how much money I was spending at the Laundromat."

Saul smiled as he hugged the clipboard to his chest. "*Ya*, you're probably right."

He had a nice smile, and she hoped to see it more often.

"What are you working on?" He stepped into the room and peered at the afghan.

"It's an afghan." She held it out for him to see. "My *mammi* taught me how to crochet when I was around Emma's age. I've found it's the only activity besides running that helps me when my nightmares get really bad."

"Nightmares?" His handsome face was full of concern. "Why do you have nightmares?"

Madeleine paused and silently debated what to share with her friend.

"I didn't mean to intrude." He stepped backward in the direction of the door. "I have your designs to show you." He held up the clipboard. "I wanted to get your approval and show you the final price before I get started. If this isn't a *gut* time, I can leave them on the kitchen table."

She didn't want him to leave. Instead, she was overwhelmed with the inclination to share her story with him. "Please stay." She pointed toward the desk chair. "Pull up a seat."

Saul paused for a moment and then steered the desk chair toward her and sat beside her. He shucked his coat and set it on the floor next to him before placing the clipboard on top of it.

She took a deep breath and studied the afghan while she considered her words. "I told you my fiancé, Travis, passed away, but I didn't tell you what happened to him." She started to crochet before going on. "He took his own life."

When Saul gasped, she looked up at his shocked expression.

"I knew he was sick," she continued, "but I thought he was getting better."

"He was sick? Did he have a disease?"

"No." Madeleine's voice thickened, and she cleared her throat. "He was suffering from depression. He told me he was seeing a counselor, but I didn't know it had gotten so bad. If I'd known he was struggling, I would've helped him. I always thought I was a good nurse, but I wasn't good enough to help my own fiancé." She thought back to the night he died. "I was working in the ER at the hospital on base that night. I knew a patient had been brought in with a gunshot wound, but I had no idea it was Travis until I saw him on the stretcher."

"I'm so sorry." Saul started to reach for her hand and then stopped, moving his hand back to his side. Was he going to touch her hand? The gesture was warm and comforting, even though their hands never touched.

"Thank you." Tears stung her eyes. "I'll never forget that image of him. It haunts me. Sometimes I dream I'm trying to revive him. Other times I dream I'm working as a flight nurse and his body is there with me on the aircraft."

"Madeleine." He whispered her name as he studied her. "I can't imagine how difficult it is for you to relive that pain over and over again. Do you know why he took his own life?"

"Yes." She sniffed and wiped her eyes. "He left me a note, taped to my door." She nodded toward the desk where she kept the letter. "I found it when I got home that night. You see, a few months earlier, he had learned he was part of a military unit that accidentally bombed an orphanage while they were fighting in the Middle East. In the letter, he told me he loved me, but he wanted to escape the heartache that had taken over his life. He said he couldn't live with himself knowing he'd accidentally killed innocent children. He said he was certain God wanted him to die because those children couldn't live."

"Did he pray about it? Did he ask God for forgiveness?" Saul asked.

"I told him to, over and over again. We went to church together, and we even prayed together. But I guess he couldn't forgive himself. So he shot himself and left me alone to try to pick up the pieces. At least his parents had already passed away, so they didn't have to suffer."

She paused and collected her thoughts.

"I couldn't work in the hospital after that. I always thought of Travis when I took care of wounded patients. It was too much for me to be around the trauma and the death. My tour with the air force was ending around that time, and I didn't sign up for more time. My mother could see how much I was suffering, and she suggested I come out here to try to find some peace, a place that *is* peaceful. That's why I love it here."

Saul's expression was full of sympathy. "Have your nightmares at least gotten any better now that you're away from the hospital and the military base?"

"I don't have them as frequently, and I've found ways to cope." She held up the afghan. "Sometimes the nightmares get so bad that running doesn't help me. One day I started making this afghan, and I felt better. Lately, I've only had them a couple of nights a week."

He nodded. "I'm glad to hear that. I hope it continues to get better."

The compassion in his expression made her feel secure, and she relished the comfort. She was surprised by how close she felt to him at that moment. They were truly becoming friends.

"You're the first person I've shared that story with, other than my parents," she admitted. "Not even with other women who've been my friends. I don't normally tell people about the letter Travis left me. I'm always afraid they'll judge Travis or that they won't understand."

"*Danki* for trusting me with your story."

The intensity in Saul's eyes caused her heart to skip

a beat. Did he feel close to her too? A moment passed between them, and she tried to think of something to say to fill the space. She looked down at the clipboard.

"You put those sketches together quickly."

He shrugged. "It doesn't take me long when I know what I want to do."

"Great." She set the afghan on her lap. "I can't wait to see them."

He handed her the clipboard. "Let me know what you think."

Madeleine flipped through the sketches and nodded. "These are exactly what I want." She tried to imagine the new cabinets in her kitchen. "Should we walk out to the kitchen to talk? I want to compare these sketches to the old cabinets."

"That sounds like a *gut* idea."

He followed her out to the kitchen, and she studied the old cabinets and the sketches. "This is perfect. I think they will look fantastic, don't you?"

He nodded.

"I think my *daadi* built the original cabinets."

"*Ya*, he did. He told me." Saul ran his fingers over the counter. "He did all of the work in the kitchen. He and his *daed* built this *haus*."

"Did you know my grandparents well?" Madeleine asked.

"I did. My best friend, Marcus, told me your grandparents were looking to sell part of their property, and he thought I might want to buy it. I didn't have enough room on the land my parents left me to build a big shop. My *dat* wasn't a farmer, and he didn't have much property at all. I already had a buyer for my land, but I hadn't found anything I liked yet." He leaned against the counter. "I came and met your *daadi*, and we struck a deal. I got to know them well over the years."

Madeleine smiled. "They were really good people. I didn't see them much once my mother remarried and I became a teenager. I got busy with school and college and then my military service. And even when I was here, I only stayed a day or two. Not long enough to meet anyone." Her smile faded. "But mostly, I miss them."

"I do too," Saul said. "After Mel passed away, I used to stop by to see Martha frequently and ask if she needed anything."

"Really?" Madeleine was overwhelmed with appreciation for him. "That's very nice. Thank you for doing that."

"Martha was a very special lady. She had a special relationship with my Emma." Saul looked down at the counter, and Madeleine wondered if it was painful for him to talk about his feelings. "After Annie was gone and Emma got old enough to venture off our property by herself a little, Emma began visiting Martha. Martha became a *mammi* to her. In fact, I'm certain you already know Emma called her 'Mammi.' I was grateful that God put a mother figure in Emma's life. We didn't have my *mamm* or Annie's *mamm* around."

He rubbed his bearded chin. "Martha taught Emma a lot of things *mamms* are supposed to teach daughters. She taught her how to sew, how to work in the garden, how to cook." He looked at her and smiled. "How to use the wringer washer."

She laughed. "Is that directed at me?"

He grinned, and Madeleine laughed again.

"In all seriousness," he continued, "Martha was a special friend to Emma. It was difficult for us when she passed away."

Tears filled Madeleine's eyes once again. "I hated that I missed the service for her, especially after I had missed my grandfather's funeral too. I was on my way home from overseas when she died, and I didn't get home in time. My mom said it was lovely, though."

"It was." He paused. "Emma was upset for a long time. She cried and cried about Martha. I didn't know how to help her. Your *mammi* meant a lot to her."

"I imagine Emma meant a lot to her too." Madeleine thought back to the time she spent with her grandmother. "Whenever I visited here as a child, my *mammi* let me stay in my mother's room. I wore my mother's Amish clothes, and I went to service with my grandparents. Sometimes my *mammi* would accidentally call me Leah. She would have tears in her eyes, and she would say I looked just like my mother."

Saul nodded slowly. "It had to be difficult for her to see you and think of Leah."

"Did she ever talk to you about my mother?" Madeleine asked.

"Sometimes she'd mention Leah and say that she missed her. I told her I understood because, well—" He paused for a moment, and she wondered if he was thinking of Annie and her abandonment. "My *bruder* had left."

Madeleine longed to ask him about Annie, but she

didn't want to say too much. She didn't want to ruin their budding friendship. "It has to be challenging for you to raise Emma alone."

Saul's expression hardened and his shoulders stiffened. He took the clipboard from her and studied the sketches. Madeleine immediately regretted her words. She'd said something that upset him, and she groped for a subject that would make it better.

"You've done a wonderful job with Emma," Madeleine continued. "She's a lovely girl."

"Let me show you the estimate," he said, flipping to the last page on the clipboard. "Does this work for your budget?" He handed the clipboard back to her.

In a flash, his warm, friendly demeanor was gone, and he was all business. Annie was a forbidden subject. Madeleine yearned to take back what she'd said. She longed for the closeness she'd felt with him while they were talking in the spare room.

"Saul." She studied his eyes. "I'm sorry."

"Take a look at the estimate." He tapped the paper. "Does this work for you?"

Madeleine craned her neck and studied the document. "This is fine. How much do you need now to start the job?"

He pointed toward the last line on the document. "There's the deposit. Does that work for you?"

"Yes. I'll write you a check." She headed into the spare room and fished her checkbook out of the desk. She sank into the desk chair and sighed. Why did she have to ruin the nice conversation she was enjoying with Saul? He had a warm heart, and he loved his daughter. She saw glimpses of the kind and gentle man he most likely had been when he was first married. She wanted to get to know him better, but he had built a wall around his heart after his wife abandoned him and Emma. She prayed that she could see beyond that wall and maybe even melt his heart.

. . .

Saul stared after Madeleine as she left the kitchen, guilt filling his heart. He knew he'd hurt her feelings when he abruptly changed the subject, but he couldn't bring himself to discuss Annie. The subject was too painful, and opening up that wound made him too vulnerable.

Yet he had immediately felt remorseful when he'd glimpsed the hurt in Madeleine's eyes. She, too, had been hurt by someone, but he wasn't ready to share his feelings about Annie's abandonment with anyone. It was best to keep those feelings close to his shattered heart.

The storm door opened and shut with a bang, and Emma stood in the mudroom doorway with a frown creasing her sweet face.

"*Dat*?" Emma's voice was shaky. "I was looking for you at the shop."

"Emma?" He opened his arms to her. "*Was iss letz, mei liewe?*"

A tear trickled down her cheek.

"*Kumm*," he said.

She stepped into his hug, and a sob broke from her throat.

"Emma?" Madeleine appeared in the doorway, holding a check in her hand. "What happened?" She turned to Saul. "Is she okay?"

Saul shook his head. "I don't know what's wrong." He looked down at his daughter and then pulled her next to him as he sat down on a chair. "What's wrong, Emma? Please tell me."

Madeleine pulled a chair up next to them. "Are you okay, Emma?" She touched Emma's arm. "Do you want me to leave so you can talk to your *dat* alone?"

"No, you can stay." Emma wiped her eyes. "It's Jacob. He made fun of me again on the playground."

"Who's Jacob?" Madeleine asked.

"He's a mean *bu* at my school." Emma's face twisted into a scowl. "He makes comments to me every day. Today was worse." Her eyes flooded with tears again. "He laughed when I fell on the playground, and then he called me a wimpy *maedel* when I couldn't hit the soft-ball. He embarrassed me in front of everyone. I yelled at him, and he kept laughing at me."

Saul felt frustration boil inside of him. He knew he couldn't shield her from all the hurt in the world, but he was determined to try.

"You should talk to Teacher Lillian," Saul said. "Tell her how much Jacob hurts your feelings. If that doesn't work, then I'll talk to Jacob's parents."

Madeleine rubbed Emma's arm. "I had a boy tease me when I was about your age."

"You did?" Emma sniffed and wiped her hand over her eyes again. "What did you do?"

"Well, I talked to my teacher, and she said she'd talk

to him." Madeleine pushed back a lock of Emma's hair that had fallen from her prayer covering. "But I found something that worked better than that."

"What was it?" Emma asked with curiosity.

"I ignored him," Madeleine explained. "That did more good than talking to my teacher or her talking to his parents."

Emma tilted her head and studied Madeleine. "Why would that work?"

"It would work because he wants to see you get angry. He's saying mean things and making fun of you to get a rise out of you. It's a game, and in his eyes, he wins when you get angry. He wants to see you upset because then he thinks he's the coolest kid in the class. If you ignore him, then he loses and you win the game." While she spoke, Madeleine took a paper napkin from the holder in the center of the table and gently wiped away Emma's tears.

The sweet gesture caused Saul's heart to warm. At that moment, he was overwhelmed with admiration for Madeleine.

"You're saying that I should just ignore him?" Emma asked.

"Right." Madeleine nodded. "That way you don't give him the power to hurt you."

"Should I still tell my teacher how he embarrasses me?" Emma asked.

"*Ya*," Saul chimed in. "I think you need to tell your teacher." He met Madeleine's gaze, and she nodded in agreement.

"You should tell your teacher, but make sure you're

in private when you tell her. Don't let Jacob hear you tell her that you're upset. He can't know how much he hurts you because then he wins." Madeleine touched Emma's shoulder. "Do you think you can be strong and not show your emotions?"

"*Ya*, I *can* do it." Emma wrapped her arms around Madeleine's neck and hugged her close. "*Danki*."

"You're welcome." Madeleine smiled. "I'm happy to help."

"Maddie," Emma said, "you're my best grown-up friend."

Saul's shoulders stiffened. He and his daughter were getting too emotionally involved with Madeleine. She was a nice person, someone who had been hurt like him, but she was making her way into their hearts, and this could only lead to trouble. He had to find a way to pull away from her—if it wasn't too late.

"*Danki*, Emma." Madeleine's eyes shimmered, and Saul wondered if she was going to cry. "That's the sweetest thing anyone has ever said to me." She wiped her own eyes and then turned to Saul. "Here's my check." She held out the small piece of paper, and her voice quaked. "Let me know when you need more money."

"*Danki*." He slipped the check onto the clipboard. "I'll get started on the cabinets right away. It should take me about two weeks to build them and the counter, and then I'll need to take these old cabinets down."

"What are we making for supper tonight?" Emma asked.

"Oh." Madeleine glanced at Saul. "I don't know if you have plans . . ."

"How about we make something at our *haus* tonight?" Emma looked at her father. "Would it be okay if Maddie and I cooked at our *haus* tonight?"

Saul hesitated as he turned to Madeleine. Her expression was tentative. Did she feel the tension clenching his jaw?

"Please, *Dat*?" Emma folded her hands as if to pray.

He felt stuck between his eager daughter and his determination not to let Madeleine worm her way any further into their lives.

"We can try for another night," Madeleine said.

"Why not tonight?" Emma frowned. "Do *you* have plans?"

"Tonight is fine." Saul stood. "I have work to do, but you two can figure out a menu. We have plenty of food at our *haus*. I went to the market earlier today."

"*Ya.*" Emma clapped. "I know exactly what we can make."

. . .

Madeleine dried the last of the dishes and placed them in a cabinet while Emma still prattled on about school and her friends. All during supper she'd wondered how she could make Saul see that she'd never meant to cross the line with him or hurt his feelings by asking about his former wife. She couldn't stand the distance between them. He'd avoided her gaze and studied his plate the whole time they were eating.

"Supper was *appeditlich*," Saul said as he stood by

the mudroom door. "I'm going to go out in the shop for a little while."

"Don't stay out too late, *Dat*," Emma said, sounding like his mother instead of his daughter. "You need your rest."

Saul's mouth turned up in a slight smile. "I promise I won't." He turned to Madeleine and gave her a half-hearted nod. "*Gut nacht*, Madeleine."

Madeleine stiffened at the sound of her formal name. She couldn't stand the awkwardness, and she wouldn't sleep until their friendship was back on track.

He disappeared through the door, and Madeleine turned to Emma.

"I think I'm going to head home," she said. "I need to do a few things before I go to bed."

"Okay." Emma smiled up at her. "I'll see you soon."

"Yes, you will," Madeleine agreed. "Now, remember what I said about the bully. Be sure to stand your ground with him, and don't let him get to you. Let me know what happens."

"Okay." Emma gave her a quick hug. "*Gut nacht*."

"*Gut nacht*." Madeleine pulled on her coat and hurried outside. She was going to talk to Saul and set things straight before she headed home.

She found Saul in the shop, rearranging piles of wood.

"Saul."

He turned toward her, and his eyebrows rose toward his hairline.

"Can we talk before I go home?" She shivered and hugged her coat closer to her body.

"*Ya.*" He leaned on the workbench.

She took a deep breath and prayed for the right words. "I'm sorry about earlier."

He shook his head. "I don't understand."

"When you came to see me this afternoon, I know I crossed a line." She hoped his expression would relax. "I was rude, and I didn't mean to be. I would never try to deliberately hurt your feelings or make you uncomfortable."

His expression remained stoic, but she thought she saw a change in his eyes. She needed to continue trying to bring back the warm man she'd glimpsed.

"You know I was hurt too," she said. "I explained it all to you earlier. I never imagined I'd wind up here in Pennsylvania and all alone. I believed I'd be married and have children of my own by now. After losing Travis, I lost my love of nursing. I lost everything." She put one hand on her chest. "Travis left a hole in my heart."

Saul looked toward the workbench, and she knew she'd hit a nerve. She did a mental head shake. Why had she managed to say the wrong thing again?

"I should go." She jammed her thumb toward the door. "Good night, Saul."

. . .

Saul saw the regret in Madeleine's eyes, and he couldn't let her go. She'd bared her soul to him earlier, and then he'd shut her out. She was trying to reach out to him, and he had to tell her the truth. After all, though few talked about divorce, the rumors about Annie when she first left had spread throughout the community like wildfire. Eventually Madeleine could run into someone who would tell her the truth about Annie.

Madeleine reached for the doorknob.

"Wait," Saul said, and her hand fell to her side. "Please don't go."

She faced him, fresh tears shimmering in her eyes.

"Thank you for sharing your story with me. Now I need to tell you the truth about Annie." He heaved a deep breath as he took a step toward her. "Annie left me and Emma."

Madeleine wiped her eyes and studied him.

He paused and stared down at the toes of his work boots. "This isn't easy for me to talk about."

"I'm sorry." Her voice was soft. "You don't have to tell me."

"No, I do." He looked up at her. "You deserve the truth."

She nodded.

"Annie loved someone else, and I knew I was her second choice." He crossed his arms over his chest as if to protect his heart. "She loved my friend Timothy, but he left and went to a former Amish community in Missouri. She was heartbroken, and I tried to console her. When I asked her to marry me, I knew she only said yes because I was her last option. I had saved up money to buy this land and build this shop after also selling my parents' land." He gestured around the room. "I knew she was marrying me out of desperation, but I never imagined she'd leave me."

Saying the words out loud twisted his insides, but he plowed through, moving his gaze back to his boots to avoid her sympathetic expression. "I don't think she expected this, but Timothy came back for her once he was settled and had a home ready for her. It was obvious she still didn't love me the way I'd hoped she someday would, but I prayed she'd make it work between us for Emma's sake." He shook his head. "But she left and never looked back. And then one day I received divorce papers in the mail. I was shattered by that. Our community doesn't believe in divorce. But I signed them because I didn't really have a choice."

A tear trickled down Madeleine's cheek. "I'm sorry."

Saul took in her kind expression and then cleared his throat to avoid showing his own raging emotions. "I told Emma her mother passed away. It was easier to say that than to tell her that her own *mamm* left her for a man. She once asked me how she died, and I said it was pneumonia. I told her Annie had gone into the hospital and never come home, and that satisfied her questions. She never asked me where her mother is buried, never asked if there was a funeral she just didn't remember because she was so young. So it's been possible to keep up the lie. I know lying is a sin, but I would do anything to protect her from the painful truth."

"I understand," Madeleine whispered.

"And that lie is the truth now." Saul leaned back on the workbench. "Timothy wrote me a little over a year ago and told me Annie died in an accident. He and Annie were spending the day on a friend's boat, and there was a collision with another boat." He shook his head. "She really is gone, and I need to tell Emma the truth someday. I'm waiting for the right time to tell her."

"That makes sense." She fingered the zipper on her coat. "I meant what I said this afternoon when I said you are doing a great job with Emma. She's a lovely young lady."

"*Danki.*" Saul fingered his beard. "Now that Annie is gone, I want to find Emma a proper mother."

"I'm certain you will." Madeleine was silent for a moment, and he felt overwhelmed by the soft expression in her eyes. "You're a good man, Saul, and you deserve to be happy. Annie was blind if she couldn't see that, but don't sell yourself short. You deserve a good woman, one who will appreciate you. You're a wonderful father, a hard worker, and you're thoughtful and kind. You're a good friend."

Saul was speechless. He'd never expected such enormous compliments to come from her lips.

"Thank you for sharing that with me," Madeleine said. "I should go."

He nodded, still not certain what to say.

She started for the door and then faced him again. "Thanksgiving is next week, and I was wondering if you and Emma have plans. I know sometimes there are weddings on Thanksgiving."

"We usually eat at my friend Marcus's *haus*."

"Oh." She frowned. "I understand. I was thinking about going home to California to see my mom and stepdad, but I'd rather save the money for the cabinets."

"You should come." He extended the invitation before thinking it through.

"What do you mean?"

"Come to Marcus's with us." He stood up straight. "You'll be my guest."

"Oh." She looked surprised. "Are you certain that would be okay?"

"Why not?"

"I don't know if Marcus would want an *Englisher* at his table on Thanksgiving." She gave him a nervous smile.

"It will be fine. I'll let him know."

"What can I bring?" she asked.

"I usually provide dessert. Maybe you can make a pie."

"Great." Madeleine's expression brightened. "I'll make a pumpkin pie. Two of them." She rubbed her hands together. "I have my *mammi's* recipe." She started for the door again. "Good night, Saul."

"*Gut nacht.*" She disappeared from the shop, and Saul hoped he hadn't made a mistake by baring his soul to his new friend.

SIXTEEN

Emma gnawed her lower lip. She had stayed just inside the schoolhouse door as the rest of the students started leaving at the end of the day, and now she was watching Teacher Lillian wave good-bye to them as they filed past. She'd been considering what she'd say to her teacher ever since she'd spoken to Madeleine last week. Today felt like the right time to talk to her.

Teacher Lillian waved to the last student and then turned toward Emma. "Emma? What are you still doing here?" She pushed her glasses farther up her nose and studied her. "Is everything okay?"

Emma fingered the handle on her lunchbox. "Jacob has been bullying me."

"*Ach* no. Let's sit and talk." Lillian made a sweeping gesture toward the desks.

Emma took a seat at her desk and faced her teacher, who pulled a chair up next to her. "He makes fun of me when I miss the ball during softball and he calls me names."

Teacher Lillian shook her head and frowned. "I'm sorry I haven't noticed he was doing that to you."

"I talked to my friend Maddie, and she gave me some *gut* advice." Emma sat up taller as confidence surged through her. "She told me she had bully problems when she was my age, and she ignored the bully. She said Jacob is just trying to get a reaction out of me, and I'll take away his power if I ignore him."

"That sounds like a *gut* plan."

"*Mei dat* said I should still talk to you about Jacob."

Lillian nodded. "I will talk to Jacob and his parents."

"I don't want him to know he upset me, though." Emma held her hands up as if to stop her teacher. "He can't know I gave him that power. I need him to think it doesn't bother me. Maddie said that's the only way to defeat a bully."

"I'll keep a better watch on the playground and do my best to catch him in the act. After I see what he's doing, I'll talk to him, and I'll also talk to his parents. Would that work?"

"*Ya*." Emma nodded with enthusiasm. "That would be perfect. *Danki*, Teacher Lillian." She stood and started for the door.

"Wait, Emma," Lillian called after her. "Who is your friend Maddie?"

"She's my neighbor." Emma smiled. "She's *English*. Her *mammi* owned the property where *mei dat* and I live before he bought it. Maddie moved into her *mammi's haus*, and we've become best *freinden*. We cook together, and *mei dat* is replacing her cabinets. We have a lot of fun together."

"Oh." Lillian grimaced. "You know it's best not to get too close to *Englishers*. They aren't like us. They live a different way, and they sometimes offer a temptation to leave our community."

"She wouldn't do that." Emma felt the need to defend her special friend. "She's very nice, and she's my *freind*."

Teacher Lillian paused. "It would be better if you didn't spend too much time with her. Just promise me you'll be careful. You don't want to get too attached to her and then wind up hurt."

"I don't understand. What do you mean by 'hurt'?" Emma contemplated her teacher's caution.

"*Mei mamm* became *English*, and I don't see her anymore. It's been very hard on me," her teacher said. "I know this must be difficult for you to understand, but I miss *mei mamm* very much. She's not Amish anymore, and it's made me *bedauerlich*. I don't want you to be *bedauerlich* if Maddie decides to move away."

"Oh." Emma smiled. "Maddie said *mei dat* has said that same thing, but I don't think she'll move away. Most people stay in their *haus* after they fix it up, right? *Mei dat* says that a lot of times people put new cabinets in so they enjoy their *haus* even more. It's a lot of money to put in new cabinets."

"Right." Teacher Lillian nodded. "You'd better go. I don't want your *dat* to worry about you. Be careful walking home."

"I will. Have a nice Thanksgiving!" Emma waved and then rushed out of the school. As she walked home, she thought about her conversation with Teacher Lillian. Maddie wouldn't leave like Teacher Lillian said. Her teacher had to be wrong. After all, Maddie was her best grown-up friend. She pushed her worries aside as she walked home. Everything was going to be fine. Jacob was going to leave her alone, and Maddie was going to stay.

. . .

Madeleine placed the two pumpkin pies she'd baked into the bottom of a large basket she'd found in the pantry. She hoped the pies tasted as delicious as they smelled and looked. She'd worried all morning about giving Saul's friends a good impression of her, and she'd changed her clothes four times before settling on a matching chocolate-brown blouse and skirt with tights. She'd styled her hair in a French twist and didn't apply any makeup.

A knock sounded, and Madeleine pulled on her coat and carried the basket to the mudroom where she could see Saul and Emma through the window on the door.

"Are you ready?" Saul asked as soon as she swung open the storm door.

"Yes, I am." She held up the basket. "I'm hoping these pies will taste as good as my *mammi's*."

"I'm sure they will." Saul took the basket from her. "I'll carry this for you."

"Let's go." Emma started toward the pickup truck. "I can't wait to see Esther."

Madeleine climbed into the driver's seat, and Emma sat in the middle with her father beside her. Emma spent the short ride to the Smucker farm discussing recipes. Madeleine nodded and agreed with whatever Emma said, but her mind was occupied with thoughts of Saul. She hoped he approved of her outfit, and she prayed she wouldn't say anything that embarrassed him or made him regret inviting her to join them for Thanksgiving dinner.

When they arrived at the farm, Madeleine parked halfway up the rock driveway and killed the engine. She climbed out of the truck and met Saul at the front bumper while Emma ran ahead toward the house. Madeleine studied the farmhouse, and doubt assaulted her mind. Why was she here at this Amish family's house? She didn't have a right to intrude on their holiday. She belonged with her non-Amish family in California.

"Are you all right?" Saul asked.

"Yes." She forced a smile.

He studied her. "I haven't known you long, but I can tell when you're not being truthful."

"Am I that obvious?" she asked.

He nodded. "You are to me."

"I'm nervous about meeting your friends." She smoothed her hands over her coat. "I don't want to embarrass you."

"You won't embarrass me, and they're looking forward to meeting you." He started for the house. "Let's go inside before we freeze out here."

Madeleine followed Saul into the two-story, white clapboard house, and she immediately inhaled the delicious aroma of turkey. They made their way through the spacious family room to the kitchen, where Emma and a little blonde girl were setting the table. She remembered her being with Emma at Carolyn's wedding.

"Hello!" A pretty blonde woman who looked to

be in her early thirties smiled at them. "You must be Madeleine. I'm Sylvia."

"It's nice to meet you." Madeleine unbuttoned her coat. "Thank you for having me for supper."

"You're welcome." Sylvia touched Esther's arm. "This is Esther." The girl waved.

"It's nice to meet you," Madeleine told the girl. "I saw you with Emma at Carolyn Glick's wedding, and I've heard a lot about you from Emma."

"*Danki,*" Esther said.

Sylvia looked at Saul. "Marcus is in the shop if you want to go see him. I'll send the girls out to get you when supper is ready."

"All right." Saul handed Sylvia the basket. "Maddie made pies."

"Oh!" Sylvia took the basket from him. "That's perfect. *Danki.*" She placed the basket on the counter.

Saul held out his hand. "Would you like me to hang up your coat?"

"That would be nice." Madeleine handed her coat to him.

He headed toward the back door, stopping to hang up her coat near the mudroom on his way out.

Madeleine glanced around the kitchen and into the family room and enclosed porch. "You have a lovely home."

"*Danki.*" Sylvia pointed toward a pot on the stove. "Would you please stir the noodles?"

"Oh yes." Madeleine moved to the stove, happy to have a job to keep her mind off how self-conscious she felt.

"Saul told us you work at the Lancaster Grand Hotel." Sylvia pulled a loaf of bread from the bread box on the counter and began to slice it.

"Yes, I work there part-time." Madeleine stirred while she spoke. "Martha Stoltzfus was my *mammi*."

"I'm sorry for your loss. I remember Martha. She was a lovely lady." Sylvia glanced toward the girls, who were placing utensils by the plates. "Esther, would you please get out the butter and then fill six glasses with water?"

"*Ya, Mamm*," Esther agreed.

"How long have you known Saul?" Madeleine asked.

"Marcus and I went to school with Saul and—" Sylvia stopped speaking as if to correct herself. "We went to school with Saul and his *bruder*."

"Oh." Was Sylvia going to say Annie instead of his brother?

Sylvia finished cutting up the bread and placed it in a basket before moving toward the oven. "Excuse me. I'm going to check the turkey."

"Of course." Madeleine stepped away from the stove and turned toward Esther and Emma, who were discussing friends at school. When Sylvia opened the oven door, the warm smell of the succulent turkey permeated the room.

"I think it's almost ready." Sylvia closed the door and spoke to the girls. "When you finish the table, please go collect your fathers."

Soon the girls pulled on their cloaks and rushed out the door.

"Esther is adorable," Madeleine said. "Emma talks about her all the time."

"*Danki*." Sylvia nodded toward a cabinet. "Would you please grab some serving bowls from there and put the noodles, vegetables, and mashed potatoes in them?"

"I'd be happy to." Madeleine gathered the bowls and began filling them, and Sylvia pulled the turkey from the oven. "Everything smells delicious."

"*Danki*." Sylvia placed the turkey onto a platter. "I'll let Marcus carve it." She faced Madeleine. "I want to talk to you quickly before the girls return."

"Oh." Sylvia's serious expression caused Madeleine's stomach to tighten. "What did you want to discuss?"

Sylvia wiped her hands on a dish towel. "I know you care for Emma and Saul. I can tell by the way you look at them."

Madeleine nodded. "I do."

"I have a feeling Saul cares for you." Sylvia's expression was full of worry. "He may seem like a strong man, but he's been hurt."

"I know about Annie," Madeleine said. "He told me what happened, and I realize he's hurting. I only want to be his friend."

"I knew Annie. What she did to Saul practically destroyed him emotionally. He's held it together all these years just for Emma's sake." Sylvia crossed her arms over her apron. "What Annie did hurt us all. She was my best friend, and I never imagined she'd leave her family for another man. I tried to stop her, but she was stubborn. Anyway, Marcus and I have done our best to help Saul. I've tried to be like a *mamm* to Emma. My point is that I don't want to see either one of them hurt."

"I don't want to see them hurt either," Madeleine

said. "I care about them, and I would never want to hurt them. It's not my intention to cause problems here."

"You seem like a nice person." Sylvia tossed the dish towel onto the counter. "I just need you to promise me you'll be careful of Saul's heart."

"I will," Madeleine said. "But we're only friends."

Sylvia seemed unconvinced, and she wondered why Sylvia had made the assumption they were more than friends. The question filtered through Madeleine's mind while they continued preparing the table for the Thanksgiving feast.

· · ·

Saul followed the girls and Marcus into the house, where he hung his coat and hat on the peg by the back door and then stopped just inside the doorway to the kitchen. He watched Madeleine help Sylvia deliver food to the table and noticed she seemed at ease when she instructed the girls to wash up for supper. He was alarmed by his strong emotions for her. Yet simultaneously, he enjoyed having her join him for the holiday. He was conflicted in his feelings, but he pushed the worry aside and decided to enjoy the day.

Marcus turned to Saul and gave him a concerned expression. "Have a seat."

Saul sank into a chair while Marcus moved to the counter and began to carve the turkey.

When Madeleine and Sylvia had finished their preparations, Madeleine sat in a chair across from him.

She gave him a tentative smile and then looked down at her plate. Why was she suddenly acting shy toward him?

"Here's the turkey." Marcus brought a platter to the table. "It's time to eat."

Marcus sat at the head of the table to Saul's right, and Sylvia sat at the other end of the table. Emma took the chair beside Madeleine, and Esther sat beside her mother. After the silent prayer, the sound of utensils scraping plates filled the air as arms reached and grabbed for the many platters and bowls.

"How do you celebrate Thanksgiving, Maddie?" Emma asked as she plopped a mound of mashed potatoes onto her plate.

"I celebrate the same way you do." Madeleine spooned some stuffing. "We have turkey and the trimmings."

"Does that mean you do exactly the same thing we do on Thanksgiving?" Esther chimed in. "Do you have any traditions that are different from ours?"

"Well, let's see." Madeleine handed the bowl of stuffing to Marcus. "When I was little, my mom and I would say what we were most thankful for before we started to eat."

"Really?" Esther and Emma exchanged smiles. "Let's do that." Esther turned to her father. "What are you most thankful for?"

Marcus stroked his beard with his free hand as he met Sylvia's gaze. "I guess I am most thankful for my family."

"You guess?" Sylvia raised an eyebrow, and Saul stifled a chuckle.

"No, I don't guess," Marcus quickly added. "I am most thankful for my family."

"That's better." Sylvia smiled. "I'm most thankful for my family and our health."

"*Ya*, that's a *gut* one." Marcus picked up the meat platter, selected a piece of turkey, and dropped it onto his plate. He passed the platter to Saul. "Who's next?"

"I am!" Esther raised her hand as if she were in school. "I'm most thankful for our home. I've heard of people who don't have a place to sleep at night, and they must be cold." She pointed toward Emma. "How about you, Emma?"

"I'm thankful for my *freinden*." Emma smiled up at Madeleine. "God has given me wonderful *freinden*."

Madeleine returned the smile, and Saul felt his heart turn over in his chest. The love between his daughter and Madeleine was overwhelming. He tried to look unaffected, however, when in his peripheral vision he saw Marcus was studying him.

"What are you most thankful for, Maddie?" Emma asked.

Madeleine glanced down at her plate and then looked over at Emma again. "I'm thankful for my new home and my new life here in Lancaster County." She then looked across the table at Saul. "What are you most thankful for, Saul?"

Saul looked into her beautiful orbs and then at Emma, who smiled over at him. "I'm most thankful for my family and my *freinden*."

Emma smiled, and he returned the gesture.

• • •

Saul thought he might burst after enjoying the scrumptious Thanksgiving meal and then delicious pumpkin pie. After dessert, Emma and Esther cleaned off the table, and Madeleine and Sylvia began washing the dishes.

Marcus touched Saul's arm. "Let's go outside and check on the animals."

Saul followed him to the back, where they pulled on their coats and then stepped out into the crisp evening air.

"What are you doing?" Marcus asked as they made their way to the barn.

"What do you mean?" Saul asked.

"I see how you look at her." Marcus shook his head. "I know you're lonely, but you know how this is going to end for you."

Saul stopped walking and stared at his best friend. "Are you accusing me of having a relationship with Maddie? We're only *freinden*. Emma enjoys visiting her, and I'm replacing the cabinets in her *haus*."

Marcus snorted with sarcasm. "Please, Saul. I'm not blind, and I'm not stupid. You call her Maddie. You only use nicknames for people you're close to. I thought it was strange when you asked if you could bring her over for supper today, but I never expected you to be this attached. I thought maybe you'd taken pity on her because she's alone. It looks to me like it's more than just pity."

Saul heaved a heavy sigh and leaned against a fence. He'd been caught with his feelings exposed.

"Saul, I've known you since we were *kinner*. I don't want you to wind up hurt. You need to take a step back before she breaks your heart. You've been through enough." Marcus stood beside him. "I'd rather see you meet someone in our community or even someone from another church district. Emma is attached to her, too, and you don't want her to experience another loss, do you?"

"No." Saul shook his head while he stared at Madeleine's truck. "You're right."

"You know I am." Marcus started for the barn.

Marcus disappeared into the barn as his words soaked through Saul. Marcus was right, but Saul didn't know how to let go of the strong and overwhelming emotions that were swelling within him.

. . .

Later that evening, Madeleine kicked off her shoes before she went to her bedroom. She was full both physically and spiritually after the day she had spent at the Smuckers' farm. The food was delicious and the company was delightful. She only wished she could get Sylvia's warning to cease echoing through her mind. Why had Sylvia felt the need to warn her? Why would Sylvia assume Madeleine would hurt Saul? They were only friends!

She was just starting to pull off her tights when her

iPhone began to buzz. She reached over to her dresser and picked it up.

"Happy Thanksgiving, Maddie!" Mom's voice sounded in her ear.

"Hey, Mom." Madeleine smiled. "How was your day?"

"It was good, but we missed you. I've been trying to call you all day. Did you get my messages?"

"Oh, I'm sorry. I went out, and I left my phone here at home." Madeleine balanced the phone between her neck and shoulder while she pulled off her tights and skirt. "I just got home, and I haven't had a chance to check my voice mail."

"Where were you all day?" Now she started pulling on yoga pants and slippers.

"I had Thanksgiving with friends."

"Which friends? Someone from work?"

"No. Saul, Emma, and their friends," Madeleine said. "I had an Amish Thanksgiving."

"What?" Her mother gasped. "I thought you were convinced Saul didn't like you."

"Oh, he's been much nicer recently. He's going to replace my kitchen cabinets." She tried to pull off her blouse but wound up tangled in it. "Hang on a minute." She placed the phone on the dresser and changed into a long-sleeve shirt. "Okay. I'm back."

"Madeleine Dawn!" her mother snapped. "Tell me about Saul and Emma."

"I will. Just calm down." Madeleine sank onto the edge of the bed. "We've been spending time together lately, and I asked them if they had Thanksgiving plans. Saul invited me to go with them to have Thanksgiving dinner with his best friend, Marcus, and his family. We had a really nice time."

"And he's replacing your cabinets?"

"Right," Madeleine said. "He's a cabinetmaker, and the kitchen cabinets are almost falling off the walls. You had to have noticed that when you were here for *Mammi's* service."

"*Ya,* I did." Her mother's voice was softer. "My *daadi* helped my *dat* build those cabinets a very long time ago."

Alarm seeped through Madeleine. She'd never heard her mother use *Dietsch* words before. "Do you want me to leave them? I can ask him to fix them instead of replacing them."

"No, no," her mother said. "It's your house now. You do what you want with it."

"No, Mom." Madeleine shook her head. "Don't be like that. I don't want to upset you."

"It's fine, really. Tell me about your day with Saul and his friends."

Madeleine shared what they ate and how much fun they had talking. "It was a great day. I'm enjoying my new Amish friends. I really feel like I belong here. I mean, I don't even miss electricity or television. I only use my phone to talk to you. And Saul is very sweet. I'm enjoying getting to know him and Emma. Emma told me I'm her best grown-up friend. I helped her figure out how to handle a bully the other day." She paused, but her mother remained quiet. "Hello? Are you there, Mom? Did we get disconnected?"

"I'm still here. I was just listening. I know you like spending time with Saul and Emma, but you need to remember that they're Amish."

"How could I forget that, Mom?" Madeleine asked while rolling onto her side and facing the wall. "I know we're from different worlds. I'm just enjoying their company."

"Well, you sound like you're really close to them."

"They are sort of like my family, even though we're not related." Madeleine shook her head. "I'm not making sense. I'm enjoying being here and being a part of their community. I think I want to go to a church service. *Mammi* used to take me to them. I might call Carolyn and see if I can go to a service with her again."

"That sounds nice," Mom said. "I remember you enjoyed going to services with your grandmother. Just be careful, okay? I don't want you to get hurt. You have to remember that Saul lives by certain rules, and those rules are strict."

"Is that why you left?" Madeleine asked.

"Yes, that's part of the reason."

"And my father was the other reason."

"Yes, I met your father, and we wanted to see the world together."

"Was it easy to leave?"

"No." Mom paused. "It was a difficult decision to leave the only life I'd ever known. I had to say good-bye to my friends and my family. But I was certain I was in love. I was too young and immature to realize the mistakes I was making. I had tunnel vision, and I only wanted to get married to your father. I was anxious to feel grown up even though I was pushing myself too hard."

"I'm sorry. I'm sure it was hard on *Mammi*. I know she missed you."

"Yes, I know it was." Mom sighed. "But your father and I were certain we'd conquer the world. We both wanted to join the military and travel, and the Amish community wouldn't allow me to do that."

"Did you ever regret leaving?" Madeleine asked.

"I missed my parents and my friends, and I often felt alone. It's a big world outside the tight-knit Amish community. I didn't appreciate how the community took care of its members until I was out on my own. It wasn't easy after your father left me, but I never regretted my choices. After all, I had you."

Madeleine smiled. "You should come and visit me. Maybe we could find some of your old friends."

"I might someday," Mom said. "I'm not sure if I'm ready yet."

"Well, you'll have to come and see my new cabinets."

Mom laughed. "That's a deal."

Madeleine sat up. "Tell me about your day."

While her mother talked about her Thanksgiving, Madeleine couldn't help smiling. Her mother was happy in California, but Madeleine had experienced a perfect day in Lancaster County. She was thankful for her new life.

SEVENTEEN

Madeleine called Carolyn Saturday morning. The phone rang several times before someone answered.

"Hello," a feminine voice said. "This is Glick's Belgian and Dutch Harness Horses. How may I help you?"

"Carolyn? This is Madeleine Miller."

"Madeleine!" Carolyn sounded surprised. "How are you?"

"I'm well, thanks. How are you doing?"

"Just great. I'm surprised to hear from you. Is everything all right?"

"Everything is fine," Madeleine said. "I was wondering if I could go to church with you tomorrow if there's a service in the district."

"Actually there is a service, and I'd love for you to come," Carolyn said. "It's going to be held at Ruth Ebersol's *haus*."

"Wonderful," Madeleine said. "I'll meet you there. What's the address?"

"Hang on one moment. Let me check my address book . . . Oh, here it is." Carolyn rattled off the address and directions. "I'll see you tomorrow."

"Great!" Madeleine disconnected the phone and smiled. She felt such a strong connection to the Amish community, and she wanted to experience more of it. She looked through her closet to find the most appropriate outfit to wear. She couldn't wait to experience another Amish church service and meet more members of the community. She was certain her grandparents would be happy to see her immersing herself in the culture again.

· · ·

Madeleine parked her pickup truck on the road beside Ruth's house Sunday morning and then slipped her keys into her skirt pocket as she walked up the driveway. Her eyes moved to the sea of buggies parked by the barn. Would Saul and Emma be at the service today?

She smoothed her hands over her skirt as she entered the kitchen where the women were gathered before the service. She hoped she looked presentable. She'd found her grandmother's cloak and pulled that over her skirt and blouse. She'd also found a Mennonite lace prayer doily and attached it to the back of her head over a tight bun.

"Madeleine!" Carolyn emerged from the circle of women and hugged her. Her eyes took in Madeleine's long black skirt and navy blue blouse. "You look *schee*." Carolyn reached around and touched the lace prayer covering Madeleine had put on her head. "Where did you find that *schee* covering? I love it."

"*Danki*," Madeleine said as she pulled off her cloak

and hung it over her arm. "I found it in my *mammi's* sewing closet. I think she used to make these and sell them to the local Mennonites."

"That's wonderful!" Carolyn pulled her toward the circle of women. "Come meet my family and *freinden*."

Madeleine smiled and shook hands as Carolyn introduced her to the circle of women. She felt a part of the community, and she was thankful for Carolyn's help. After she met everyone in the room, Carolyn led Madeleine over to a quiet corner.

"How have you been?" Carolyn asked. "I haven't had time to talk to you at work."

"I've been fine," Madeleine said. "How was your Thanksgiving in your new home?"

"It was *gut*." Carolyn pushed the ribbons from her prayer covering behind her shoulders. "We had Joshua's parents over, and my family stopped by for dessert. We had a *gut* time. How was yours?"

"It was very nice. Saul and Emma Beiler invited me to eat with them at Marcus Smucker's *haus*. I really had a lovely time. I took two homemade pumpkin pies."

"How fun!" Carolyn smiled. "Did you enjoy your first Amish Thanksgiving?"

"I really enjoyed spending the day with Saul, Emma, and their friends. They made me feel comfortable and welcome. It was perfect." Madeleine considered telling Carolyn what Sylvia had said to her, but she decided not to. She didn't want to give Carolyn the wrong impression about her friendship with Saul.

"I'm glad you're getting to know Saul and Emma." Carolyn's smile suddenly faded. "I want to tell you something, but I don't want anyone else to hear." She moved closer to Madeleine and lowered her voice. "Josh still wants me to quit the hotel, no later than spring. I really don't want to quit yet. I want to keep working there, maybe even longer than spring. But he's insistent."

"Oh." Madeleine studied her friend. "Why do you want to keep working there? Doesn't he need your help with the horse business?"

"He does, but the job at the hotel was all I had for a long time. It doesn't feel right to give it up. Not yet."

"But you're his wife now. Aren't you expected to be home and helping him?" Madeleine asked. "Aren't you supposed to be his helpmate?"

Carolyn sighed. "I know you're right. I want to be his helpmate, but I also want to help our family by bringing in my own little salary. I can save that money for Benjamin. I can help him buy his own *haus* when he's old enough."

"I'm certain Joshua will help him buy a *haus*. Isn't Joshua going to adopt him?" Madeleine asked.

Carolyn smiled. "*Ya*, he is. Benjamin will be a Glick soon."

"You don't need to worry about Benjamin as much now." Madeleine touched Carolyn's arm. "Josh is going to take care of you both. You know he will."

The kitchen clock started to chime nine.

"It's time to head into the barn." Carolyn pointed toward Madeleine's cloak. "You're going to need that."

"Madeleine!" Ruth approached them with a wide smile and hugged Madeleine. "What a nice surprise."

"It's great to see you too," Madeleine said. "I called

Carolyn yesterday and asked if there was a service today."

"I'm glad you came. Would you like to sit in the back with me?" Ruth asked.

"I'd love that." Madeleine followed Ruth and Carolyn as they made their way toward the large barn where the backless benches were set up.

Carolyn touched Madeleine's hand. "I'm going to go sit with my sister-in-law. I'll see you after the service."

"Okay," Madeleine said. As soon as she was sitting in the back beside Ruth, she scanned the congregation and spotted Emma with the other young girls, sitting beside Esther. Emma met her gaze and waved. Madeleine smiled as she waved in response.

She looked over to the area where the married men— and obviously men who had been married—sat. Saul was leaning over and talking to Marcus beside him. Saul was handsome in his Sunday best. The thought took her by surprise. Was she attracted to Saul? Did she have a crush on him? She thought of Sylvia's warning, and suddenly it made sense. Had Sylvia noticed an attraction between Madeleine and Saul? She swallowed a groan. Any relationship between Saul and her would be forbidden. She couldn't tempt him to break the rules, which was what her mother had been trying to tell her on the phone Thursday night.

Madeleine had to dismiss any romantic feelings she may have for Saul. Besides, after losing Travis, she didn't need another broken heart. She was better off alone.

Soon the congregation began singing, and Madeleine followed along in the *Ausbund*. She lost

herself in the beauty of the Amish service and thought
of her grandparents. She would have loved to worship
with them in her adult years.

. . .

Saul followed along with the opening hymn. But soon
the sound of the congregation singing was only background noise to his churning thoughts. He'd spent the
past couple of days working on Madeleine's cabinets
and thinking of her. Marcus's warning echoed in his
mind constantly. He needed to find a way to get her out
of his thoughts, but it seemed impossible.

His eyes scanned the congregation, and when he
spotted her in the back row, he froze.

"Saul?" Marcus whispered. "*Was iss letz?*"

"Nothing," Saul muttered.

"Something is wrong. You look upset," Marcus
prodded.

"No, no." Saul looked down at the *Ausbund*. He
tried to join in the singing, but his gaze was drawn to
Madeleine as if she were a magnet pulling him to her
without his consent or control. She was beautiful with
her cloak over a navy blue blouse, and her hair was
pulled back in a bun. His heart thumped in his chest.
She followed along with the hymn, and her mouth
moved in time with the rest of the congregation. She
could actually read and understand the words to *Lob
Lied*? This left him stunned.

Saul tried to imagine Madeleine as a member of
the church, but the idea was preposterous. How could

someone who'd grown up *English* and had even served in the military make the ultimate sacrifice of giving up all her worldly possessions and joining an Amish church district? She could never settle for the plain life after seeing the world. Conversions rarely happened, and he didn't expect her to be the first *Englisher* to join his church district.

But if she were to join, then we could be together.

He shook his head. Madeleine wasn't going to join the church, and he had to stop taunting himself with the idea. He needed to stay loyal to his church and his beliefs and also be the best example possible for his daughter. He would finish Madeleine's cabinets and then go back to being only a neighbor to her. They would wave if they saw each other outside and leave it at that.

Saul trained his eyes on the *Ausbund*, but he couldn't bring himself to sing. Instead, his thoughts were stuck on Madeleine and the temptation he felt when he was near her. The women he allowed in Emma's life had to be proper influences. Perhaps Marcus and Sylvia would help him find a widow or unmarried woman who would consider dating him.

Throughout the service, Saul didn't hear the minister's or the bishop's words; instead, he was thinking of his daughter.

His thoughts were interrupted when the minister recited a verse from the book of James. "'Therefore confess your sins to each other and pray for each other so that you may be healed,'" he said. "'The prayer of a righteous person is powerful and effective.'"

The verse felt like a punch to Saul's chest. *I need God to lead my life in the right direction.* When he thought about Madeleine and her beauty, he was allowing himself to be just as sinful as Annie. *I have to stop this before it's too late. It's my job to lead Emma toward the plain life, and I need God's help.*

Saul closed his eyes and prayed for God to cleanse his thoughts and his prayers.

. . .

Madeleine helped Ruth and Carolyn deliver food to the tables after the service before moving around the long tables to fill coffee cups and greet the members of the congregation. She smiled at everyone.

She was filling the last cup when she noticed Saul sitting with the other men at one of the tables. She had tried to catch his eye during the service, but he was so engrossed in the service that he never looked her way. When he finally met her gaze, she smiled at him. He returned the gesture with a tentative smile and then turned back to Marcus. Why wasn't he as friendly as he'd been on Thursday? She hoped to talk to him privately later.

"Maddie!" Emma appeared behind her. "It's *gut* to see you here at church."

"Hi, Emma." Madeleine held up the empty coffeepot. "I'm heading back to the kitchen. Would you like to walk with me?"

"*Ya!*" Emma fell into step beside her. "I can help you fill cups if you'd like."

"We'll see what Ruth needs us to do," Madeleine said. "It was a nice service."

"Could you understand it?" Emma asked.

"I understood most of it," Madeleine said as they stepped into the kitchen.

Madeleine and Emma helped deliver more food for the men and then ate lunch with the women. Afterward, they assisted with cleaning up the kitchen.

Once the kitchen was clean, Madeleine found her cloak and pulled it on as she moved to where Carolyn and Ruth were talking. "*Danki* for including me in the service today. I had a really nice time."

"We loved having you," Carolyn said. "I'm *froh* you could come."

"Absolutely," Ruth agreed. "I'll see you at work on Tuesday."

"Have a nice afternoon," Madeleine said before stepping out to the driveway.

She was almost to her truck when she saw Saul standing outside with Marcus, Sylvia, and the girls. She waved, and she was certain that Saul and Marcus exchanged concerned expressions. What did those expressions mean? Certainly they had nothing to do with her.

Saul said something to Emma, and they began walking toward her.

"Maddie!" Emma ran over with Saul following closely behind.

"Hi, Emma!" Madeleine hugged her and looked to where Saul stood. "Hi, Saul. I didn't get to talk to you much today."

"I was surprised to see you here." His expression was devoid of the usual warmth. He glanced down at Emma. "Go to the buggy. I'll be there in a moment."

Emma gave him a curious expression and then turned to Madeleine. "I'll see you later."

"I look forward to it," Madeleine told her before she headed off. She looked back at Saul. "I was hoping you and Emma could join me for supper tonight. I was going to make something special."

Saul cupped his hand to the back of his neck and frowned. "I'm sorry, Madeleine, but I don't think that's a *gut* idea."

"Oh?" Her stomach twisted with worry. "Why not?"

"Look, I like you, Madeleine. I like you a lot, but I don't think you're the best influence for Emma. It's better to keep our relationship neighborly."

"Neighborly?" She shook her head. "I don't understand."

His expression was cold, as if they'd just met, but his eyes seemed sad again. "I'm going to have your cabinets ready for installation in a couple of weeks. Until then, I don't think we should see each other."

"But we had such a nice time on Thanksgiving." Madeleine groped for an explanation to his sudden coldness. "What's changed?" She glanced past him to where Marcus was watching them. "Is it Marcus? Does he disapprove of our friendship?"

"I'm sorry, Madeleine. It's better this way. I can't risk losing my *dochder* to the outside world. She's all I have left."

"I don't want to take your daughter or tempt her to

leave the Amish church." Madeleine's voice was thick with disappointment and hurt.

"I'm sorry," he repeated.

They stared at each other, and tears stung her eyes.

Without uttering another word, Saul turned and started for his buggy.

She wiped the tears that splattered her cheeks.

What have I done to make him reject me as if I were a total stranger? I'm not even worthy of Saul's and Emma's friendship. I've failed again, just like I failed with Travis. I'm not worthy of the Amish community.

· · ·

Lillian saw Ruth across the kitchen talking to her aunt Carolyn and an *Englisher* woman. She'd longed to talk to Ruth all day, but she wanted to get her alone to keep their conversation private. She waited until Carolyn and the *Englisher* left, and then she crossed the kitchen and stopped next to Ruth.

"Ruth," Lillian said. "I was hoping to talk to you."

"Lily!" Ruth smiled at her. "How are you?"

"I'm fine, *danki*." Lillian looked around the kitchen at all the women talking and laughing. "Could we please speak privately?"

"Of course, dear." Ruth pointed toward a doorway. "Let's go into my sewing room."

"That would be perfect." Lillian followed the older woman into a small room containing a treadle sewing machine, two chairs, and a table cluttered with piles of material.

"You look troubled." Ruth sank into a chair and motioned for Lillian to sit beside her. "What's on your mind?"

"I've been struggling with something." Lillian's voice was thick with her emotion. "I tried talking to *mei mammi*, but she doesn't understand. I thought you might be able to help me sort through my feelings."

"Of course, *mei liewe*. What is it?"

"I used to believe I was supposed to completely shun *mei mamm* and not have anything to do with her." Lillian's eyes filled with tears. "I thought I should punish her for leaving me. But now I don't know what I'm supposed to do." She stared down at her lap, plucking some fuzz off her apron. "I found out that *mei mamm* is going to have a *boppli*."

"She is?" Ruth gasped. "What a blessing!"

Lillian looked up and Ruth smiled with tears glistening in her eyes. "I know," she whispered. "A *boppli* is always a blessing, and I want to be a part of my new sibling's life."

"Of course you do." Ruth touched Lillian's hand. "That *boppli* is your family, just as your *mamm*, Amanda, Andrew, and even Trey are your family."

"But I don't know how to forgive *mei mamm*." Tears trickled down her hot cheeks, splattering her glasses. "I don't know how to let go of the anger I have about her leaving me. Like I said, I tried to talk to *mei mammi* about this, but she doesn't understand how I feel stuck in the middle. She says *mei mamm* doesn't deserve to be forgiven for taking my siblings away from her and also for leaving the church. I want to have my family, but I also want to stay Amish."

Ruth nodded. "I understand how you feel."

"You do?" Lillian asked. "How can you understand?"

"My son left Paradise," Ruth said. "He moved to a former Amish community in Missouri."

"I had no idea." Lillian removed her glasses and wiped her sleeve over her face before rubbing a corner of her apron over the lenses. "When did he leave?"

"It's been about seventeen years ago now." Ruth had a faraway look in her eyes. "I miss him every day, but I'm also angry and hurt that he left."

Lillian nodded slowly. "That's exactly how I feel. I still love *mei mamm*, and I miss her. But I'm angry and hurt that she left me."

"But we have to remember what the Lord says in the book of Matthew. 'If you do not forgive others their sins, your Father will not forgive your sins.'"

Lillian contemplated the Scripture verse. "You're saying I need to forgive her."

Ruth nodded. "Yes. It's not easy, but you need to forgive her. I've forgiven my son, even though it's been hard." She patted Lillian's hand. "Think about it, and pray about it, Lily. Let the Lord guide your heart."

"*Danki.*" Lillian stood and hugged her friend.

"*Gern gschehne.*" Ruth patted Lillian's back. "You can talk to me anytime you need to."

EIGHTEEN

Guilt rained down on Saul as he guided his horse toward his house after the church service. He hadn't been able to stand the sadness and disappointment in Madeleine's eyes when he told her they couldn't be friends anymore. He still couldn't. He had to sever their close relationship, but saying the words out loud to her cut deeply into his soul. He hadn't experienced such a deep attachment to a woman since he was a young man. Yet he had to suppress those feelings and concentrate on raising his daughter the right way, teaching her to live within the confines of the *Ordnung*.

"Emma," he said while keeping his eyes trained on the road ahead, "we need to discuss something serious."

"What's that, *Dat*?" Emma asked while sitting beside him.

"I need you to stop spending time with Madeleine."

"But you said I could go to her *haus* while you were working on her cabinets."

"I made a mistake. I should've stuck with my original decision to keep our distance," Saul said. "I was wrong. You need to be with other Amish."

"But she was Amish at one time."

"No, she wasn't. Her grandparents were Amish. She was raised *English*, and you know that, Emma."

"But she's my best *freind*," Emma said, her voice raising an octave.

"No, she's not your best *freind*. Esther Smucker is your best *freind*. It's not right for you to spend all your free time with an *Englisher* adult."

"But, *Dat!*" Her voice pitched even higher. "She's my best grown-up *freind*. I like being with Maddie."

"Please don't whine, Emma. You know I can't stand it when you whine." He stared at the road ahead. "I was wrong to allow you to spend so much time with Madeleine. I need you to remain at home."

"I don't understand." Emma crossed her arms over her cloak in defiance. "We had a lot of fun with her. You like being with her too. If you didn't like her, then you wouldn't have invited her for Thanksgiving at Marcus's *haus*."

Saul knew he'd been caught, but he was the parent. He had to lay down the law. "I was wrong, and now we need to stop breaking the rules. We need to stay with the Amish."

"I'm going to miss her." Emma sniffed. "She was going to teach me how to make more of *Mammi's* recipes."

"You can learn to cook from Sylvia. Maybe you should go and spend more time at their *haus*."

"It won't be the same," Emma muttered while staring out the window with her back to Saul.

His daughter's disappointment was breaking his

heart, but he had to stand firm. "I need you to respect my rules, Emma. If I catch you over at Madeleine's *haus*, then you will be in trouble."

"*Ya, Dat.*"

Saul guided the horse into the driveway just as Madeleine walked out to the small barn behind her house. He quickly moved his gaze toward his house and tried to pretend Madeleine wasn't there, even though he already felt himself missing her friendship.

. . .

Madeleine tried to concentrate on dusting a hotel room, but her mind kept wandering back to the painful conversation she'd had with Saul on Sunday. She'd tried to erase it from her mind and ignore how much he'd hurt her, but there was no avoiding it.

Her nightmares had also returned in full force. When she closed her eyes both Sunday and Monday night, she found herself back on the C-130, trying to keep wounded military personnel alive while working alone without enough medical supplies. Travis was there too—dying in her arms as she begged him to stay and tried to revive him. She thought being in Amish Country had finally healed both her broken heart and her nightmares, but losing Saul and Emma's friendship had brought them back.

"Madeleine?" Ruth's voice rang into the room.

She turned to see Ruth standing in the doorway with a concerned expression. "Hi, Ruth." Madeleine pushed her long ponytail behind her shoulder. "I didn't see you there."

"Do you realize it's after one?" Ruth pointed toward the digital clock on the nightstand. "You missed lunch."

"Oh." Madeleine shrugged and tried to smile. "I was very busy and didn't realize what time it was."

"You need to eat." Ruth stepped into the room. "You can finish your work later."

"I'm not hungry." It wasn't a lie. Her painful encounter with Saul on Sunday had stolen her ability to sleep and eat.

"What's going on?" Ruth sank onto a corner of the king-size bed. "You seemed *froh* on Sunday. What happened to you to change your mood during the past two days? Talk to me, Madeleine."

Madeleine pulled out the desk chair and sat across from Ruth. "I don't know how to explain it because I don't really understand it." She placed the duster cloth on the dresser behind her. "I'd been spending a lot of time with Saul and Emma. We were sharing meals, and he even invited me to Thanksgiving dinner at Marcus Smucker's house."

Ruth nodded. "What happened?"

"He seemed to be avoiding me on Sunday, and I finally had a chance to talk to him after the service was over and right before I left." Madeleine slumped back in the chair. "He basically told me I am a bad influence for Emma, and I can no longer be friends with him or his daughter."

"And this hurts you." Ruth filled in the blanks.

"I'm crushed," Madeleine said. "Saul and I were becoming close. I had told him about my fiancé committing suicide, and he had shared with me what happened with Annie."

Ruth cupped her hand to her mouth. "I had no idea your fiancé had committed suicide. I'm very sorry."

"Thank you." Madeleine cleared her throat as a lump swelled. "That's why I moved here. I needed to start over and try to find a way to cope with the loss."

"I can't imagine the pain you've felt after losing him."

"I was finally feeling better, but then . . . I never imagined Saul would cut me off like this." Madeleine pointed toward the clock. "That's why I missed lunch. I feel like my heart has been punched. Saul and Emma have come to mean a lot to me. They were like my surrogate family. I shared things with Saul that I had never told anyone. In fact, in some ways, I've felt closer to Saul than I did to Travis. When I talked to Saul, I knew he was truly listening to me. Travis was distant, especially after he returned from serving overseas. I think I connected with Saul on a deeper level because we both had experienced a great loss. Saul's friendship meant so much to me, but now it's gone."

Ruth frowned. "I'm sorry, Madeleine. I don't know what to say."

"Why would he do this?" Madeleine asked. "We had such a nice time on Thanksgiving. I was wondering if they would consider having Christmas dinner with me, but I guess I'll be alone on Christmas."

"You don't need to be alone. I would be happy to invite you over for Christmas."

Madeleine shook her head. "You don't need to do that. I might look into a flight home to see my mom and stepdad." She paused. "How can he go from inviting me to spend a holiday with him and his daughter to telling me he doesn't want his daughter to visit me because he's afraid I'll tempt Emma to leave the community?"

"I think he's scared of getting too close to you," Ruth explained. "He lost Annie, and that made him leery of getting too close to any woman. And he's afraid Emma will want to learn more about your *English* background and then consider leaving the church."

"I'm a good person, Ruth." Madeleine shook her head. "I adore Emma. We had a lot of fun cooking together. I thought maybe she'd help me plant a garden in the spring." She considered her home. "I'm almost living like an Amish person. I don't have any electricity, and I went to a service on Sunday. How can I be a bad influence?"

Madeleine stared toward the large, sliding-glass door that led out to the balcony a moment before turning back to her friend. "My mother told me to be careful, and Sylvia Smucker asked me to be careful with Saul's heart. I didn't understand then why they warned me, but now I do. I care for Saul too much."

"I'm sorry, Madeleine." Ruth shook her head and frowned. "He can't be with you unless one of you makes a sacrifice."

"I know. Thanks for listening. I'll just have to learn

to live without them in my life." Madeleine stood. "I'd better get back to cleaning."

"Madeleine," Ruth began. "Give him time. Maybe he'll realize you can be friends without crossing a line into dangerous territory."

Madeleine nodded. "I think I need to just go about my business and let him come to me. Maybe it will get easier."

"It will." Ruth touched her arm. "Pray for him."

"I will," Madeleine promised. "I always do."

. . .

The two weeks since Saul had told Madeleine they could no longer be friends had passed at a painful snail's pace for him. Not only had Saul hammered his fingers more than once while building her cabinets, but the project had also kept Madeleine in the forefront of his mind. The mental picture of her dressed plainly at the church service stayed in his head almost constantly.

Truth be told, he'd wanted to get the cabinets finished as quickly as possible because he looked forward to working in her kitchen again. But now on this Monday afternoon, he'd finally completed his work and told himself he needed to get the installation over and done with. He had to keep his resolve to sever the ties they'd built over the last couple of months.

Saul stepped outside his shop, spotted Madeleine's truck in the driveway, and started toward her house. He hoped to work on installing the cabinets even while she was at work so he could keep their contact to a minimum. He prayed he could install them in a couple of weeks' time at the most.

Saul climbed the steps to Madeleine's back porch and knocked on the door. When she appeared, clad in jeans and a long-sleeved shirt, he couldn't help but notice how beautiful she was. Her thick, dark hair cascaded past her shoulders, and he couldn't take his eyes off of it for a moment. He longed to feel the texture of her hair. Was it as soft as it looked? What did it smell like?

"Saul," she said, her eyes open wide. "Hi."

"Uh, I have your cabinets ready to install," he said. "I was wondering if I could get a key so I could work even when you're at the hotel."

"That would be fine. My days at the hotel are usually Tuesdays, Thursdays, and Fridays, so I work tomorrow." Madeleine opened the storm door and motioned for him to step into the house. "Come on into the kitchen. I'll find the spare key."

She went on through to the hallway, and he stood in the kitchen, glancing around and remembering the meals they had shared there. He missed those times, but he needed to forget them. It was better that way.

She reappeared a few minutes later and handed him a single key on a round key chain with an *M* hanging from it. Her fingers brushed his, and he felt a spark ignite between them. He quickly jammed the key into his pocket.

"*Danki.*" Saul cleared his throat. "I'll start by removing your old cabinets tomorrow. Would you please empty them out tonight?"

"Sure," Madeleine said, her determined eyes boring into his. "How's Emma?"

"She's *gut*." He gave her a stiff nod. "I'll get started first thing tomorrow. What time do you leave for work?"

"I normally leave around seven, but you can come over anytime. It's not a problem."

"I'll be here after seven." He started for the door.

"Saul," she called after him.

He faced her, anxious about what she wanted. Would she say something that would melt his heart and cause him to be tempted again?

"How long do you think the installation will take?" she asked.

He shrugged. "Approximately two weeks. I'll do it as quickly as I can, and I'll see when the plumber can come in and take care of your sink. I also wondered if you wanted me to paint before I put up the new cabinets. I can go by the home improvement store and pick up some white to match what you currently have on your kitchen walls."

"That sounds fine. I'm okay with any shade of white." She looked down at the table where a stack of papers sat. "Whenever I'm here, I'll do my best to stay out of your way so you can finish without any interference from me."

"Oh." He wasn't sure how to take her comment. "That will be fine. But I'll do my best to finish quickly and before you return home on the days you work."

"Fine. Have a good night. Tell Emma I said hi." Madeleine stayed at the far end of the kitchen while he headed out through the mudroom.

Saul fingered the key in his pocket as he walked

home. He was glad she'd given him the spare key. Now he had a way to avoid Madeleine, at least on the days she was at work. The intensity in her eyes was almost too much to bear. He missed her friendship. He longed for their special talks. Every day he thought of something he wanted to share with her, but he knew he couldn't dare take the chance. His feelings for her went much deeper than what he ever felt for Annie. He could never open his heart to her.

He gripped the key in his pocket. With that key he would lock his heart away from Madeleine. He didn't want to work on the cabinets with her in the house. He was better off working alone whenever he could, when she wasn't there to remind him of how much he longed to be with her.

. . .

The following afternoon, Madeleine returned home from work and was surprised to find Saul still there in her kitchen. His back was to her as he pulled another of the old cabinets down. His shoulders were broad, and his back was muscular as he moved. She stood in the doorway of the mudroom in awe.

When he turned to face her, she quickly looked away and pulled off her coat.

"I didn't hear you come in," Saul said. "I got a late start, but I'm almost done."

"Take your time. I'll stay out of your way."

Madeleine put her keys in her coat pocket, hung up her coat, dropped her tote bag on the floor, and started for the hallway. She quickly moved past him, careful not to trip over the broken cabinets or the pile of tools.

She hurried to her bedroom, forcefully closing and locking the door behind her. She quickly changed into running pants and a long-sleeve workout shirt, hung up her work clothes, and grabbed her phone. As she sat down on the bed, she punched in her mother's number. She had made a decision about the holidays today, and it was time to tell her parents the news.

After four rings, her call went to voice mail, and she heard her mother's voice. "You've reached Leah McMillan. I can't come to the phone right now. Please leave me a message. Thanks!"

"Hey, Mom." Madeleine flopped onto her back, allowing her head to hit the pillow. "I'm coming home for Christmas. I hope that's okay. I really miss you and Jack, and I thought it was the best time to come." She paused, gathering her confused thoughts. "I know this is really last minute, but I hope it's okay. I'll fly home on the 23rd and then come back on the 29th. Give me a call when you get this message. Bye, Mom."

Madeleine disconnected the call and dropped her phone onto the bed. She closed her eyes and rubbed her forehead. She missed her parents, but truthfully she just couldn't bear to spend Christmas alone. Going home to her family made the most sense, even though she was going home with her tail between her legs. Even though she'd told her mother she was certain she belonged here in Amish Country, now she knew she'd failed. Still, she wasn't giving up. She'd regroup and make this place her home. After the holidays.

Madeleine rolled onto her side and stared at the wall. She couldn't go back out to the kitchen with Saul there. Seeing him was torture. Instead, she would hide in her room until he left. It was childish, but hiding was easier than looking into the face of the person who had caused her such heartache.

. . .

Madeleine disappeared down the hallway. After getting a late start because of some new orders that came in that morning, Saul had been so engrossed in his work that he hadn't heard the door open, and she'd surprised him. But then she was gone in a flash. Her bedroom door slammed, and then the lock clicked.

After several minutes, her voice sounded through the door. He didn't mean to listen to her conversation, but the small house made it difficult not to overhear.

His mouth dropped open when she said she was going home to California for Christmas. The news was like a knife slicing into his heart. Why would she go there after she said she had to save her money for the cabinets? Why had she decided to go at the last minute? The questions continued to echo through his mind while he took down the last of the old cabinets before preparing the walls for painting.

What was she was doing back there? Was she upset? Did she need someone to talk to?

Why did he care? He couldn't be her friend. He needed to do his job and not worry about her. This was strictly business. He had been hired to do a job, and he was going to do it.

. . .

Madeleine stared at the ceiling while she listened to Saul working in the kitchen. After several minutes, she pulled her Bible from her nightstand and began to read it. Reading her Bible always provided her comfort and strength when she was serving overseas. She found her way to the second book of Thessalonians, and two verses in the second chapter seemed to speak to her. She read them out loud.

"'May our Lord Jesus Christ himself and God our Father, who loved us and by his grace gave us eternal encouragement and good hope, encourage your hearts and strengthen you in every good deed and word.'"

The Scripture verses rang through her. She needed to keep Jesus in the forefront of her thoughts and not worry about her friendship with Saul. Jesus would take care of her and lead her down the correct path.

She closed her eyes. *Lord, please help me. I thought my heartache after losing Travis had healed, but now I have a brand-new one. I miss Saul and Emma more than I ever imagined I would. It hurts to see them. Please help me navigate through this heartache. Only you can give me the strength I need to find happiness. I thought you had led me to Amish Country to start over again, but now I'm lost and hurting once again. Where do I belong, God? Will I ever find anyone who will love me? Am I even worthy of love? Help me, Lord. Amen.*

After she prayed, she continued reading. Soon the noise in the kitchen subsided, and she assumed Saul was gone. She needed to go figure out what to make for supper.

When she entered the kitchen, she saw that all the old cabinets had been removed from the wall, but only a couple of them were on the floor. Where were the others? Why was it so cold in there?

She found the storm door propped open and saw Saul positioning the old cabinets outside. He had taken them out on the porch, seemed to be making room for the last one, and was sure to come right back in. Madeleine went back to the kitchen and examined the last two cabinets. She lifted one in an attempt to take it out to the porch for him. She was prepared to do anything to get him out of her house for the day.

She hefted the cabinet into her arms, and her eyes widened. It was much heavier than she had imagined. She wasn't certain how she was going to get to the door without injuring her back.

"Stop." Saul came up behind her. "I'll take that."

"I've got it," she muttered.

"Don't be stubborn," he snapped. "I'll carry it. I'm taking all of them out to the porch so I can get out of your way. I need to hurry. It's cold with the storm door propped open."

Saul reached around her and took the cabinet. As he grabbed it, his arm rubbed up against hers, and she felt his body heat radiate through her sleeve. His sinewy arm moved down hers, and she shivered at the contact, not at the cold air coming in from outside. She quickly stepped aside and averted her eyes, trying to recover from the thrill of his touch. Why was she attracted to someone she couldn't have? It was pure torture.

He carried the cabinet out to the porch and then walked back into the kitchen, his expression full of determination.

"Where are you taking the old cabinets?" she asked, rubbing her arms against the cold air.

"To my shop, if that's okay with you. I can make something out of them."

"That's fine. Why don't you load them into the bed of my truck, and I'll drive them down to your shop?" she offered.

He shook his head. "I was going to go get a wagon and a horse."

"Don't be silly." She pointed toward the door. "I'll back my truck up to the porch, and we can load up the cabinets. It's no trouble at all. Then I'll come hold the storm door open for you while you take out the last cabinet."

He gave her a quick nod. "Fine."

His curt response and stoic expression cut her to the bone. How could he have gone from being her good friend to treating her like a stranger in only a few days? He could turn his emotions on and off like a light switch. How could he be so unfeeling? She could never turn her emotions off the way he did. She'd never understand Saul, and she was only hurting herself by trying to analyze him.

"I'll get my truck," she said as she moved past him before grabbing her coat and closing the storm door behind her.

Madeleine backed her truck up to the porch and then climbed the steps to the row of cabinets, shelves, and doors. She opened the storm door for Saul to bring out the last cabinet.

"Do you want me to start loading them into the truck bed?" she asked as she closed the door behind him.

"You can't lift them." He set the cabinet down. "I'll load them."

"I'm a nurse. I used to lift patients and equipment." She pointed toward the cabinet doors. "I'll load the doors and shelves."

"Fine," he said.

Madeleine placed the doors and shelves into the bed of the truck while Saul loaded the cabinets. She tried her best to avoid touching him, but they brushed past each other a couple of times. Once all the cabinets were loaded, she climbed into the driver's seat, and Saul got in beside her.

They drove the short distance in silence. When they reached the shop, Madeleine unloaded the shelves and doors and placed them on a workbench while Saul carried in the cabinets and set them at the far end of the large room. After everything was unloaded, she went outside, slammed the truck's tailgate, and glanced across the property. Was Emma home? If so, then was she instructed to avoid all contact with Madeleine?

"I'll start painting tomorrow, and once it's dry, I'll start installing the new cabinets."

Madeleine glanced over her shoulder to where Saul stood in the shop doorway. "Sounds great." She started for the driver's side door and then faced him. "Tell Emma I said hi."

He nodded and then disappeared into the shop.

NINETEEN

Saul's shoes crunched the rock driveway, and the crisp morning air tickled his nose as he headed toward Madeleine's house. His gaze fell on her pickup truck, and he scowled. Although he knew she didn't work on Wednesdays, he'd hoped she would be out running errands this morning, maybe even for the whole day. He gripped the cold metal handle of his toolbox in one hand and a can of paint in the other as he climbed the steps leading to her back door. After opening the storm door and knocking, he waited for her to come.

Through the door's windowpane, he could see Madeleine enter the mudroom. She was clad in tight black running pants that stopped at just above her ankles and a snug-fitting pink, long-sleeve, athletic-looking shirt that accentuated her thin but healthy body.

"Good morning," she said after she wrenched the door open.

Her lips formed a smile, but the sentiment didn't reach her sad eyes. He hesitated just a moment as she quickly slipped on a matching windbreaker and zipped it, and he noticed her hair was pulled back in a thick ponytail that flittered around her shoulder as she moved. As his eyes took in her beautiful face and fit body, he felt his resolve crumbling. He needed a distraction before he broke his vow to stay away from her.

"Hello." Saul moved past her and placed the toolbox on the floor of the kitchen. "I'm going to get started installing the cabinets tomorrow." He kept his back to her and began pulling out tools. "Today I'll paint and then let it dry overnight. Tomorrow I'll work on getting the walls ready for the installation, and then I'll load up the cabinets and bring them over."

"That's fine. I have a bag of new paintbrushes and other painting supplies in the spare room. I'm going for a run. There are drinks in the refrigerator if you get thirsty." Madeleine stepped back to the still-open back door. "See you later."

"*Ya*," he said, turning toward her. "See you."

She headed out, closing the door hard and letting the storm door slam shut behind her with a loud bang.

Saul shook his head. Why was it this difficult for him to maintain his composure when she was around? But looking into her dark eyes nearly melted his restraint. She was beautiful, more beautiful than any woman he'd ever met. If he was reading her expressions correctly, she felt an attraction too.

Saul had spent more than an hour last night lying in bed, staring at the ceiling, and contemplating Madeleine. He remembered the spark of electricity when they'd accidentally brushed against each other yesterday. He analyzed the emotion in her eyes when they'd said good-bye last night. He mulled over the phone call he'd overheard. Was she going to California for the sole purpose of getting away from him? He couldn't stand the thought of her leaving. He wanted to be with her, but it was impossible. He longed to be her friend. *At least* her friend.

I'm a mess. I need help, and only God can provide the help I need, he thought. He needed to pray more and listen for God's responses.

As he headed to the spare room to find the painting supplies, he sent up a silent prayer to God, begging him to help keep his emotions in check and guide him. He needed God to help him stay true to his beliefs.

· · ·

Madeleine's feet pounded the pavement as she pushed her body to run, run as fast as she could away from her house. She'd hoped to be gone from the house before he'd arrived this morning, but things didn't work out the way she'd planned. Instead, she'd had to be civil and then exit as quickly as she could.

She followed her usual path through Paradise, jogging past the beautiful farms that were a part of the place she considered home. As she rounded a corner, she saw the sign for the Heart of Paradise Bed-and-Breakfast. Madeleine had run into Hannah a few times at the market, and she had promised to visit her. She wondered if Hannah was busy or if she could take some time to talk with her this morning.

Madeleine picked up speed and headed toward the

bed-and-breakfast. A black sedan sat in the driveway. Hopefully Hannah was home. She climbed the front steps and rang the doorbell. A few moments later, the door opened, and Trey greeted her as he swung open the storm door.

"Hi, Madeleine."

"Hi, Trey. I wasn't sure if you'd remember me."

"Oh, of course I do. How are you doing?"

"I'm fine, thanks." Madeleine worked to catch her breath. "I was wondering if Hannah is home."

"She is. Come on in. Hannah will be happy to see you."

"Thank you." Madeleine followed him through a small sitting area decorated with poinsettias, holly, ivy garland, and red-and-green candles. A porcelain nativity scene sat on a bookshelf.

"Hannah," Trey called. "You have a visitor."

Hannah hurried in from the hallway. "Madeleine! It's good to see you. I've been thinking of you. I'm so glad you came by."

"Hi, Hannah." Madeleine gave her a little wave.

Trey turned toward Madeleine. "It was nice seeing you. I'm going to head into town." He grinned at Hannah. "I need to do some Christmas shopping."

Hannah wagged a finger at him as she gave him a facetious smile. "Don't spend too much money."

"I can't make any promises." He kissed her cheek. "I'll be back soon. Enjoy your visit," he called back as he headed out through the kitchen.

"I hope this isn't an inconvenient time," Madeleine said. "I'm sorry to just stop in, but I was literally jogging by." She glanced down at her outfit. "You must think I don't own any presentable clothing."

"Don't be silly." Hannah motioned toward the kitchen. "Would you like a cup of tea?"

"That would be wonderful." Madeleine pointed toward the nativity scene. "I love your Christmas decorations. They're lovely."

"Thank you." Hannah glanced around the room. "Trey wants me to put up a tree, but I'm not sure about it. We never put up Christmas trees in the Amish tradition, and I have mixed feelings. We're still learning how to best blend our cultures."

Madeleine considered that observation as she followed Hannah into the kitchen. "Blending your cultures must be a challenge."

"We've hit a few snags, but we're both willing to compromise." Hannah filled a measuring cup with water, added two tea bags, and then put the measuring cup in the microwave. "Christmas shopping is a good example. I'm used to being thrifty and only buying small, practical gifts, while Trey wants to spoil me with jewelry, expensive clothes, and what I think are unnecessary appliances. Neither one of us is right or wrong. It's just a different way of thinking and living." She pulled a box of donuts out of a cabinet. "Would you like one?"

"Yes, please," Madeleine said. "Thank you. I didn't expect you to feed me."

"Oh, I don't mind." Hannah brought the box to the table. "I always have food around for our guests. We had two couples leave this morning, so it's nice to have a little break. Another couple is arriving Saturday."

"It's wonderful that you're staying busy. May I grab some mugs or cups for you?"

"Yes, please." Hannah pointed toward a cabinet. "You can find mugs in that cabinet next to the sink."

Madeleine took out two mugs and then found spoons in a nearby drawer. She placed the mugs and spoons on the table and sat down.

"How have you been?" Hannah asked as she brought sweetener and creamer to the table. "It was nice to see you when we were at the market at the same time last week."

"Well, I want to talk to you about something." Madeleine tugged a paper napkin from the holder at the center of the table and began to fray the edges. "It's interesting that you brought up the differences between the Amish and *English* cultures." Her voice became thick. "An issue has come up with my Amish neighbor."

Hannah studied Madeleine. "Are you okay? You look upset about something."

"I don't know if you know that my house is located by Saul Beiler's property. He's a widower, and he has a daughter," Madeleine said. "His daughter used to come to see me frequently, and we cooked together."

"That's nice. I know who Saul and Emma are from church services, when I was still a part of the community. I'm sure she appreciated that with her mother being gone." The microwave beeped, and Hannah brought the tea to the table. She filled the mugs and then placed the measuring cup on the counter. "How old is his daughter again?" she asked as she sat across from Madeleine.

"She's eleven." Madeleine mixed in sweetener and

cream as she talked. "She's a really special young girl. I got to know Saul and Emma very well, and they even invited me to join them for Thanksgiving at his best friend's house."

"Oh." Hannah looked surprised. "That's very nice."

"But then everything changed after Thanksgiving." Madeleine shared Sylvia's warning on Thanksgiving and then how cold Saul had been at the church service. "He told me not to spend time with Emma, and he's been standoffish while working on my kitchen cabinets. It's as if he changed overnight."

Hannah frowned as she chose a donut from the box in the middle of the table. "I think I understand how he feels."

"You do? Could you please explain it to me?" Madeleine asked before sipping her tea.

"Madeleine, do you have feelings for Saul? You can be honest with me. I won't judge you or tell you how wrong you are to feel something for an Amish man."

Madeleine nodded as her eyes filled with tears. "They were like my surrogate family."

Hannah touched Madeleine's hand. "You know the position he's in, right?"

"That's why he's pushing me away." Madeleine plucked a cream-filled donut from the box, even though her appetite had disappeared when Saul told her he couldn't be her friend. She thought she might have even lost some weight.

"Absolutely." Hannah's expression was serious. "He knows if he crosses the line, he'll be excommunicated until he confesses his sins and repents."

Madeleine stared down at the donut. "I've been doing my best to avoid him ever since he told me he can't be my friend. But he's at my house right now working on installing new cabinets, which is why I made a point of going for a run this morning. Yesterday I came home from work and found him in the kitchen, and I hid in my room until I thought he'd left. Everything is so awkward now."

"I'm sorry." Hannah broke her glazed donut in half.

"I actually asked for unpaid time off work and made a flight reservation to go home to California for Christmas. I'm running away to avoid sitting in my house alone on Christmas Day, staring across the field toward his house. I left my mother a message yesterday and told her I'm coming. She called me back last night, and she was almost in tears because she was so delighted. I couldn't bear to tell her the truth—that I'm really spending Christmas with her and my stepdad just to avoid feeling sorry for myself here."

Madeleine cradled the warm mug in her hands. "You were talking about being thrifty at Christmastime. Well, booking a trip to avoid seeing someone is probably the biggest waste of money you've ever heard of."

Hannah shook her head. "I'm not judging you. At least you'll be with your family, right?"

"Yes, that's true." Madeleine sipped her tea again and then took a bite of her donut. Although it was filled with sweet, smooth cream, the taste did little to brighten her sour mood.

"Saul probably received a warning from a friend.

You mentioned that you had Thanksgiving at his best friend, Marcus's, house. Maybe Marcus said something to him?" Hannah lifted her mug. "If his wife said something to you, then she must have discussed it with Marcus before you visited them."

"I'm sure that's it." Madeleine wiped her mouth with a napkin. "Saul has to obey certain rules, but I had hoped we could be friends. I moved around most of my life, but this place represents the best parts of my childhood. After I met Saul and Emma, I felt as if this was going to be my permanent home. That's why I'm investing in the cabinets. Now that I've lost their friendship, I don't want to give up, but I don't feel secure."

"Why don't you feel secure?" Hannah asked.

Madeleine explained about her nightmares and how she lost Travis. "Now that Saul has pulled away from me, my nightmares and sleeplessness have returned. I'm back to grieving for Travis constantly. It's as if I've lost Travis all over again. I feel like I'm losing what I've loved about this place—that feeling of home."

"Oh dear." Hannah shook her head. "Please don't give up on Paradise. You love other things here, right? You have other friends. You have Carolyn, Linda, Ruth, and me. And you have the house you love. I'm sure memories of your grandparents give you comfort."

"Yes, that's very true." Madeleine considered Saul and his sad eyes. "I just don't know how to get over this pain I feel when Saul is around." She heaved a sigh. "I hope he's done with the cabinets by the time I get back from California. After that I won't have to see him much—unless I go to church service with Carolyn and

Ruth again." Tears trickled down her cheeks. "My emotions are a mess."

"I know that feeling well," Hannah said. "That's how it was when I met Trey. I wanted to see him, but I also prayed for God to remove that longing out of my heart because I knew it was going to put me in such a difficult position with my community. Falling in love with Trey was both the most wonderful and the most challenging emotion I ever had to sort through."

Madeleine sniffed and wiped her eyes with a tissue from the pocket in her windbreaker. "I wonder if that's how Saul feels. He shields his emotions behind his stony expression. But I also see sadness in his eyes."

"He probably knows how to hide his sadness after losing his wife." Hannah broke another piece off the donut. "I did the same thing after I lost my first husband."

"How did you decide to leave the community for Trey?"

"It wasn't easy, and it's still not easy. I left everything I'd ever known, but I believe that's the path God wanted me to choose. I prayed a lot, and I'm still praying my daughter Lillian will forgive me and become a part of my new family." Hannah patted her abdomen. "I'm going to have a new family member in the spring."

"Oh, Hannah." Madeleine smiled. "That's a beautiful blessing from God."

"You're right." Hannah's green eyes glistened with tears. "God has wonderful days in store for you too. Just pray and be patient."

"I will," Madeleine promised.

• • •

Hannah's advice rang through Madeleine's mind while she jogged back to her house. When she came in the back door, Saul was painting the walls, and the aroma of paint filled her nose. She stood in the kitchen doorway while he worked, enjoying the view of both the crisp white wall and the self-assured way he worked.

He looked over his shoulder at her, and his expression softened slightly.

"It looks nice," she said as she pulled off her windbreaker. "The kitchen really needed a new coat of paint."

"*Danki*." Saul raked his hand through his dark brown hair. "How was your run?"

The thoughtful question caught her off guard for a brief moment. "It was fine." She moved to the table and picked up her shopping list, the one she'd made as an excuse to leave the house again. "I'm going to the store now. Did you and Emma need anything?"

"No, *danki*." His eyes lingered on her for a moment, and then he moved back to painting the wall.

"Oh, by the way, I'm going to California for Christmas. Do you want me to give you a check for the remaining balance before I leave?"

"That won't be necessary," he said without looking back at her. "You can pay me when you get back."

"Okay. You can keep working while I'm gone. Would you mind bringing in the mail for me?"

"That won't be a problem." He kept his back to her. "I'll watch out for your *haus* and leave your mail on the kitchen table."

The sight of his back caused her frustration to flare. Why couldn't he look at her? Did he find her that revolting? Or was sidestepping her stare another coping mechanism to avoid facing the feelings he had for her?

"Would you ask Emma to look after the cats in my barn too?" she asked.

"*Ya.*" He nodded.

"Thank you." She folded up the shopping list and shoved it into her purse. "I'm flying back to Pennsylvania on December 29. Do you think you'll be done by then?"

"*Ya,*" he repeated. "I should be finishing up by then. I'll be sure my mess is all cleaned up too."

"Great." She moved past him and stepped into the hallway. "I'm going to get changed and then head to the market."

He grunted a response as she moved down the hallway. After a stop to wash up in the bathroom, she moved into her bedroom, closed the door, and leaned against it.

"Lord, give me strength," she whispered.

As she stripped off her running clothes, Madeleine considered how she could show Saul that he and Emma still meant a lot to her. An idea popped into her head while she pulled on her jeans. She would leave special Christmas presents on the table the day she headed out to California. In keeping with the Amish tradition, she would find something meaningful but not extravagant. She pulled on her shirt while pondering what the gifts would be. She'd find something special, and maybe then Saul would be convinced to be her friend.

The idea was superb! Now she just had to find the perfect gifts.

flip through the book. His words were stuck in the lump swelling in his throat. Emma looked up at him.

"What are you waiting for, *Dat*?" She pointed to the box. "Open yours!"

He nodded and removed the card from the box.

"Open the card!" Emma picked it up. "Want me to read it to you?"

He nodded again.

"Let's see." Emma pulled out a card with a photograph of a poinsettia on the front. "'Dear Saul, I know my grandparents meant a lot to you and Emma, and I thought you'd enjoy something that belonged to my *daadi*. *Frehlicher Grischtdaag!* Fondly, Maddie.'" She clapped her hands. "I can't wait to see what it is! Open it, *Dat*! Open it!"

Saul ripped off the paper and found a plain cardboard box. He opened the flaps and spotted a set of screwdrivers he remembered Mel using on many occasions when they worked on home improvement projects together.

"Wow." Emma touched one of the screwdrivers. "These belonged to her *daadi*?"

"*Ya*." He fought to hold back his threatening emotions by clearing his throat. "I remember them."

"How nice." Emma gnawed her lower lip. "I need to think of something to give Maddie."

"That won't be necessary." Saul closed up the box. "We don't need to give her anything."

"That isn't right. If Maddie gave us something, then the proper thing to do is to give her something. I'll think about it at school."

"You need to feed the cats before you go to school."

"I know." She grabbed a scoop of dry cat food from the pantry and then glanced past him. "The cabinets are *schee*. Maddie will love them. I'll be right back." She rushed outside.

Saul studied the card while trying to comprehend why Madeleine had left gifts for Emma and him. Why would she want to give something to them after he'd shunned her friendship?

Because she cares about you and Emma.

The response came from deep in his soul, and he tried to suppress the sentiment attached to it. Tears pricked his eyes.

Emma hurried into the kitchen again and dropped the scoop in the pantry before picking up her school bag. "I'm heading off to school. Bye, *Dat!*" She waved as she rushed out again.

"Have a *gut* day." After she was gone, he moved to the counter and surveyed the remaining cabinets he had to install. But then he turned toward the refrigerator and found an envelope with his name on it stuck to the door with a magnet.

He opened the envelope and pulled out a check along with a note from Madeleine that said, "Saul— Here is the remaining balance for the cabinets. Thank you for your hard work. I'm certain that my kitchen will look brand-new. Fondly, Maddie."

He studied the note and leaned against the refrigerator. Pretending only to be her acquaintance was much more difficult than he'd ever imagined. Even her hand-writing conjured up strong feelings within him. How could he continue to be aloof when she returned from California? He already missed her, even though he'd seen her in passing a few times before she'd left for her trip. He needed strength to continue to maintain this facade.

Saul placed the check on the table beside the Christmas gifts and then started on his installation. And while he worked, he prayed, begging God over and over again to renew his heart and set his spirit right.

. . .

On Christmas Eve, Madeleine sipped a mug of eggnog while sitting beside her mother in front of her parents' tree. She'd arrived late yesterday and spent most of the afternoon shopping with her mother, right up until the shops closed to let their employees go home to be with their families. Although she was keeping a smile plastered on her face, she couldn't get Saul and Emma off her mind. What were they doing? Were they visiting Marcus and his family today? Had they found her gifts? If so, did they like them? And, most important, did her gifts change Saul's feelings about her?

"Are we going to the midnight service?" Mom's voice broke through her mental tirade.

"Yes," Madeleine said quickly. "It's been a long time since I've gone to a Christmas Eve service."

Mom studied her. "You don't seem to be too excited to be home. What's going on, Maddie?"

"Nothing." Madeleine forced a yawn. "I think I'm just suffering from a severe case of jet lag."

"Hmm." Mom continued to study Madeleine while looking unconvinced. "Well, we should get ready for church then. Let me go and see what Jack is doing."

"Sounds good." Madeleine finished the eggnog and then headed to the guest room to change into a dress and fix her hair.

Madeleine sat in the backseat of her stepfather's SUV and took in the colorful lights and inflatable Christmas decorations during the drive through town.

Once they arrived at the church, Mom looped her arm around Madeleine's waist as they walked through the parking lot. "Are you certain you're okay?"

"I'm fine, Mom." Madeleine smiled at her. "It's great to be home with you and Jack at Christmas."

Mom squeezed Madeleine to her. "We're glad you're here too."

Madeleine enjoyed singing the traditional Christmas carols during the service. She had tears in her eyes when the congregation lit candles and sang "Silent Night" at midnight. Although this was the kind of church she'd been accustomed to since she was a child, she couldn't help but think of her Amish friends. She missed the Amish service—the plain and simple way of worshiping God without the flowers, candles, and musical instruments.

When they returned home, it was close to one in the morning, but Madeleine and her parents gathered around the tree once again.

"Are we going to keep with tradition and open one gift?" Jack asked as he picked up a small box from under the tree.

"What do you think, Maddie?" her mother asked. "Do you want to open one gift for old time's sake?"

"Sure." Madeleine yawned as the time difference and lack of sleep drowned her. She longed to curl up in the guest room bed, but she didn't want to disappoint her parents. Opening one gift on Christmas Eve was a tradition going back to her early childhood when Madeleine and Mom lived alone.

"This is for you, sweetheart." Jack handed her mother a small box. "Merry Christmas, Leah."

"Oh, Jack." Mom took the box and then handed him a small box as well as he sat down beside her. "This is for you. Merry Christmas, honey."

Madeleine hugged a sofa pillow to her chest while she watched her parents open their gifts. Her mother gasped as she opened the jewelry box, revealing a sparkling diamond solitaire necklace. "It's gorgeous. Thank you." She leaned over and kissed Jack.

He opened his package and held up an expensive-looking watch. "I love it, Leah. Thank you."

Madeleine yawned again and imagined how warm and comfortable the bed would be when she finally crawled into it.

"This is for you, Maddie." Her mother handed her an envelope. "We thought you could use this right now."

"Thank you." Madeleine opened the envelope containing a $200 gift card to a home improvement store. "Jack. Mom. This is too much."

"We know you're working on your house, and we want to help," Jack chimed in. "You can buy whatever you need."

"Thank you." Madeleine stood and hugged each of them. "You really didn't need to spend that much money. It's extravagant."

Mom raised an eyebrow in disbelief. "We want to help you out. We're happy to do it."

"I really appreciate it." Madeleine yawned again. "I need to go to bed."

"Good night, dear," Mom said. "Merry Christmas."

Madeleine walked to the guest room and changed into her pajamas. As she snuggled down in the bed, she closed her eyes and then fell asleep wondering how Saul and Emma were.

. . .

Madeleine poured herself a cup of coffee in her mother's kitchen. She'd spent nearly an hour opening gifts with her parents. Her mother had showered her with new clothes, more gift cards, and jewelry. Madeleine was overwhelmed by her parents' generosity. Was the Amish way of being thrifty but thoughtful already rubbing off on her? Why did she even bother thinking the way the Amish did? After all, she wasn't worthy of their community. She would never be accepted as one of them.

Mom stepped into the kitchen and smiled. "May I have a cup of coffee with you, Maddie?"

"That would be nice." Madeleine poured a cup for her mother and handed it to her. "Merry Christmas." She sat down at the table.

"Yes, Merry Christmas." Mom sat across from her. "Thank you for the gift card and the sweater."

"You're welcome." Madeleine sipped her coffee. "I feel bad for not giving you and Jack as much as you gave me."

Mom waved off the comment. "Don't be silly. You spent all of that money coming out here to see us. Besides, it's the thought that counts. We're just happy you're here."

A news anchor on the television sounded from the family room where her stepfather sat on the sofa.

"I'm happy I'm here too." Madeleine said the words, but she felt as if she'd left her heart in Pennsylvania.

"Tell me the truth. Why did you really come out here?" Mom asked.

Madeleine studied her mother. "What do you mean?"

"Maddie, I know you. You're not quite as impulsive as you pretend to be. Normally, when you make up your mind about something, you follow through. You told me more than a month ago that you wanted to spend your first Christmas in your new house. You even said you didn't care that the house didn't have central heat and you had to deal with that coal stove." Mom studied her. "Why did you change your mind?"

"I just wanted to be here." Madeleine pushed her hair back from her shoulder. "I wanted to have another Christmas in California."

Mom frowned. "Something is bothering you. What is it?"

"I'm fine." Madeleine sipped her coffee. "Everything is great."

"Does it have something to do with your neighbors?"

Madeleine knew she was caught. She nodded and sighed. "Yes, it does. It has everything to do with them." She told her mother the whole story, starting with the church service after Thanksgiving and ending with the gifts she'd left on her kitchen table for Emma and Saul. She'd managed to share her feelings without getting emotional, but the heartache swelled within her.

Mom listened with sympathy in her eyes, and Madeleine was thankful for her mother's patient silence.

"But honestly, I didn't come out here just to get away from Saul and Emma. I also didn't want to be alone on Christmas. It only made sense to come and see my family." She gestured dramatically. "That's it. That's my messed-up life in Amish Country. You told me to be careful, but I wound up getting hurt." She held her breath while waiting for her mother's response.

"I know how Saul feels," Mom finally said.

"You do?"

"I don't know if I ever told you, but I had been participating in baptism classes before I met your father. I wasn't in the exact same position Saul is in. However, I was preparing to give my heart to the church when I met someone who wasn't a part of the church. Your father had no intention of becoming Amish." She gave a wry grin. "He had no intention of being true to me or to any church. I was too young and naive to realize the kind of man he was."

Madeleine nodded. She'd heard the stories before about her father's lack of loyalty to anyone but himself.

"Saul is confused, and he doesn't know what to do. He feels caught between his loyalty to the church and his feelings for you." Mom's expression was sad. "He has a child to think of, and I doubt he's going to choose you. I'm sorry, Maddie. I think you need to try to forget him."

Madeleine gripped the cup in her hands. "I thought we were close, and then he rejected me. I never expected this to hurt that much."

"You grew attached to him and his daughter." Mom touched her hand. "I understand. Maybe it would be better if you sold the house and came back here. Maybe Amish Country isn't right for you."

"No, that's not true." Madeleine shook her head.

"I worry about you being out there alone. You've been through a lot, losing Travis the way you did." Mom's eyes glistened with tears. "I hate that you're all alone."

"I'll be fine, Mom. I promise," Madeleine insisted. "I love it there. It feels like home. I just need to find a way to let go of these feelings for Saul and Emma."

"You have to forgive Saul, and then yes, let it go." Mom squeezed her hand. "Leaving the community was the most difficult decision I've ever made. I knew I was breaking my parents' hearts, and I felt guilty for leaving my friends. At the same time, however, I believed God was leading me on a new path."

"Did you think you misread God's plans for you after my father left?" Madeleine asked.

"No." Mom shook her head, and her hazel eyes still glistened with tears. "You are the greatest blessing in my life. I believe I was supposed to have you. You're my blessing, and you were a blessing to your grandparents."

Madeleine smiled as tears filled her eyes too. "Thank you, Mom."

"I mean that, but you have to appreciate Saul's position in the community. You told me his wife left him, right?"

Madeleine nodded. "His wife left him for another man and divorced him."

"See, that's even more devastating for him because he's Amish. When she left, she broke her vow to him and to the church. And to make matters worse, she divorced him, which the Amish believe is a sin. He can't possibly consider leaving the church to be with you after his wife abandoned him and their child—even though she's dead now."

"I understand that." Madeleine nodded. "I'm not asking him to leave the church for me."

"I know you're not asking him to do it, but he may feel tempted by you. Your giving him space is a good plan."

"That's one of the reasons I'm here." Madeleine lifted her cup. "I'm giving him a chance to finish the cabinets. Once he's done, we won't have to see each other except in passing."

"It will be fine," Mom insisted. "Just give him time. Maybe he'll find a way to be your friend after he sorts through his feelings." She stood. "How about some coffee cake? I'll put a fresh pot of coffee on too."

"That sounds good." Madeleine sent up a silent

prayer for Saul and Emma. She prayed they were enjoying a nice Christmas and that God would find a way to heal her broken heart.

. . .

Later that evening, Emma rushed into the family room and ran over to the small pile of gifts Saul had given her that morning. Christmas Day had been exciting for her.

"I love my new ice skates!" Emma pulled off her shoes and straightened her socks. "I can't wait to use them. Do you think the pond will be frozen by the weekend? Maybe Esther and I can skate together."

"It might be." Saul sat down in a chair across from her and watched her pull on one of the skates. All the way home, he'd been thinking about how thankful he was that Marcus and Sylvia invited them over on Christmas every year to make sure they weren't home alone.

"I wonder if Maddie is having a nice Christmas," Emma said as she pulled on her second new skate. "I miss her, *Dat*."

I do too. I miss her smile. I miss her sense of humor and the way she likes to tease me. I miss her laugh. I miss everything about her.

The mental response caught Saul off guard, and he frowned.

"She's with her family, which is where she belongs," he said, even though he didn't truly believe the words. He'd eventually move past the feeling of loss that haunted him. After all, he'd gotten used to being without his parents and his brother. He still missed them, but the pain wasn't as bad. The loss eventually transformed into a dull ache that loomed in the back of his mind. Surely losing Madeleine would get easier as the years wore on.

"I made her a card." Emma laced up the skates while she spoke. "It's on my dresser in my room."

"You did?" he asked. "I told you not to give her anything."

"It's just a thank-you card." Emma examined her white skates. "It's only proper to give her a thank-you note after receiving a gift from her. That's what Sylvia says."

He nodded. "Fine, but I'll leave it at her *haus*. I'm going to finish installing the cabinets and countertop and try to get the plumber there before she gets home."

"I'll put my note in the kitchen when I feed the cats tomorrow. You know I love spending time with them. Her kittens are just as cute as the ones in our barn." Emma moved her feet back and forth and studied her skates. "These are very *schee. Danki, Dat. Frehlicher Grischtdaag.*"

"*Frehlicher Grischtdaag.*" He looked at the clock on the wall. "We need to go to bed. It's late, Emma."

"I know." She started unlacing the skates. "I can't wait to try these out."

"I'm certain you'll have plenty of opportunities to skate this winter."

"I wonder if Maddie likes to ice-skate." Emma looked up at her father. "I'm just wondering. I'm not going to ask her to skate with me."

"It's bedtime, Emma." Saul stood and watched her remove the skates. How could he convince Emma to stop thinking about Madeleine when he couldn't stop himself from thinking about her?

TWENTY-ONE

Madeleine pulled her wheeled suitcase up the back porch steps, and before unlocking the back door, she glanced back toward Saul's house. She saw a dim light flicker in his kitchen window. Saul and Emma were probably getting ready for bed. Although she'd only been gone for six days, it felt more like a lifetime.

She pulled open the door, closed it behind her, and stepped through to her kitchen, which greeted her with the sweet smell of new wood and stain. She flipped on the two lanterns on the table and looked at the beautiful new countertop and cabinets lining the far wall. She blew out an excited gasp. Saul's creations were more beautiful than she'd ever imagined!

After letting go of her suitcase and setting her bag on the table, she rushed over to the cabinets. She ran her hands over the smooth wood and opened a door, then another. She was stunned to find all her dishes, cups, and bowls lined up perfectly.

Madeleine shook her head. Even though he was

acting cold and aloof, Saul had taken the extra time to arrange things for her. She studied the cabinets and countertop for several minutes, taking in the beautiful artistry of Saul's work.

She stepped over to the table to sift through the stack of mail, sorting out bills and advertisements. She thumbed through an advertisement for the home improvement store where her parents had bought her gift card before placing it back on the table. Then she spotted an envelope with her name handwritten on it, and her heart thumped in her chest. She picked up the envelope, wondering if Saul had written her a note. Had he been touched by her gift and felt compelled to write her a letter?

She opened the envelope and found a letter inside that said:

Dear Maddie,

Thank you for the cookbook. You were very generous to give it to me. I'm excited to try *Mammi's* favorite recipes. I'll let you know how the oatmeal cookies and chocolate cake come out. Maybe I can sneak over and give you some. *Mei dat* appreciates the screwdriver set. I saw him using them in his shop yesterday. I think it means a lot to him that you gave him those special tools. He loved *Mammi* and your *daadi* too. I wanted to make you something as a gift, but *mei dat* said it was best if I kept my distance.

Even though I'm not supposed to be your friend, I want you to know that I miss you. *Mei dat* does too,

but he won't admit it. I hope you had a nice Christmas
with your family. We miss you.

> Love,
>
> Emma (and Saul too!)

Madeleine read the letter over and over until she
practically had it memorized. She was touched to hear
the gifts had meant something special to Emma and
Saul. Maybe she could find a way to prove to Saul that
she had no intention of threatening his world, that she
just wanted to be a part of his and Emma's life. She
couldn't just let them go and act as if they were only
strangers who lived on the adjacent property. She had
to show him how much she cared.

· · ·

Emma hummed to herself as she made her way out
to her father's shop. She was excited to tell him what
she'd made for supper. All by herself, she'd followed
Mammi's recipe for crepes! They were actually easy
to make—easier than she'd thought they would be.
Now she had to convince *Dat* to come in from working. She couldn't wait for them to enjoy her delicious
creation!

She picked up her pace as she approached the shop
door and then stepped into the showroom where her
father was sanding a long piece of wood. "*Dat!*" she
yelled. "Supper is ready. I made crepes." She stood up a
little taller and hugged her cloak to her body to try to
shield herself from the early January cold. "It's ready."

"Emma." *Dat* looked over at her, frowning. "Would you do me a quick favor?"

"*Ya.*" She nodded.

"I think I left my favorite work gloves on my dresser." He pointed toward the house. "I need them so I can finish up this one piece of wood."

"But supper is ready." She jammed her hand on her small hip. "Can't you look for them after we eat? I worked hard on this meal for you. I want to show you how much I've learned about cooking."

"I know you did, *mei liewe*, and I appreciate it. You're a *gut* cook. I just want to finish this one piece of wood. I promise I won't take long."

"All right. I'll be right back." Emma rushed into the house and upstairs to her father's bedroom.

She searched his dresser and didn't find the gloves. She sank to her knees and looked under the bed in case he had dropped them and they'd fallen underneath it. She spotted something under the middle of the bed, and she crawled under and grabbed what turned out to be a metal box. She gripped its handle and yanked it out from under the bed.

She crossed her legs under her and examined the small, cold box. She'd never seen it before. Why would *Dat* keep it under the bed? Had he forgotten about the mysterious box? Or had he accidentally pushed it under there and been searching for it?

After turning the box over in her hands, she clicked open the latch. She lifted the lid and found a stack of papers. While pulling them out, her eyes focused on a tattered envelope at the bottom of the stack. The envelope, which had already been ripped open, was addressed to her father and contained a letter. She pulled out the handwritten letter, and even though it was wrong to snoop in her father's things, she had to read it.

Dear Saul,

I hope this letter finds you well. I know you never expected to hear from me, but I thought it was only right for me to inform you of the sad news. Annie has passed away. She died tragically in a boating accident almost two months ago. I've spent the past two months grieving, and I felt you had a right to know about it.

She and I liked to spend our weekends during the summer months boating with friends. We had been out for the day when our boat was involved in a collision. Annie fell and hit her head, and she died from massive head trauma after two weeks in a coma.

I know there is a lot of bad blood between us, and I'm sorry. I was wrong to come back for Annie and steal her away from you and Emma. At the time, my focus was only on my own needs, and I never considered that I had broken up a family. Now that she's gone, I know what it's like to experience real loss. I never thought about how much I had hurt you and your daughter until now. I guess I'm also writing to say I'm sorry. I've been selfish and hurtful.

I know I can't fix the past, but I wanted to at least tell you I'm sorry. I've lost Annie now, but you and Emma lost her years ago. Please forgive me.

Sincerely,
Timothy

Emma read through the letter two more times, trying to comprehend it. Who was Timothy? And what did he mean that Annie had died? Annie . . . Was this letter about her *mamm*? And didn't her *dat* say she had pneumonia and died in a hospital? If her *mamm* was the Annie mentioned in this letter, then why was she in a boat? It didn't make sense.

She read the letter for a fourth time and then examined the envelope. According to the postmark, it had been mailed more than a year ago from Missouri. If Annie was her *mamm* and she was in Missouri, then . . .

Emma gasped. *My* mamm *was alive?*

Then it hit her like a thousand bales of hay falling from the loft in the barn: Mamm *didn't die more than seven years ago. She abandoned* Dat *and me!*

"No, no, no!" Emma yelled. "This can't be true! It can't be!"

Tears gushed from her eyes like powerful waterfalls. Emma needed answers. She needed to hear the truth from her father, and she needed to hear it *now*.

Emma jumped up and ran down the stairs, gripping the letter in her hand.

By the time she'd reached her father's shop, she was sobbing and the letter was crumpled in her fist.

"Emma? What happened?" *Dat's* eyes were wide. "Emma, *was iss letz?*"

"What is this?" She shook the letter in front of his face. "What does this mean? Who is Timothy? Why did he write this to you?" And then she found the courage to ask the question that was burning through her. "Did *mei mamm* leave me? Did she leave us?"

Dat took the letter from her, and his expression hardened. "Where did you find this?"

"Answer my questions!" Her voice croaked on her sobs. "Tell me the truth, *Dat*. Did *Mamm* leave us?"

He gave her a quick nod. "She left the Amish."

"Why?" Emma's question came out in a wail. "Why?"

He stared at her. "She just . . . left."

"Why did she leave?" Emma demanded. "Where did she go? Who's Timothy?"

Dat blew out a heavy sigh and shook his head.

"Tell me, *Dat*. I need to know why she left." She wiped at her tears with the back of her hand. "Why didn't she come and see me? Why didn't she call me?" Her questions thundered through her like a midsummer storm. "Why didn't she write to me? Didn't she love me at all?"

"We're not going to talk about this now. You need to calm down. Let's go eat supper."

Dat reached for her, but Emma stepped away. "I can't eat." Emma shuddered as more tears filled her eyes. "I need to know why *mei mamm* left me."

"Just go in the *haus* and wash up. I'll be right there." He patted her arm. "I'll be right behind you in a minute."

Emma stepped out into the cold evening air and shivered as confusion and frustration nearly overcame her. Large, fluffy snowflakes danced down from the sky and wet her cloak. She wiped away the snowflakes that pelted her cheeks while considering the news that had just shattered her heart. She needed to know the truth, and she wanted to hear it from her father.

Why wouldn't he answer her questions? How could

her mother leave her and never contact her again? None of this made any sense! Everything her father had told her since she was four had been a lie. How could he lie to her? He was the one person she'd always trusted the most, and he'd lied to her!

She looked at her house and couldn't bear the thought of sitting down to supper as if nothing had happened. She needed time alone. She had to have some quiet time to think and try to figure everything out. Instead of following her father's instructions, she began to run.

. . .

Emma rushed out of his shop, and Saul blew out a deep, shuddering breath. He knew he'd have to tell her the truth about her mother someday, and he'd always been afraid someone else would tell her. But he'd never expected her to find out on her own. Several times he'd considered burning Timothy's letter, but instead he'd kept it in case she wanted proof that her mother had left of her own accord. He was certain his hiding place had been sufficient, but it had only proven to be a painful way for Emma to find out the truth without his guidance and support.

He studied the crumpled letter and shook his head. Did Annie have any idea how much pain she'd caused when she'd walked away from their daughter? It was one thing for her to hurt Saul; he was an adult and he'd found a way to recover. But the pain in Emma's eyes was enough to crush his heart and his spirit. Now he had to pick up the pieces and try to console her. He'd needed a few minutes alone to collect himself before he could help her.

He folded up the letter, shoved it into his pocket, put his tools away, and set the wood aside. After extinguishing the lanterns, he left the shop. Large, wet snowflakes peppered his coat and hat as he strode toward the house in the dark.

"Emma?" Saul stepped into the mudroom. "Emma? Where are you? Let's sit down and have supper. We'll talk after you've calmed down." He moved into the kitchen and found the table set with a platter of crepes and trimmings in the middle. "Emma Kate?" He walked through the kitchen to the family room. "Emma Kate? Where are you?"

He stood outside the bathroom door and gently knocked. "Are you in there?" He knocked again. "Emma, please answer me."

The house remained deathly silent. He stuck his head into the laundry room and still didn't see her. With a lantern in his hand, he climbed the stairs to the second floor and stepped into her bedroom, hoping to find her sitting on her bed, maybe reading her Bible for comfort.

"Emma Kate, where are you?" He stalked down the hallway, glancing into the sewing room and spare room on his way to his bedroom. "Emma! Where are you?"

When he found his bedroom also empty, Saul's mind began to race. He rushed down the stairs and outside with a lantern. He held the lantern out in front of him and moved through the now blinding snow toward his barns and shops. He searched the horse barn and the area by the chicken coops while calling out her name. He walked behind the house and yelled into the field.

"Emma!" he screamed. "Emma, come out now! Where are you?"

As the curtain of snow falling down from the heavens intensified, terrifying visions flashed through Saul's mind. Had Emma run off toward Marcus's house and gotten hit by a car? Had she fallen into a ditch by the side of the road? Did a passerby kidnap her?

The worries slammed through him, and his heart pounded against his rib cage as he rushed toward his largest shop, where he kept a phone. He needed to call his friends and neighbors and ask them to help him find his precious daughter.

While dialing Marcus's number, he prayed someone would hear the phone ringing in their barn.

"Please answer, please answer," he muttered. After nearly two dozen rings, someone finally did.

"Hello?" Marcus's voice sounded through the receiver.

"Marcus!" Saul almost yelled. "I need help. Emma is missing. I can't find her anywhere. I've searched my *haus*, my barns, and my shops, and now it's getting dark. And the snow is falling heavily, and I—"

"Whoa," Marcus said. "Slow down. How long has she been missing? Where was the last place you saw her?"

"It's been about twenty minutes," Saul said. "I sent her to look for something in my room, and she found the letter from Timothy. She read it, Marcus." His voice quavered. "She knows the truth now about Annie. She brought the letter out to me in the shop. She was really upset, and she asked me several questions I wasn't prepared to answer. I told her to go back into the *haus* and that we'd talk after supper. I went in to find her, and she was gone. She may be on the way to your *haus*."

"All right. I'll ask Sylvia to look around our property, and I'll head your way in a horse and buggy. I'll also tell Esther to call a few neighbors," Marcus said. "You call neighbors too. We'll organize a search party."

"*Danki*." Saul nodded. He was grateful his best friend had taken control of the situation, because he didn't seem to have the presence of mind to do it.

"I'll be there soon. We'll find her." Marcus hung up.

Saul called two of his surrounding neighbors and asked them to help him search for his daughter. While he waited for his neighbors to arrive, Saul gazed across the field and spotted a light shining at Madeleine's house. He jogged down the driveway and hurried up her back porch steps.

Her door opened before he even had a chance to knock. She must have been looking out the window and seen his lantern.

"Saul?" Madeleine asked, her eyes round as she swung open the storm door. "Is everything all right?"

"I'm looking for Emma. Is she here?"

"No." She shook her head. "I haven't seen her since I got back from California. What's going on?"

"I can't find her," Saul said while working to catch his breath. "I think she ran away."

"Oh no." Madeleine started to reach for him and then stopped. "Why would she run away?"

"She found the letter telling me about her mother's death. She knows the truth now, and she was so upset . . ." Madeleine gasped again. Saul couldn't go on.

"Let me get my boots, and I'll help you. Just give me a minute." She opened the storm door wider. "Step inside. It's freezing out there." Madeleine hurried down the hallway toward her bedroom.

He waited in the kitchen, his mind racing with worry. Madeleine reappeared a few minutes later clad in a heavy coat, scarf, and boots.

She held a large flashlight toward him. "Would you like to use this? I have two of them."

"*Danki.*" Saul took the flashlight, and their hands brushed. "I've called a few friends and neighbors, and they are going to help."

"Do you want me to call the police?" Madeleine pulled out her phone. "I can dial 9-1-1 right now."

"*Ya,*" he said. "You call them, and I'll go organize the neighbors."

"I'll be out as soon as I can and find you."

"*Danki.*" Saul headed out the door and prayed he'd find his daughter soon—before it was too late.

. . .

Madeleine's heart raced with panic after she disconnected her call to the police. The emergency dispatcher promised to send out an Amber Alert and send police officers to Saul's farm. The worry and panic in Saul's eyes had cut right through Madeleine's soul. She couldn't bear the thought of something happening to his sweet little girl.

Armed with her large flashlight, Madeleine hurried outside and up the driveway toward Saul's house, where she found him standing with a group of Amish men.

"The police are coming," she said as she approached. She recognized Marcus. "How can I help?"

"We're going to knock on doors and search the fields," Marcus said. "We need someone to stay at the *haus* in case she comes back."

"I want to help you search for her," Saul said, his eyes shining with worry. "Someone else can stay here and talk to the police."

"I'll stay," an older man said. "I'll sit on the porch and wait for the police. I'll also call for Emma."

"*Danki*," Saul told him.

"I'll help you go door-to-door," Madeleine said.

"No, you should drive your truck around and shine your headlights into the fields," Marcus said. "We'll go door-to-door."

Madeleine glanced at Saul, who nodded in agreement. "I'll do it," she said.

"Let's go. It's getting colder, and the snow isn't letting up at all." Marcus gestured for the group of men to follow him toward the road.

She stepped over to Saul and took his cold hands in hers. She wished they both had gloves, but that didn't matter as much as finding Emma.

"We'll find her, Saul. I promise you."

"*Danki*." His eyes filled with tears.

Unable to speak, Madeleine nodded and then hurried toward her truck.

For more than two hours, Madeleine drove around the surrounding area in search of Emma. The hum of the windshield wipers was the only sound she heard as she combed the dark roads, struggling to see past the glare of her headlights reflecting off the snow. She prayed constantly, begging God to bring Emma home safely. She prayed for him to give Saul strength and to help Emma accept her mother's actions without allowing them to break her heart.

After Madeleine had driven through Paradise three times, she turned around and steered her truck toward her house. She parked in the driveway and then jogged up the driveway toward Saul's house. She found two Amish men standing on the porch and talking to a police officer.

"Did she come home?" Madeleine clasped her hands together.

The same older Amish man shook his head. "We haven't seen her."

Madeleine's heart sank. "Where's Saul?"

"He's still out searching," the older man said.

"What can I do to help?" Madeleine asked. "I've driven through Paradise three times."

"Miss, I think you've done all you can do," the officer said. "We're handling things now."

Madeleine frowned. "Please let me know when you've found her." She pointed toward her house. "I live right there."

"We will," the officer promised.

Madeleine walked through the raging snow toward her house. She put a kettle of water on the stove, wrapped herself in a blanket, and stared out her window toward Saul's house while she continued to silently pray for Emma.

After drinking a cup of tea, she read her Bible and then climbed into bed fully clothed, the best way to keep warm on a night like this. Her thoughts were still with Emma and Saul as, despite her efforts not to do so, she was drifting off to sleep.

A thought hit her, and Madeleine bolted up.

"The kittens in my barn!" She leaped out of bed.

TWENTY-TWO

Madeleine hurriedly pulled on her coat, scarf, and boots and then grabbed her flashlight before rushing outside to her barn. When she got there, she climbed up into the loft and found Emma asleep and curled up on the quilt Maddie had left next to the mother cat and kittens. Her heart melted at the sight of the little girl snuggled next to the animals.

She slowly sank into the hay and brushed Emma's hair back from her face. Emma sighed and rolled over onto her back, and Madeleine could see tearstains on her pink cheeks.

"Emma," Madeleine whispered. "Emma, wake up. Emma?"

Her eyes fluttered open. "Maddie?" She rubbed her eyes.

"Everyone is looking for you. The whole community and the police are searching." Madeleine continued to run her fingers through the hair that had fallen out from underneath Emma's prayer covering. "You've scared us all to death."

Emma sat up, and her lip quivered. "I had to come

here to be alone. I found out *mei mamm* didn't die when I was four. She left me." Tears flooded her pale blue eyes, and Madeleine pulled her into her arms.

"It's okay to cry," Madeleine murmured against Emma's prayer covering. "Let it all out, sweetie."

"I always thought *mei mamm* died because she was sick. Now I know she left because she hated me, and she wanted a better life without me."

"No, no," Madeleine said while rocking her. "That's not true. She didn't hate you."

"*Ya*, she did." Emma sniffed. "If she didn't hate me, then she wouldn't have left. Instead of staying and being *mei mamm*, she moved away and went on boat rides with a man named Timothy. That's all she cared about. She never cared about me."

"Now, I need you to listen to me, and then we have to go tell everyone you're safe." Madeleine rubbed Emma's back. "Your mother didn't hate you. But some people in this world don't know how to be parents. Your mom was one of those people. My father was like that too. My mother told me a long time ago that my father didn't know how to be a daddy, and that's why he left. I used to think he hated me, but my mother told me he didn't. He just was too selfish to be a father. It takes a very special person to be a good parent."

Emma sniffed again.

Madeleine looked down at Emma. "Your father is a very good *dat*. He loves you with all of his heart. I can tell by the way he talks to you and by the way he takes care of you. Has your *dat* given you everything you needed?" She lifted Emma to her feet as she spoke.

Emma nodded. "*Ya*, he always has taken care of me."

"He gives you food, and he provides your clothes. He keeps you safe, right?" Now Madeleine was preparing to take steps toward the ladder, ready to lead Emma with her arms still around the little girl's shoulders. She had to let Saul know his daughter was safe.

Emma wiped her eyes with her fingertips. "*Ya*, he's always been there for me."

"Exactly. Your *dat* loves you enough for a *mamm* and a *dat*." Madeleine pointed to the mother cat. "It's sort of like a *mamm* cat. She makes sure her babies are fed and warm. We give them some food, but they're really getting all they need from their mama. The food we give them is keeping their mama healthy so they can nurse from her. She's keeping them safe up here, away from other animals and the cold snow."

Emma reached down and stroked one of the kittens. "I just don't understand why *mei mamm* would leave me. Why didn't she ever call me or write me? Did she wonder how I was? Did she want to know what I look like?" Fresh tears glistened in her eyes. "Did she even care that I have her eyes and her hair?"

Madeleine's heart splintered at the sadness in Emma's eyes. Keeping her arms tight around the little girl's shoulders, she gently steered her toward the ladder. "I don't know the answer to that. I used to wonder why my father didn't want to get to know me too. I used to think that someday he'd come back to see me, and he'd be a part of my wedding or spend time with my children. I eventually gave up that dream because he never reached out to me. He paid child support to my mother until I turned eighteen, but we never heard from him. He would just mail the checks."

She rubbed Emma's arm and then guided her down the ladder as she continued. "I know it hurts, sweetie, but you have to listen to me. Many, many people love you. Sylvia and Esther love you. I'm certain Marcus loves you too. My grandparents loved you, and the rest of the community loves you. They love you to the moon and back, as my mother used to say."

When they'd both landed on the barn floor, Emma smiled at Madeleine and wiped her eyes.

"And I love you too, Emma," Madeleine went on as she pushed another lock of hair away from Emma's face. "I love you very much."

"I love you too, Maddie. But you're not Amish." Emma frowned. "*Mei dat* doesn't want me to get too attached to you. He's probably afraid that you'll leave me just like *mei mamm* did. My teacher even told me not to get too close to you because you might leave."

Madeleine shook her head. "No, they're both wrong about me, Emma. I promise you with my heart that I won't leave you."

"Prove to me that you won't leave." Emma's expression was serious.

"All right." Madeleine nodded slowly. "I'll find a way to prove to you that I won't ever leave you."

"*Danki.*" Emma hugged her again, and she shivered as Madeleine wrapped her in her arms and walked them to the barn door.

"We need to get you home. Your dad is so scared."

Madeleine took Emma's hand and led her out into the snow.

They hurried across the field toward Saul's house. She could see the same group of Amish men standing with the police officer. Even with little light, she could see that Saul was there too.

"Saul!" Madeleine yelled. "Saul! I found her!"

"*Dat!*" Emma yelled. "*Dat!*"

Saul broke into a run and met them halfway through the field. He lifted Emma into his arms and spun her around. "I've been worried sick about you. Where were you?"

"In Maddie's barn." Emma pointed to Madeleine. "She found me."

"She was asleep with the kittens." Madeleine hugged her coat to her body. "I was falling asleep when I realized we hadn't checked the barn."

"*Danki.*" Saul's voice was thin and shaky. "I can't thank you enough."

"You're welcome." Madeleine studied his eyes, wishing they were friends again. She longed to hug him and console him. It was going to be hard for him to answer all Emma's questions.

The Amish men and police officer hurried over and surrounded Saul and Emma. Madeleine slowly backed away from the group and walked home.

As she put on pajamas and climbed back into her bed, she contemplated her conversation with Emma. She wanted to prove to the girl that she would be a part of her life, but she also wanted to finally have roots in a place she could call home. She closed her eyes and prayed, asking God to lead her to the right decision in her life. How could she become a part of Emma's community?

And then the answer appeared in her mind—she could become Amish.

Madeleine loved everything about the Amish culture—the simplicity, the focus on God and family, the community. The answer was right there before her, clear as a cloudless blue sky. It was as if God was speaking to her and directing her thoughts. For the first time since she'd lost Travis, she felt God's presence holding her and comforting her. This was the answer she'd been searching for. This was where God had been leading her all along, but she couldn't see past her own insecurities to see the answer that was right before her eyes. She was supposed to come to Amish Country and start again. She was finally home.

The thought settled comfortably in Madeleine's mind, and she fell asleep with a content and warm feeling in her heart. She slept soundly without any nightmares. And she dreamed of her baptism.

• • •

After everyone else had left, Saul tucked Emma into bed. Although he was now furious that she had run away, he was thankful she was home and safe again.

"I'm sorry for running away." Emma pulled the quilt up to her chin. "And I'm sorry for scaring you."

"I forgive you, but you can't ever do that again." Saul

touched her pink cheek. "The whole community was worried about you."

"I know." Emma nodded. "Maddie told me everyone was scared. Especially you."

Saul's heart turned over in his chest at the mention of Madeleine's name. "I'm grateful she thought to look in the barn. I was so frantic that I never thought to check with the kittens."

"I went there to think. I like going to see the kittens and thinking by myself." Emma frowned. "I told Maddie I was upset and that I thought *mei mamm* hated me. Maddie explained that *Mamm* didn't hate me. She said that some people aren't *gut* at being parents. She said her *dat* was the same way. He left before she was born, but he didn't hate her. He just didn't know how to be her *dat*."

Saul nodded slowly, overwhelmed by Madeleine's wisdom.

"Maddie said you love me enough for two parents, and the community loves me too," Emma continued. "And Maddie said she loves me, and she'll never leave me."

Tears filled Saul's eyes, and he couldn't speak. Instead, he leaned down and hugged her.

"*Ich liebe dich, Dat,*" Emma said. "Thank you for being my *dat* and taking such good care of me."

Tears flowed from Saul's eyes as he held on to her.

"Are you okay, *Dat*?" Emma asked.

"*Ya.*" He sat up and wiped his eyes. "We're both tired. I think we need to get some rest. We'll talk in the morning." He kissed her forehead. "*Ich liebe dich. Gut nacht.*"

"*Gut nacht.*" Emma rolled over onto her side and extinguished the lantern on her nightstand.

Saul sauntered to his bedroom and sank onto the edge of the bed. He placed his lantern on the nightstand and then stared up at the ceiling. How had the evening taken such an emotional turn? Not only had Emma learned the truth, but Madeleine had helped her sort through it so quickly. It was all so surreal.

His feelings for Madeleine were stronger than ever, and he didn't know how to stop them from growing. He needed God's help to sort through all the confusing emotions surging through him.

He closed his eyes and prayed. *God, thank you for delivering my* dochder *back to me safely. Thank you for the wonderful members of my community who surrounded me and helped me search for her. Thank you also for Madeleine, who found Emma and brought her home.*

Lord, I'm confused. I know I need to stay true to my baptism vows, but I can't stop how I feel about Madeleine. She was there for Emma and me in our time of need, and she even helped Emma cope with the truth about her mother. How do I stop feeling close to someone who has done so much for my dochder *and me? I've asked you repeatedly to help me sort through all of these confusing feelings, and I'm not hearing your answers.*

Are you listening to me, God? I know I need to wait for your perfect timing, but these feelings are getting stronger by the day. I need your help now, Lord. Are you hearing me? Why aren't you answering? Please help me stay true to my beliefs. Please lead me to your perfect path. I can't do this alone.

Saul stripped off his clothes and pulled on his pajamas before climbing into bed. As he fell asleep, his thoughts turned to Madeleine and how thankful he was that she saved Emma—in more ways than one.

. . .

Madeleine awoke refreshed the following morning. Now her decision to become Amish had settled not just in her mind but in her heart, and she couldn't wait to talk to a friend about it. She was thankful she had already scheduled a personal day from work.

She ate a quick breakfast and then dialed Carolyn's number, hoping Carolyn would be somewhere near where they kept their phone so she wouldn't have to leave a message. After several rings, Carolyn answered her phone.

"Carolyn," Madeleine gushed into the phone. "It's Madeleine. Would it be all right if I came to visit you today?"

"*Ya*, that would be fine." Carolyn's voice was tentative. "It's Tuesday, though. Don't you have to go to work?"

"I took the day off."

"Oh. I'd love to see you. Come by anytime."

"Wonderful," Madeleine said. "I'll be right over."

Thirty minutes later, Madeleine was sitting in Carolyn's kitchen and sipping coffee with her.

"I heard what happened with Emma Beiler last night." Carolyn shook her head. "That is scary. I'm thankful she's okay."

"Yes, it was scary." Madeleine shivered as she remembered how worried she'd been. "I drove around searching for her for more than two hours. It didn't occur to me until I climbed into bed that Emma might be in my barn because she likes to visit the cats there. I don't know why I didn't think of that earlier."

"I think sometimes when we're panicking the most obvious solutions don't occur to us." Carolyn lifted her mug. "How have you been?"

"I'm doing well." Madeleine took a deep breath. "I've made a decision, and I want you to be the first person I share it with."

"Oh?" Carolyn raised her eyebrows. "What is it?"

"I want to become Amish." At saying the words aloud for the first time, she smiled. The decision felt so right that it warmed her soul. She no longer felt alone, and the tight grip of grief that had strangled her heart was slowly letting go. The Lord had spoken to her, and she heard his words loud and clear. This decision was certainly divine.

Carolyn's eyes widened. "Are you certain?"

"I'm positively certain. I've wanted to find a home, and I believe God has been leading me here all along. What do I need to do?"

"Well, you'll need to meet with the bishop. He's a very kind man, and I know he'll be more than willing to talk to you." Carolyn smiled. "And you'll need a proper dress, apron, and prayer covering. I can help you make those."

"When can we get started sewing?" Madeleine asked.

"How about right now?" Carolyn stood. "I have plenty of fabric in my sewing room. We can start on a dress and apron this afternoon."

"Thank you very much. I'll pay you for it." Madeleine clapped her hands together. "I can't wait to get started."

By the time Madeleine left later that afternoon, she had a dress and apron half made. That evening she searched through her grandmother's sewing room and found fabric to make more dresses and aprons. She also found two of her grandmother's prayer coverings.

Madeleine worked late into the night, finishing the dress and the apron and then starting on another dress. She spent the next day sewing and finished the second dress too. While she sewed, she thought about her grandparents and her happy memories of being with them. She wondered what they would think if they were alive and knew about her decision to become Amish. The thought warmed her heart. She knew her grandparents would be happy for her. She wondered how her friends at work would take the news.

. . .

Madeleine found Ruth and Linda eating in the break room at lunchtime on Thursday. She sat down at the table and unpacked her bag.

"How's your day going?" Ruth asked Madeleine.

"It's going fine, thank you." Madeleine pulled out her sandwich and bottle of water. "How about yours?"

"The usual." Ruth turned to Linda. "And yours?"

Linda shrugged. "Dirty rooms and unmade beds."

Madeleine smiled. "I wanted to tell you something. I've made a decision."

Ruth raised an eyebrow. "What decision is this?"

"I'm going to become Amish." Madeleine waited for their reaction.

Linda nodded slowly, and Ruth studied Madeleine. Then Linda frowned. "Do you realize what you have to give up? You can't use your cell phone or drive your truck."

"I know." Madeleine nodded. "I'm comfortable with that."

"Why do you want to be Amish?" Ruth asked. "Does it have to do with your neighbors?"

Madeleine nodded. "Partly it does. When I say I want to be a part of the community, I *am* thinking of Emma Beiler. I made a promise to her, and I intend to keep it. But I also want to be Amish for myself. I want to feel closer to God, and I think being a part of this community of faith will help me do that."

"What promise did you make to Emma?" Ruth asked.

"Does this have something to do with when she went missing the other night?" Linda asked. "I heard about that when I stopped at the market yesterday."

"Yes, it does." Madeleine opened her bottle of water. "Emma was upset, and I promised her I would never leave her."

"Have you spoken to the bishop?" Linda asked. "You'll need to talk to him about joining a baptism class and living as an Amish person for a certain amount of time."

"I'm planning to go see him this weekend." Madeleine sipped her water.

"Do you want me to go with you?" Ruth offered.

"No, but thank you." Madeleine smiled at Ruth. "I need to do this myself." She looked at Ruth and then Linda. "Do I have your blessing?"

"Of course you do." Linda touched her hand. "You have my blessing. And if you change your mind, I'll still support you. Becoming baptized is a big decision, and you might change your mind after you start the classes."

"I don't think I'll change my mind." Madeleine turned to Ruth. "How do you feel about this, Ruth? I really value your opinion."

"If you feel God is leading you to this, then I support it." Ruth smiled. "I have a feeling he *is* leading you, and I'm glad to hear it. If you feel this is your home, then you belong here."

"Thank you." Madeleine hoped the bishop would feel the same way.

TWENTY-THREE

Saul was staining a cabinet when he heard a knock on the door frame behind him. He looked over his shoulder and saw Marcus standing in the doorway. He stepped back from the workbench and pulled off his respirator.

"Marcus," Saul said. "*Wie geht's?*"

"I was in the neighborhood, and I thought I'd stop by." Marcus stepped into the shop, closed the door behind him, and craned his neck to look at the cabinets. "Nice work."

"*Danki.*" Saul pointed toward two stools across from the workbench. "Would you like to have a seat?"

"*Ya.*" Marcus hopped up on a stool. "Sylvia and I have been worried about Emma. How is she doing?"

"She's fine." Saul grabbed two bottles of water from the cooler by his workbench and handed one to Marcus. "She's actually taken the news a lot better than I thought she would. I feel bad for keeping it from her for this long, but I was afraid of how much it would hurt her."

Marcus sipped the water and shook his head. "I

don't think you did anything wrong by waiting to tell her. She's just a little girl."

"But she had a right to know." Saul sat on the bench across from Marcus. "I guess I need to give the credit for how well Emma is doing to Maddie. She's the one who helped Emma understand that her mother left because she couldn't handle being a mother. That's what matters, not that Annie left me—though I'm sure questions about her mother choosing another man will eventually come up."

"Why was Madeleine the one talking to her?" Marcus asked.

"Maddie comforted Emma as soon as she found her and told Emma that although Annie left her, she has plenty of people who love her. She told Emma that I'm the only parent she needs because I can love her as much as two parents would." Saul sighed. "Maddie knew how to say all the right things because her father left her before she was born. She knows how it feels to be abandoned by a parent. She was there when Emma needed her most. I feel God put Maddie in Emma's life because he knew Emma was going to need her."

Marcus eyed Saul with suspicion. "You still have feelings for that *English maedel*."

"I just appreciate what she did for Emma. She's the one who found Emma. And she talked to her and calmed her down too. I don't know if I could've done that."

"*Ya*, you could've. You're her *dat*." Marcus scowled. "You know her best. I'm grateful that Madeleine found Emma before it got any later or colder, but don't give her all the credit. You're doing the best you can with Emma, and you're doing a fantastic job as *mamm* and *dat*."

Saul took a long drink of water. "I don't know. I still feel Maddie was helpful. Emma seems much more content knowing the truth than I thought possible."

"You're treading on dangerous territory." Marcus's eyes were full of concern. "You really do have feelings for her, don't you?"

"No, I don't." Saul knew he was lying to his best friend, but he couldn't admit the truth out loud. He wouldn't dare confess that he'd been thinking of Madeleine nonstop ever since she'd found Emma. He couldn't tell Marcus he was starting to wonder if he should take another chance with Madeleine and invite her over for supper.

"You need to be careful," Marcus warned. "You don't want to risk losing Emma to the outside world. If Emma thinks that much of Madeleine, then she may start asking questions. She might want to know what it's like to join the military or drive a car. You don't want to lose her like you lost your *bruder*."

"I know. I know." Saul shrugged. "I'm not going to lose Emma. I'm just thankful Maddie is our neighbor. That's all I meant."

"You have to be careful. Emma is at a very impressionable age." Marcus stood. "I need to get home. Tell Emma hello for us."

"I will." Saul waved to his friend. "*Danki* for stopping by."

• • •

"I saw Maddie outside earlier," Emma said while washing dishes later that evening. "I waved to her, and she waved back."

"What was she doing?" Saul brought a bowl to the counter.

"She was carrying grocery bags into her *haus*." Emma scrubbed a pot while she spoke. "I was going to go and help her carry in her bags, but I didn't want you to be upset with me."

Saul nodded as Marcus's warning rang through his mind. "That was a *gut* choice. It's best that you leave her alone."

"I miss her." Emma frowned up at him.

"I know." Saul touched her arm. *I do too.* "We appreciate all she did when she found you, but we need to give her some privacy."

"But she said she'll always be here for me." Emma's eyes were determined. "Why can't I be her friend?"

Saul sighed. He felt torn between the Amish community and the outside world. "I know it doesn't make much sense, but I'm only trying to do what's best for you. Right now I need you to follow my rules. You'll understand why when you're older." He paused, waiting for her to argue with him. Instead, she simply nodded.

"Okay, *Dat*," she said before turning her attention back to the dishes.

He breathed a sigh of relief. For now, the argument was settled, but he knew she would keep asking him

why she couldn't be friends with Madeleine. And soon
he would run out of explanations.

. . .

Madeleine parked her truck in front of Bishop Elmer
Smucker's house the following afternoon. She climbed
out and then smoothed her hands down her cloak.
She'd dressed in her new purple dress and apron that
she'd completed with Carolyn's help. Her hair was
styled in a traditional Amish tight bun and covered
with a prayer *kapp* she'd found in her grandmother's
closet. Wearing the prayer covering made her feel
closer to both God and her grandmother. She only
hoped the bishop would see that her intentions were
pure.

She walked up the front path leading to the bishop's
white, two-story house and knocked on the door. She
folded her hands in front of her cloak and shivered in
the cold breeze.

The front door opened, and Elmer Smucker stood
inside the storm door with a confused look on his face.
Madeleine estimated he was in his late seventies. He
was short and stocky with a long, graying beard. After
a moment, he held open the storm door. "Hello. May I
help you?"

"Good afternoon," Madeleine said. "I'm Madeleine
Miller. I'm Martha Stoltzfus's granddaughter."

"Oh, Madeleine. How are you?" He opened the
storm door wider. "What can I do for you?"

"I'm well, thank you. I was hoping I could talk to

you. Is now a good time?" She paused while gathering her thoughts. "It's a personal matter."

"Of course." Elmer made a sweeping gesture. "Please come in. Would you like to have a seat?"

"Thank you." Madeleine followed him into a large family room. She removed her cloak and folded it in half. She sat on a sofa and placed the cloak beside her while Elmer sat across from her in a wing chair. "I guess I should've called first."

"It's no problem," Elmer said. "What can I do for you, Madeleine?"

Madeleine paused for a moment and then decided to plow forward with the full truth. "I've been doing a lot of thinking and praying, and I want to know what I need to do to become Amish."

"*Ach*." The bishop's eyes flew open as if he were startled by an unexpected noise. "You want to be Amish?" He asked the question slowly, as if trying to comprehend the words.

"Yes," Madeleine said. "I inherited my grandparents' house, and I spent a lot of time with them when I was a child."

"They were *gut* people." He suddenly smiled. "Now that you say it, I recall seeing you with them. Martha was always *froh* when you were here."

Madeleine nodded. "I was *froh* too. I cherish those times. Becoming Amish and a part of this community would give me the chance to have a real home."

The bishop studied her while fingering his beard. "This is something you've been considering for a while?"

"Yes," she said. "I've spent the past several months in prayer about my life, and the other night I realized I belong here. I believe God has told me to become a part of the Amish church."

"But your mother left before you were born." The bishop's expression was pointed. "It's rare an *Englisher* joins our community. What are your true intentions?"

"I work with the Amish at the hotel, and my closest friends are Amish." She paused and considered what else was in her heart. "I learned *Dietsch* from my grandparents, and I understood the language when I went to Carolyn Glick's wedding and when I went to church with Carolyn." She cupped her hand to her chest. "My heart belongs in this community, and I'm ready to start living like a true member."

The bishop's expression softened. "Are you certain your reasons are pure?"

Madeleine paused, thought of Emma, and knew she needed to be honest with the bishop. "I'm sure you heard about Emma Beiler running away. The truth is, I made a promise to her that night when I found her. I told her I love her, and she asked me to prove that I'll never leave her. By becoming Amish, I will not only join your community, but I will prove to Emma that I'll never leave her."

Elmer studied Madeleine. "You're saying you want to convert to keep a promise to Emma Beiler?" He raised one of his bushy gray eyebrows. "It's not my place to judge, but I'm not certain that's a strong enough reason to become Amish."

"My reasons are pure because it was God who brought

me to this decision after months of praying. This wasn't a hasty decision," Madeleine said. "I've searched my heart and soul, and I know I need to convert to feel whole again. When I'm at home in *mei mammi's haus*, I feel as if I belong here." She folded her hands as if to pray as her thoughts turned to Travis. "I lost my fiancé tragically, and that caused me to refocus my life toward God. I believe *mei mammi* left me her *haus* because she knew how much I loved this community, and it's as if she's calling me back home."

The bishop rubbed his beard and was silent for a moment. "You truly believe God put this decision in your heart?"

"Absolutely," she said, emphasizing the word. "I could never have decided this without his guidance."

Elmer paused. "I believe you. Now, back to your request to join the church. What would your family say about your decision to convert?"

"My parents will understand." Madeleine fingered her apron. "I plan to call my mother tonight and tell her."

Elmer fingered his beard. "And your *mamm* left the faith before you were born, right?"

"That's right. She hadn't joined the church before she left, but she told me that she always felt as if she were shunned." Madeleine sat erect, hoping to look serious and respectful. "Her relationship was strained with her parents until I was born, after my father left her. I have a great love and respect for the Amish faith. Now it seems God is leading me to the faith more than ever."

Elmer nodded while contemplating her words.

"I know this seems sudden, but I truly have thought this through." She nodded emphatically.

"You realize you can't simply decide to be Amish and then quickly convert," Elmer said. "You'll need to live as we do without any of your modern conveniences. And you must complete baptism classes."

"I understand," Madeleine explained. "My house is already an Amish home. I'll stop my cellular phone service, and I'll sell my truck. I'll find a ride to work. I'll have the phone in the barn hooked up and use that to make calls. I've already been worshiping in your district, and I've made some Amish clothes." She glanced down at her dress and apron. "Carolyn Glick helped me make this dress and apron, and I found prayer coverings in my *mammi's* closet. I'm ready to make a full commitment to this community and to my new life right away, and I'll be ready for my instruction."

"Wonderful." Elmer stood and crossed the room, coming to a stop in front of her. "I'd like to welcome you to the Amish community." He shook her hand "You're invited to join the baptism class in the spring."

"Oh, thank you!" Madeleine clapped her hands together. "I mean, *danki*! This is wonderful. I'm so grateful. I appreciate your time."

Elmer chuckled. "*Gern gschehne*. I'll see you at church."

"Yes, you will." Madeleine pulled on her cloak. "Have a good afternoon."

· · ·

Madeleine finished her supper at the kitchen table that evening before pulling out her cellular phone and dialing her mother's number. Anxiety coursed through her while she awaited her mother's voice on the other end of the line.

"Hi, Maddie," Mom said. "How are you doing today?"

"I'm doing great, Mom. How are you and Jack?"

"We're fine. I was just trying to figure out what to make for supper. What did you eat?"

"I had veggie burger and corn." Madeleine chuckled. "It was a gourmet meal."

"Yes, it was." Mom laughed. "What's new with you?"

"Well, I met with Elmer Smucker today." Madeleine gathered up her dirty dishes while she spoke, her phone between her shoulder and neck. "He's the bishop for this church district."

"Why did you meet with the bishop?"

"I've decided that I want to convert." She placed her dishes in the sink. "I want to become Amish."

"What did you say?"

"You heard me." Madeleine leaned against the sink. "I want to be Amish. I love this community, and I want to be a part of it."

"Are you certain?" Mom asked.

"I'm positive."

"You realize what you have to give up, right?" Mom continued. "You need to get rid of your truck, and you love that truck. And what about your phone? And the Internet, music, and movies."

Madeleine smiled. "Mom, I can live without the

truck. I'll have to pay for rides, but I'll eventually get a horse and buggy. I already have a barn and a fenced pasture for a horse. There's a phone in the barn, and I'll just have to have it hooked up again. I'm living without music, movies, and the Internet now. I've thought this through. I know what I'm doing."

Mom was silent for a few moments. "Are you doing this for that man next door? For Saul?"

Madeleine shook her head. "No, I'm doing this for me."

"Are you sure, Maddie?"

"I am doing this in part for his daughter. But deep in my heart, I've always felt as if I belonged here." Madeleine paused to gather her thoughts. "I hope you support my decision, Mom. This is very important to me."

"If this is really what you want, then I will support you. But I hope you're not doing this to win a man's heart. You need to do what's right for you, not some-one else."

"I know that, Mom." Madeleine began to fill the sink with hot water. "I feel closer to God when I'm in this community. This is what I want to do."

"When will you be baptized?" her mother asked.

"I'm going to join a baptism class in the spring. I'm going to shut my cell phone off soon. I'll have the out-side phone hooked up next week, and then I'll call you and give you the number."

"Okay." Mom sniffed. "I never expected this. I'm really surprised. My mother would be so proud of you, Maddie. She really would. And I'm proud of you too."

"Thank you, Mom. That means a lot."

"Well, I'll let you go. Call me next week."

"I will." Madeleine disconnected the call and smiled. She was thankful for her mother's support.

TWENTY-FOUR

Madeleine was sweeping her kitchen floor when she heard squealing tires and a crash. She dropped the broom and ran to the front window, where she spotted a buggy twisted at the side of the road, at the end of the driveway and near a sedan with a smashed front end.

"Oh no!" Madeleine grabbed her first aid kit from under the bathroom sink and her phone before rushing out the door with her coat thrown over her shoulders. She ran to the buggy and pried the door open. She found Marcus slumped over the seat and moaning. His head was bleeding profusely.

"Oh, Marcus." Her hands trembled as she gently held his head to protect his neck and spine from injury. She snapped into trauma nurse mode, mentally clicking through the list of procedures she'd learned while serving in the military. "Talk to me, Marcus. Stay with me."

Marcus continued to moan.

"Miss?" A man walked up behind her. His face was pasty white and his hands were shaking. "I didn't mean to hit him. I didn't see him at first, and when I did, I couldn't stop. The roads are icy from the snow we got yesterday." His voice quavered. "I didn't mean to hit him. I really didn't. Is he okay? Is he alive?"

"He's alive, but he needs help." Madeleine pulled out her iPhone, unlocked it, and handed it to the man. "Call 9-1-1 right now." She used one hand to open the first aid kit and fish out gauze pads. "Marcus? Stay with me, buddy. Marcus? Can you hear me? Answer me if you can hear me."

"*Ya*." Marcus's voice croaked, but his eyes remained closed while blood poured from his forehead.

She pushed the pads up against his head while silently saying a prayer for him.

"Where are we?" The driver stuck his head back in the buggy. "I have the paramedics on the phone, but I have no idea where I am."

Madeleine rattled off the address. "Tell them to hurry."

The driver moved away with her phone still against his ear.

"Marcus?" Madeleine pressed the gauze against his head, and it was immediately soaked with blood. She applied pressure to the wound while continuing to stabilize his neck. "Stay calm, Marcus. I'm here with you." Sirens blared in the distance, and she swallowed a sigh.

"My leg." Marcus breathed the words. "It hurts."

"The paramedics are on their way. They'll take good care of you. I promise you."

"What's happened?" Saul's voice boomed nearby. "Oh no. Marcus?"

"He'll be okay," Madeleine called. "We've called for help." She looked over her shoulder as Saul approached.

"How is he?" Saul's eyes were full of worry.

"He's hanging in there," she said. "He has a head wound. I think his leg is injured, and the paramedics will have to put it in a splint when they arrive."

"What can I do?" Saul asked.

"You might want to take care of his horse. He looks awfully scared over there. And the driver of the car could use a kind word. He doesn't look hurt, but he's shaken up." She turned back to Marcus. "Just breathe and relax, Marcus. Everything will be okay."

. . .

After Saul made sure the driver of the car was all right, Saul moved back by the buggy and lingered behind Madeleine for a moment, marveling at how she was caring for his best friend. She was gentle but confident as she tended to Marcus's wounded head and assured him that help was on the way. He was overwhelmed by the Christian love in her eyes and her nurturing heart. For the second time in less than a week, Madeleine was taking care of someone he loved.

Sirens sounded as an ambulance barreled down the road, shaking him from his thoughts.

Neighbors from nearby farms began to gather in their shared driveway.

"Saul?" A young man from a neighboring farm appeared behind him. "Who's in the buggy?"

"It's Marcus Smucker," Saul said. "He was on his way to see me. He must have just been turning into the driveway when the car hit him."

"Is he going to be all right?" the young man asked.

"*Ya*." Saul nodded. "It looks like he will."

"Can I do anything to help?" the young man asked.

"*Ya*." Saul pointed toward the horse. "Would you take his horse to my pasture?"

"*Ya*." The young man walked over to the horse. "I'll make sure he's okay."

"*Danki*," Saul said as a crowd gathered around him.

"Is that Marcus Smucker?" a neighbor asked.

"Who's caring for him?" a second asked.

"What happened?" someone else yelled.

"My neighbor, Maddie, is taking care of him," Saul said. "She's a nurse."

The ambulance stopped in front of the buggy, and two paramedics jumped out. Saul stood with his neighbors while the paramedics talked to Madeleine. A fire engine blared its sirens and horns as it roared down the street and stopped near the ambulance. Soon a group of firefighters and emergency medical technicians were caring for Marcus and the driver of the car, and a police car arrived as well.

Madeleine finished talking to the emergency responders and then joined Saul. His eyes moved down her gray blouse and blue skirt, which were both stained with blood.

"How is he?" Saul asked her.

"Marcus has a gash on his head, and I suspect his leg or ankle may be broken." Madeleine crossed her arms over her blouse. "He was talking when the paramedics came. They're going to take him out of the buggy on a board just to make sure he doesn't have any back or neck fractures."

"Oh." Saul studied her, taking in her beautiful face and eyes. He was thankful for her and for her caring heart. "*Danki* for taking care of him."

She gave him a strange expression as if she were shocked by his words. "You're welcome."

One of the police officers asked if anyone in the crowd had seen the accident happen, but no one had. Then a woman with an EMT uniform came over as well.

"Does someone know this man's name?"

"*Ya*, he's Marcus Smucker. He was on his way to my farm." Saul pointed behind him. "*Mei haus* is back there. He was going to help me with a project."

"Would you mind helping with some paperwork?" the woman asked. "Would you also inform his family?"

"*Ya*." Saul turned to Madeleine. "Then would you give me a ride to get Sylvia and take us both to the hospital?"

"Of course." She glanced down at her blouse. "Let me just get changed. I'm a bit of a mess."

The EMT touched Madeleine's arm. "Miss, you did a wonderful job keeping Mr. Smucker stable before we arrived."

"Thanks." Madeleine gave her a shy smile. "I've had a lot of experience with trauma patients, and I'm glad I was here to help."

"I am too," Saul told her.

She turned toward him, and her gaze locked with his. It was as if they were the only two people in the world. His heart turned over in his chest. He longed for her friendship. *I miss you, Maddie. I miss you so much I ache.*

"I'll go get changed." Madeleine's voice wrenched him back to reality. She walked over to the EMT vehicle, retrieved her phone from the driver of the car, and then picked up her first aid kit. After jogging to her house, she disappeared through the front door.

. . .

Madeleine changed into a black skirt and plain blue blouse before pulling on her coat. She checked her hair in the mirror to make sure her hair was still secure in the tight bun she'd fixed earlier in the day. When she returned to the scene of the accident, she found Saul still talking to the EMT who was filling out paperwork on a clipboard. She stood back by the crowd of neighbors and waited until he was done.

Saul walked over to her as the ambulance pulled away with the lights flashing. She had been surprised by the tenderness in his eyes earlier when she was helping Marcus. Had he felt a spark between them? Or was he only worried about his friend? She had to have misread the heat in his eyes. Certainly he was only concerned about Marcus.

"You don't need to worry," she assured him as he stood next to her. "He was lucid when the EMTs arrived."

He nodded. "The woman told me the same thing. She thinks he'll be okay. I pray she's right."

"Do you want to go get Sylvia now?" Madeleine pointed toward her truck.

"*Ya*, please." He looked up the driveway. "Why is there a For Sale sign in your truck?"

"I've decided to get rid of it." She pulled the keys from her coat pocket.

"Why?" he asked as they walked side by side toward the vehicle.

"I need a change." She opened the door and hopped into the driver's seat. Although she knew he'd find out soon that she was going to become Amish, she didn't want to tell him just yet. She was more concerned about Marcus and his family.

"Oh." Saul climbed in next to her in the passenger seat.

They drove to the Smucker farm in silence. What was going through Saul's mind? Although he was stoic, there was something different about him. The cold vibe she'd felt from him before she went to California was gone. Was the way he felt about being her friend changing? Was he ready to be her friend? The questions echoed through her mind while they steered through Paradise toward Marcus's home.

When they pulled into the Smucker driveway, Madeleine hopped out of the truck and followed Saul to the front door.

Sylvia opened her inside door, then the storm door, and stepped out onto the porch before they even knocked. "*Was iss letz?*" She looked at each of them. "Where's Marcus?"

Madeleine touched Sylvia's arm. "Marcus was in an accident, but he's going to be fine. I just need to take you to the hospital."

"An accident?" Tears filled Sylvia's eyes. "What happened?"

Madeleine looked at Saul. "Tell her what happened, and I'll go get her things. Where are your coat and purse, Sylvia?"

"By the back door in the mudroom," Sylvia said before turning to Saul. "Is Marcus okay?"

Madeleine rushed into the house and grabbed Sylvia's things. When she returned to the porch, Sylvia was sniffing and wiping her eyes with the back of her hand.

"Madeleine took *gut* care of Marcus until the paramedics arrived," Saul said. "He will be fine. I promise you."

"*Danki.*" Sylvia hugged Madeleine. "You're a blessing, Madeleine. *Danki* for taking *gut* care of my husband."

"You're welcome." Madeleine met Saul's gaze, and her pulse skittered. "Let's get you to the hospital."

Sylvia sat between Madeleine and Saul in the truck. When they arrived, Madeleine steered up to the emergency entrance.

"Do you want me to stay with you?" Madeleine asked.

"That won't be necessary," Saul said as he climbed out.

"I'll call my driver when Marcus is ready to go home," Sylvia said. "*Danki*, Madeleine, for all you've done."

"You're welcome. Do you want me to call anyone?" Madeleine offered. "Do you need me to take care of the girls?"

"I'll call my mother-in-law," Sylvia said. "She'll meet the girls at the school and take them home."

"Okay." Madeleine nodded. "Saul, you have my number if you need anything. I'll be home today."

"*Danki*," Saul said.

"That's what neighbors are for," Madeleine said.

. . .

Later that evening, Madeleine noticed headlights reflecting off her family room wall while she was reading her Bible. She rushed to a window and saw a van parked by Saul's house. She pulled on her coat and hurried up the rock driveway, then waved at the van as it steered back down the driveway toward the road.

Madeleine climbed Saul's back porch steps and knocked on the storm door.

Emma pulled open the inside door and then smiled as she swung open the storm door. "Maddie! How are you?"

"I'm fine," Madeleine said. "How are you?"

"I'm *gut*." Emma looked over her shoulder. "*Dat*! It's Maddie!"

Saul came to the door. His eyes were tired. "Maddie. We just got home."

"I saw the van, and I came right over," Madeleine said. "I don't mean to intrude, but I want to know how Marcus is doing."

"He's fine." Saul unbuttoned his coat. "He has a sprained ankle, and he has stitches in his head. They ran all sorts of tests to make sure his injuries weren't any worse than they appeared. He'll be as *gut* as new in a few weeks."

"Good." Madeleine breathed a deep sigh. "I'm relieved to hear that. Are Sylvia and Esther okay?"

"*Ya*, they're fine. Sylvia and I stayed at the hospital with him, and her mother-in-law took care of the girls." Saul gestured toward the kitchen behind him. "Do you want to come in?"

"Oh no, thank you." Madeleine backed away from the door. "I'm letting the cold into your house, and I'm certain you're tired and hungry."

"Come in," Emma insisted. "I made some *brot* that you have to try. Esther and I baked with her *mammi*. We had a lot of fun."

"Oh no, thank you. Maybe I can try it some other time." Madeleine shook her head. "It's late."

"*Danki* for the cookbook," Emma said. "I love it."

"You're welcome." Madeleine looked at Saul. "I never got a chance to tell you that the cabinets and countertop are gorgeous. Thank you."

"I'm glad you like them." His expression softened. "And thank you for the screwdrivers."

"You're welcome." Madeleine jammed her thumb toward her house. "I'd better go. I'll see you soon."

"Good night!" Emma called after her.

Madeleine hurried down the driveway and sent a prayer up to God, thanking him for protecting Marcus. She then asked him to give her strength as she prepared her heart to begin living as a member of the community.

· · ·

"How are you feeling?" Saul stood with Marcus after the worship service the following Sunday.

Marcus shrugged while leaning on crutches. "I'm all right. I'm just very sore. I feel like I've been thrown from a horse."

"I know that feeling," Joshua Glick chimed in. "I've been thrown a few times, and it's rough. I hope you feel better soon."

"*Danki*, Josh." Marcus frowned. "It's not easy to work when I have to stay off my ankle."

Saul glanced across the barn to where a pretty young woman was talking to Emma while they delivered platters of food for lunch. The young woman had dark hair peeking out from under her prayer covering, and she was dressed in a traditional purple dress and black apron. While the woman seemed vaguely familiar, he couldn't put his finger on how he knew her.

"Josh." Saul leaned toward the other man. "Who is the *maedel* talking with Emma?"

Joshua glanced over at the woman and then turned to Saul. "That's Madeleine Miller. You don't recognize her?"

"That's Maddie?" Saul asked, surprised. "But she's dressed Amish."

"Are you sure that's Madeleine?" Marcus asked. "I was trying to figure out who she was too."

"I'm certain it's Madeleine. She was talking to Carolyn before the service started," Joshua said. "I guess she's converting?" He looked across the room to where Carolyn was waving at him. "*Mei fraa* is calling for me. I'd better see what she wants."

Saul's mouth gaped open as Madeleine smiled and talked to Emma and Esther. Madeleine was a vision of beauty in her traditional Amish clothes. Although he'd always found her beautiful, this was different. Seeing her in the raiment of his community made her more appealing than ever. It was as if his heart opened up and he could finally allow himself to feel close to her. She was no longer forbidden. His heart and soul warmed at the thought of her becoming Amish.

He loved her. Truly loved her. He was ready to trust another woman, and Madeleine was the one who had shown him how to let someone into his heart again. He'd seen glimpses of Madeleine's heart when she talked to Emma after she'd run away and also when she helped Marcus after the accident. She was the woman he wanted to marry; she was the woman who would be a proper mother to Emma. But Madeleine would also be a wonderful wife, someone with whom he'd want to share his life.

Instead of being selfish and cold like Annie had been, Madeleine was warm and caring. This love was different and deeper than anything he'd ever felt for Annie. He had never felt secure with Annie because he wasn't her first choice. But when he was with Madeleine, he was certain he was her first choice. She made him whole; she made him feel loved. Madeleine would be his partner, his helpmate.

The realizations settled in his soul, and the wall he'd built around his heart finally shattered.

Emma grabbed Madeleine's hand and pulled her toward Saul. "*Dat!*" she called. "*Dat!*"

Madeleine smiled and laughed as they weaved through the knot of people and headed toward Saul. His gaze was glued to Madeleine's beautiful face.

"*Dat*," Emma said as she brought Madeleine to a stop in front of him. "Look at Maddie! She's decided to become Amish."

"Hi, Saul." Madeleine gave him a shy smile. "*Wie geht's?*"

"Maddie." He shook his head, unable to express the words in his heart. "You look *schee*."

"You think so?" Madeleine smoothed her hands over her apron. "I'm still getting the hang of sewing, but I'm practicing."

"Maddie is keeping her promise to me." Emma looked up at Madeleine. "She promised she wouldn't leave me, and she's going to be Amish like us. She'll be a member of our church district."

"That's right." Madeleine looked down at Emma with love shimmering in her eyes. "I made a promise to you, and I will keep it."

"Maddie," Saul said. "Can we talk somewhere alone?"

"*Ya*, of course." Madeleine touched Emma's arm. "I'm going to go talk to your *dat* for a few minutes. Would you please help Carolyn fill coffee cups?"

"*Ya*." Emma rushed off toward the women who were serving the meal.

Saul and Madeleine headed toward the barn door. She picked up her cloak from the back of a chair, and he pulled on his coat before they walked out into the cold air. They walked together toward a pond at the back of the property.

"You're surprised," Madeleine finally said.

"*Ya*." Saul nodded. "I'm shocked, but I'm *froh*." He stopped walking by the icy pond, which glistened in the afternoon sun. "When did you decide to convert?"

She looked out over the pond. "I spoke to the bishop last week."

"That's why you put a For Sale sign in your truck."

She nodded. "*Ya*. I actually sold it yesterday and got a ride here today. I'm going to turn off my cell phone at the end of the month, and I'm having the phone in the barn hooked up. I'm going to join the next baptism class in the spring. I'll be baptized in the fall after I complete the classes."

"Why didn't you tell me?"

Madeleine's expression became unsure. "I guess I was afraid."

"Why would you be afraid to tell me?" He searched her eyes.

"I didn't want you to think I was converting for the wrong reason. I want to be Amish because I love this community. After dreaming of a place I could call my home, I've finally found it. I also want to keep my promise to Emma. She's very important to me."

"You're very important to both of us." He took her hands in his. "Maddie, I'm sorry I've been cold to you. When Annie left, I built a wall around my heart. I didn't know how to let someone past that wall because I was afraid of being hurt again. I also was overprotective of Emma because she was all I had left." He paused and stared deep into her eyes. "You've changed me. You've taught me how to love again.

You've awakened feelings in me that I haven't felt in years."

Madeleine sniffed as tears filled her eyes.

"Marcus once said I was too scared to take risks, and he was right. But I'm not scared anymore." He took a deep breath and mustered all of his strength. "Maddie, seeing you today has made me realize that I'm ready to give my heart away again. God has given me a second chance to love someone by bringing you into my life. I'm thankful for you."

Madeleine wiped her eyes with one hand.

"I want you to be a part of my life, Maddie. I also want you to be in Emma's life. Would you give me a chance to show you how much you mean to us?" He squeezed her hands. "I'd like to get to know you, and then we can officially start dating after you're baptized. Does that sound *gut* to you?"

"*Ya.*" She sniffed, and a tear trickled down her cheek. "That would make me so *froh*. I thought I would never love again after losing Travis the way I did. My heart was ripped out of my chest when he killed himself. I felt guilty for not seeing the signs that he needed more help than he was getting. After he died, I felt all alone, but you and Emma have become my family. God gave me another chance at love too. I'm so blessed to be here with you and Emma."

"*Ich liebe dich,*" he whispered as he wiped away her tear with the tip of his finger.

"*Ich liebe dich.*" She repeated the words, and they were like a sweet melody to his ears.

. . .

Madeleine couldn't stop smiling as she and Saul walked together back to the barn. She knew that joining the church was the right decision and that God had put that decision in her heart. She not only had found a home, but she'd also found a family with Saul and Emma Beiler.

"Madeleine!" Linda Zook rushed over to Madeleine and Saul as they approached the barn. "Ruth is in the hospital."

"What?" Madeleine gasped. "I was wondering why she wasn't here this morning. What happened?"

"Her husband just called to say she's had a stroke. She told me on Friday that she wasn't feeling well and she was going to go home and rest. I never imagined it was this serious." Linda's eyes were wide. "We have to get to the hospital."

Madeleine looked up at Saul. "Could we call your driver?"

"*Ya.*" Saul nodded. "I'll call right away."

. . .

Madeleine, Saul, Carolyn, Josh, and Linda walked into the hospital that afternoon. Madeleine rushed to the front desk and asked where she could find Ruth, and they hurried to Ruth's room.

"Do you think we should take turns going in?" Linda asked. "We might overwhelm her if we all go in at once."

"*Ya*, that's a *gut* point." Carolyn looked at Madeleine. "You go first. We'll wait in the sitting room down the hall."

Madeleine turned toward Saul, who nodded in agreement. Madeleine knocked on the door and then opened it. Ruth's husband, Jonas, sat beside Ruth's bed with his hands folded in his lap. His gaze was frozen on Ruth, who had an oxygen tube in her nose. Machines next to her beeped and hummed.

"Jonas," Madeleine whispered as tears filled her eyes. "How is she?"

The older man shook his head and frowned. The sadness and worry in his eyes caused the tears to sprinkle down Madeleine's cheeks.

Ruth stirred, turned toward Madeleine, and reached out her hand. "M–Madeleine. *K–kumm*."

"Ruth," Madeleine took her hand. "How are you?"

Ruth's eyes were wide as she weakly pulled Madeleine toward her. "I n–need to s–see A–aron. You h–have to g–get h–him. You have to t–tell him to c–come."

Tears streamed down Jonas's cheeks as he rushed out of the room.

The machines hummed and clicked while Madeleine gnawed her lower lip. *What should I do? How can I find Aaron? What should I tell Ruth?*

"M–Mad–eleine," Ruth said again, her words slow and garbled. "I n–need to s–see Aa–ron. He l–left a l–long t–time ago, and I n–need h–him to c–come b–back to m–me. I have to t–talk to h–him."

Madeleine nodded. "*Ya*, I understand, Ruth. I will try to find him."

Ruth squeezed Madeleine's hand. "I h–have to s–see h–him r–right a–away." Her voice rose. "*D–dummle!*"

"Okay." Madeleine felt her heart breaking as she studied Ruth. She looked different. She wasn't the same strong and steady Ruth who had been a pillar of wisdom and patience. This woman was agitated and excitable. The stroke had changed Ruth, and it was difficult to accept.

The door opened, and Jonas reappeared with a man in a white coat.

"I'll give her something to calm her down," the doctor said. "We'll take care of her, Mr. Ebersol." The doctor approached Ruth. "Mrs. Ebersol, I need you to rest now."

"I n–need to s–see Aaron! He h–has to c–come b–back."

"Miss," the doctor said, addressing Madeleine. "We need to restrict Mrs. Ebersol's visitors for now. You can come back and see her later on when she has calmed down."

"I understand." Madeleine cleared her throat. "Good-bye, Ruth." More tears rolled down her cheeks. "I'll pray for you." She glanced at Jonas, and he gave her a solemn nod.

Madeleine hurried out of the room and down the hallway to where Saul, Josh, Carolyn, and Linda were waiting. She tried to calm her frayed nerves and stop her tears, but they continued to flow.

When she reached her friends, Saul stood and reached for her. "What happened?"

"Ruth isn't herself." Madeleine sat down beside Saul.

"She's weak, and her speech has been affected by the stroke. She's also upset and agitated. She's asking for Aaron. She begged me to find him and make him come home to see her. She was insistent."

"*Ach*, no," Carolyn gasped, and Joshua rubbed her arm.

"That's *bedauerlich*," Linda said.

"*Ya*," Carolyn agreed. "We need to do something for her."

"We do. She was very upset. She told me to hurry, that she needed to see him right away." Madeleine looked at Saul. "Can we help her? Can we find a way to contact Aaron?"

"I'll have to look into it," Saul said. "I'll do my best to find him."

"The doctor has restricted her visitors, which means we can't go in to see her right now." Madeleine sighed. "I'm very upset to see her this way."

"It will get better." Saul touched her arm. "The doctors will take *gut* care of her."

"I hope so." Although her heart was breaking for her friend Ruth, Madeleine felt comforted with Saul by her side.

. . .

Later that evening, Saul tucked Emma into bed and then went into his room and sat on the edge of his bed. He'd told Madeleine he would do his best to find Aaron, and he intended to keep that promise. All afternoon he'd tried to think where Aaron could possibly be and how he could find him. He'd heard Aaron had gone to a former Amish community in Missouri, but he had no idea how to find him there. His thoughts kept going back to the letter he'd received from Timothy.

He retrieved the metal box that was now in a drawer in his nightstand, sifted past the legal documents Annie had sent him, and found the postmarked envelope that had held Timothy's letter. He studied the crumpled envelope, and then the solution hit him like a ton of bricks—the embossed return address on the envelope said Paradise Builders. He suddenly remembered a conversation he'd had with Aaron when they were fifteen.

They were spending time with friends at a youth gathering and discussing their dreams for the future. Aaron told Saul that someday he hoped to open his own construction business and call it Paradise Builders. Could this company be the one Aaron Ebersol had dreamed of when he was a child? Had Aaron moved to Missouri and started his own company? If so, did Timothy work for Aaron?

Saul's pulse accelerated while he stared at the Paradise Builders logo. Now he had to figure out a way to contact the company and confirm that his hunch was right. The best way to confirm it was to call the company, but how would he find the phone number? He'd heard that the Internet was the best place to find information quickly. Perhaps Madeleine still had Internet access on her fancy cell phone.

Saul stuffed the envelope into his pocket and headed down the hallway to Emma's room. After knocking, he opened the door and stepped through the doorway.

"*Ya, Dat*?" Emma sat up in bed. "Is something wrong?"

"No, no, *mei liewe*. Everything is fine. I just need to step outside for a few minutes. Will you be okay here alone?"

"I'll be fine. Be sure to wear your coat. It's cold out there."

Saul smiled. "I promise to wear my coat. I'll be back soon. You get to sleep." He rushed downstairs, pulled on his coat, and hurried down the driveway to Madeleine's house. He was glad to see a light glowing in her kitchen. He knocked on her storm door, and she quickly opened both doors when she saw him through her inside door's windowpane.

"Saul?" She tilted her head. "Are you okay?"

"*Ya*, I just need to talk to you."

"Come in." They sat down at the kitchen table. "What's going on?"

"Do you still have Internet on your phone?"

"Yes. I just charged my phone at work the other day." She took the phone from her purse. "What do you need?"

"Can you find an address for a company in Missouri?" He fished the envelope from his pocket and smoothed it out on the table. "I think I found Aaron Ebersol."

Madeleine glanced at the envelope and then looked up at Saul. "You think he works there?"

"No, I think he owns that company." He tapped the

envelope. "This is the envelope Timothy's letter came in. I was trying to figure out how to find Aaron earlier, and intuition told me to look at that letter. When I saw the envelope, I felt like this was the sign we needed. When we were kids, Aaron told me he wanted to open up his own construction business and call it Paradise Builders."

"Oh, Saul!" Madeleine grinned. "You're a genius!"

"No, I just have a really *gut* memory." He pointed to the phone. "So can you find a phone number?"

"I can try." She typed with her fingertips, and soon she smiled and turned the phone around so he could see. "Look at what I found."

The company name, address, and phone number were displayed on the screen.

He smiled. "Now you're the genius."

Her cheeks flushed bright pink, and she was adorable.

"Would you please dial the number?" he asked. "I'll do the talking if you'd like. I'm the one who knew Aaron."

"Let's hope the phone number is current." She pushed on the screen and then handed him the phone. "Hopefully it will ring."

Saul took the phone and nodded. "It's ringing."

After the third ring, a recording began. "You've reached Paradise Builders. We're not in the office right now, but if you leave a message, we will return your call as soon as possible."

After a beep, Saul said, "This message is for Aaron Ebersol. This is Saul Beiler in Paradise, Pennsylvania.

Your mother needs you now. Please call me." He left his phone number and handed the phone back to Madeleine. "Now we'll have to pray that he calls me back."

Madeleine looked determined as she turned off the phone. "He will call you back. I can feel it."

"I hope so." Saul stood. "It's late, so I'd best let you get to bed. *Danki* for your help."

Madeleine touched his arm. "Ruth will be thrilled that you found Aaron."

"That's only if I found him. We won't know unless he calls me back." Saul sighed. "Let's keep this to ourselves until we hear something."

"I agree. Good night, Saul." She smiled. "I'll see you and Emma tomorrow."

As he headed back toward the house, Saul lifted up a prayer to God, asking him to soften Aaron's heart toward his mother. He prayed Aaron would call back before it was too late. But no matter what was going to happen, he knew in his heart that God was and would always be in control.

DISCUSSION QUESTIONS

1. Toward the end of the book, Madeleine realizes she longs to convert to the Amish way of life. Have you ever longed to make a huge change in your life? If so, did you follow through with that change? How did your family and friends react? What Bible verses helped you with your choice? Share your experience with the group.

2. Saul feels God is giving him a second chance when he falls in love with Madeleine. Have you ever experienced a second chance?

3. Ruth quotes Matthew 6:15: "If you do not forgive others their sins, your Father will not forgive your sins." What does this verse mean to you?

4. Saul has been nursing a broken heart since his wife left and divorced him, leaving him to raise Emma alone. At the beginning of the book, he wants to find someone who'll simply be a good mother for Emma because he doesn't believe he will ever love again. Think of a time when you felt lost and alone. Where did you find your strength? What Bible verses helped during this time? Share with the group.

5. Saul believes he's shielding Emma from hurt when he keeps the truth about her mother from her. In the end, it's still painful when Emma finds out the truth. Do you think Saul's decision to withhold the truth was justified? Have you ever found yourself in a similar situation? If so, how did it turn out? Share with the group.

6. Carolyn is happy that she finally has her dream— her own home, a husband, and a father for Benjamin. Although she's content with her new life, she still feels the pull of two worlds—working on the farm for her husband and keeping her job at the hotel. She wants to be a good, dutiful wife, but she also wants to contribute to the family by making money on her own. If you were in her situation, would you give in to Joshua's request and quit the part-time job at the hotel?

7. In *A Hopeful Heart* and *A Mother's Secret*, Lillian is convinced her mother is selfish and betrayed her by leaving the Amish community. In this book, we see Lillian still struggling to forgive her mother, but she's also beginning to accept her mother's decision to leave. Do you think it's time for Lillian to forgive her mother and move on? Share what you think with the group.

8. Which character can you identify with the most? Which character seems to carry the most emotional stake in the story? Is it Madeleine, Emma, Saul, or someone else?

9. Saul grows as a character throughout the book. What do you think caused him to change throughout the story?

10. What did you know about the Amish before reading this book? What did you learn?

Acknowledgments

As always, I'm thankful for my loving family, including my mother, Lola Goebelbecker; my husband, Joe; and my sons, Zac and Matt. I'm blessed to have such an awesome and amazing family.

I'm more grateful than words can express for my patient friends who critique for me, including Margaret Halpin, Janet Pecorella, Lauran Rodriguez, and, of course, my mother. I truly appreciate the time you take out of your busy lives to help me polish my books.

I'm thankful for the people who helped me with research, especially Ginger Annas, Stacey Barbalace, Jason Clipston, Mark and Rebecca Hefner, Kimberly Moity, and Janet Pecorella.

Special thanks to my special Amish friends who patiently answer my endless stream of questions. You're a blessing in my life.

Thank you, my wonderful church family at Morning Star Lutheran in Matthews, North Carolina, for your encouragement, prayers, love, and friendship. You all mean so much to my family and me.

To my agent, Sue Brower—you are a blessing to me.

I'm thankful that our paths have crossed and our partnership will continue long into the future.

Thank you, Becky Philpott, my amazing editor, for your friendship and guidance. I'm grateful to Julee Schwarzburg and Jean Bloom, who helped me polish and refine the story. Julee and Jean, I hope we can work together again in the future.

I also would like to thank Laura Dickerson for tirelessly working to promote my books. I'm grateful to each and every person at HarperCollins Christian Publishing who helped make this book a reality.

To my readers—thank you for choosing my novels. My books are a blessing in my life for many reasons, including the special friendships I've formed with my readers. Thank you for your e-mail messages, Facebook notes, and letters.

Thank you most of all to God—thank you for giving me the inspiration and the words to glorify you. I'm grateful and humbled you've chosen this path for me.

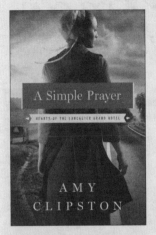
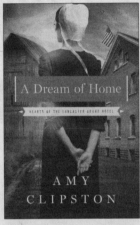
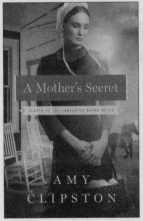
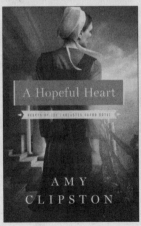

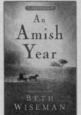

ENJOY NOVELLAS FROM FOUR OF YOUR
FAVORITE AUTHORS IN THE AMISH
COLLECTION *AN AMISH HARVEST*

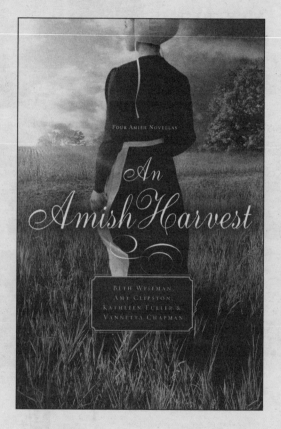

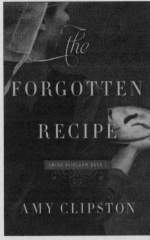
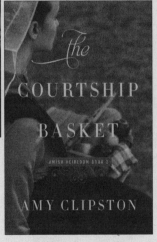
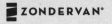

THE FORGOTTEN RECIPE

PROLOGUE

Jason Huyard had to be dreaming. The whole scene
playing out in front of him was surreal as he stood
in the Lapp family's kitchen doorway and peered into
their large family room. People, mostly strangers from
other church districts, paraded in and out of the house,
seemingly in slow motion. They walked through the
family room, shaking hands with other visitors before
expressing their condolences to his friend Seth's
mother, Margaret, and his younger sister, Ellie.

Seth's body lay motionless in the coffin behind his
family, and Jason's stomach twisted and bile rose in his
throat as he looked at his best friend.

No, it wasn't a dream; it was a nightmare, one of the
worst nightmares imaginable. It couldn't be possible
that only two days ago he and Seth were talking as they
built a shed together for the Lancaster Shed Company.
Jason's world came to a screeching halt when a board

broke, causing Seth to fall from the rafters, breaking his neck when he plummeted to the concrete floor.

In an instant, Seth was gone.

If only I hadn't walked away to grab those bottles of water . . .

Jason tried to push the thought to the back of his mind and moved into the family room to join his family. But he couldn't take his eyes away from Seth's mother. She was sobbing in the arms of a woman with graying hair peeking out of her prayer covering. Ellie, standing nearby, wiped tears from her rosy cheeks.

Jason must have told them a dozen times that he longed to go back in time and break Seth's fall.

It's my fault Seth is gone and his family is devastated.

Watching them cry was too much for him. The depth of their grief was palpable even from across the large room. Jason's chest constricted, and he felt as if he couldn't breathe. The heat in the room closed in on him, stealing the air from his lungs. He had to get out of there before he was sick or passed out.

He turned and weaved through the knot of people on his way back to the kitchen and mudroom, excusing himself whenever he bumped into someone.

"Jay?" his younger brother, Stephen, asked as Jason pushed past him. "Jason. Where are you going?"

"I need some air," Jason breathed out, pushing on the old, wooden back door, which moaned in protest as it opened.

"Wait," Stephen called after him.

Jason stepped out onto the wide, covered back porch, and the cool April air hit his face like a wall.

Finally! I can breathe! He moved to the railing and leaned over it. Staring down at the wet grass below, he took long, gasping breaths in an attempt to settle his violent stomach. He was glad no one else was there.

"Jay?" Stephen's brow furrowed with concern. "You're as white as a sheet."

Jason lifted his hat and raked his fingers through his hair. "I'll be all right. Just give me a minute."

Stephen pointed toward a group of people talking just inside open barn doors. "I see a couple of guys from work out there. I'm going to talk to them. Do you want to come with me?"

"No, *danki.*" Jason shook his head. "I'm going to stay here for a few minutes and enjoy the quiet."

"Okay. I'll be back in a minute." Stephen headed down the porch steps and dashed across the yard.

Jason turned and leaned back against the railing, crossing his arms over his chest as the cool wind seeped in through his black jacket. He moved his gaze upward. Puffy gray clouds strangled the sky, and the mist that had threatened all day finally transformed into steady raindrops. The weather was a fitting complement to the hundreds of community members who had journeyed to the Lapp home to say good-bye to Seth.

The back door creaked open, and a choked sob followed. Two women stepped out onto the porch as they supported a third woman, who seemed to be holding on to them with all her strength. They all shared similar facial features and looked to be in their twenties. The woman crying was dressed in black with wisps of blonde hair escaping her prayer covering. Her beautiful face crumpled with anguish and her ice-blue eyes, rimmed with dark circles, were clouded with tears.

The sobs grew louder as her legs seemed to buckled, causing the other two women to grasp her more tightly. Jason started to move across the porch to help them, but they successfully steered her toward a nearby bench and ordered her to sit down. The woman obeyed, and the other two young ladies sat on either side of her, cooing softly while holding her hands.

The door banged open, and a middle-aged couple rushed out and hovered over the three women.

"Veronica?" The older woman addressed the crying woman.

Jason's eyes widened as he whispered, "Veronica." *Seth's fiancée!* Seth had spoken of her so often that Jason felt as if he knew her.

"Veronica? Please take a deep breath. You need to calm down or you're going to pass out again." The woman bent down to meet her eyes. "Do you want to leave?"

Veronica shook her head and dabbed her wet eyes with a tissue. "No, I promised Margaret I would stay."

"She would understand if you left," the young woman with light-brown hair said. "You've been here all day."

"Rachel is right," the one with blonde hair chimed in. "You've been here since the crack of dawn, and I heard you pacing last night. You haven't slept since . . ." Her voice trailed off and she cleared her throat. "*Mamm's* right. You're going to pass out again if you don't calm down. And you need to sleep."

"I can't sleep." Veronica's voice was gravelly. "I need to be here. I *have* to be here for him. I can't leave him." Her voice broke, and sobs racked her body anew.

The agony in her eyes fueled his guilt. Why hadn't he saved Seth? Why wasn't he there when Seth fell? He could've broken his fall or warned him if he'd heard the board start to give way.

Now the blonde was rubbing Veronica's back. Tears still streamed from Veronica's eyes, and Jason gripped the railing behind him. He needed to apologize, tell her he was so sorry for her loss. He knew how much Seth loved Veronica. Seth talked about her incessantly. Seth acted as if Veronica was all he ever thought about.

Stephen sidled up to him. "Do you know them?"

"No, but I feel like I do."

"What do you mean?"

"Stephen, Jason." *Mamm* stepped out the door and onto the porch with *Dat* in tow. "I didn't realize you were out here." She turned toward the sound of crying, and a look of compassion crossed her face.

"I needed some air," Jason said.

"Are you ready to go?" *Dat* asked.

"*Ya,*" Stephen said. "Jason looks like he needs to go home and rest." He patted his brother's shoulder. "Let's go."

His parents walked toward the porch steps, but Jason lingered behind. He turned back to Veronica, who was speaking softly with the women he now assumed were her mother and sisters. He couldn't stop watching her. He longed to take away her pain. He felt responsible for her suffering.

"Jay?" Stephen asked. "It's time to go. We've been here nearly all afternoon."

Jason nodded. "I'm coming."

"No, you're not, actually. You're still standing here." Stephen leaned closer. "Why are you staring at that *maedel*?"

"She was Seth's fiancée. They were supposed to be married in the fall."

"That's Veronica?" Stephen blew out a breath. "Oh no."

Veronica's eyes met Jason's for a quick moment, and his breath caught. No matter how much he needed to talk to her, he couldn't do it now, not when her emotions—*his* emotions—were so raw. He was sure he'd fall apart if he tried to speak. He had to wait until he was strong enough to tell her he felt responsible for Seth's death, that he would never forgive himself.

"Jason?" Stephen nudged him. "*Mamm* and *Dat* are ready."

He nodded and followed his brother down the squeaky porch steps. When he reached the bottom, he looked over his shoulder one last time and took in the sight of Seth's beautiful fiancée and her obvious grief. He was going to find a way to talk to her soon, and he would tell her just how sorry he was for not being able to save her future with Seth.

. . .

The story continues in
The Forgotten Recipe by Amy Clipston.